# THE SPRING CLEANING MURDERS

VIKING
Mystery
Suspense

*Also by Dorothy Cannell*

NOVELS

The Thin Woman

Down the Garden Path

The Widows Club

Mum's the Word

Femmes Fatal

How to Murder Your Mother-in-Law

How to Murder the Man of Your Dreams

God Save the Queen

SHORT STORIES

The January Sale Stow-Away

The Family Jewels

# THE
# SPRING
# CLEANING
# MURDERS

## DOROTHY CANNELL

VIKING

VIKING
Published by the Penguin Group
Penguin Putnam Inc., 375 Hudson Street,
New York, New York 10014, U.S.A.
Penguin Books Ltd, 27 Wrights Lane,
London W8 5TZ, England
Penguin Books Australia Ltd, Ringwood,
Victoria, Australia
Penguin Books Canada Ltd, 10 Alcorn Avenue,
Toronto, Ontario, Canada M4V 3B2
Penguin Books (N.Z.) Ltd, 182–190 Wairau Road,
Auckland 10, New Zealand

Penguin Books Ltd, Registered Offices:
Harmondsworth, Middlesex, England

First published in 1998 by Viking Penguin,
a member of Penguin Putnam Inc.

10   9   8   7   6   5   4   3   2   1

PUBLISHER'S NOTE
This is a work of fiction. Names, characters, places, and
incidents either are the product of the author's imagination or
are used fictitiously, and any resemblance to actual persons,
living or dead, events, or locales is entirely coincidental.

LIBRARY OF CONGRESS CATALOGING-IN-PUBLICATION DATA
Cannell, Dorothy.
    The spring cleaning murders / Dorothy Cannell.
      p.   cm.
    ISBN 0-670-87571-6 (alk. paper)
    I. Title.
    PS3553.A499S67      1998
    813'54—dc21      98-2827

This book is printed on acid-free paper.
∞

Printed in the United States of America
Set in Fairfield Medium
*Designed by Betty Lew*

*To my son Jason,*

*who by always asking for his own,*

*personal bedtime story, kept the hope*

*alive that I would one day be a writer*

*With loving appreciation—*

*to Chad Michael Brewer,*

*who once gave me a gift,*

*that gave me the idea*

# THE
# SPRING
# CLEANING
# MURDERS

# Prologue

IN SPRING A YOUNG WOMAN'S FANCY LIGHTLY TURNS TO thoughts of scrubbing down walls, turning out cupboards, taking up rugs, and doing the hundred and one other jobs that make her feel at one with Mother Earth. Oh, the joy of routing woodworm from the back-bedroom bureau! (What a recharging of the female batteries at discovering enough dirt under the sofa to plant pansies!) A time for re-birth. A new day dawning in which to repaint the kitchen, hang freshly ironed curtains, and make a pilgrimage to the attic to sort out the clutter of yesteryear. The bliss of knowing one is geared to set the house, if not the world, to rights even if for the moment it is impossible to tell if you are moving in or moving out.

I was feeling on top of the world—partly because I was standing halfway up a stepladder. Another cobweb swatted with an expert flick of the wrist, another stain blotted from the face of the ceiling. Ellie Haskell, housewife extraordi-naire! Then, ruining the moment, two small voices in-quired sweetly: "Can we go and look for fairies at the bottom of the garden?"

"Not now, dears!" I smiled benignly down at my three-year-old twins, daughter Abbey and son Tam. "Mummy is very busy."

"Please!" Their little faces fell.

"Perhaps later," I said, "but right now I have to make the house all shiny and clean so we can live happily ever after."

"I want Daddy!" Tam dug his knuckles into his eyes.

"Me too," wailed his sister.

"Daddy's at work, which is where good children get to go when they grow up," I told them. "Not," I added quickly, "that Mummy doesn't have the most marvelous time when she is home looking after you and making everything nice."

"You don't look nice, Mummy." Tam scowled up at me. "Actually"—this was his word of the week—"you look like a witch."

"No, she don't!" Abbey, always quick to my defense, gave him a push that landed them both on the floor. And suddenly I wavered, which may have been partially due to one of the stepladder's legs being shorter than the other. All morning I had been picturing myself as an Amazon. I hadn't realized that seeing me with an old cloth tied around my head and a feather duster resembling a diabolical magic wand in my hand might end up giving my children nightmares.

I'll admit that when I glanced up and noticed another cobweb dangling brazenly from the corner above the Welsh dresser, I considered sending the children outside to play by themselves. There is a walled area that was once the herb garden, so I didn't have to worry about them wandering through the gates and out onto the cliffs. And I could keep an eye on them from the kitchen window. But then I remembered the picture book I had found in the attic that morning. It related the sad and sorry tale of a band of brigand goblins who once upon a time holed up in the rockery of a sweet old lady's garden. Horrid, knobby little people, all cleverly disguised as crocus bulbs.

I came down off the stepladder and, as the children wrapped themselves around my knees, surveyed the up-ended kitchen. Surely it would be the height of irresponsibility to grab up a bottle of milk and a handful of apples, slap some cheese between slices of bread, and head with this makeshift picnic out into the garden. But birdsong drifted in through the open window on the back of a sweet-scented breeze, and I remembered how that morning I had barely restrained myself from dusting off Miss Vienna Miller's legs when she came to discuss an upcoming Hearthside Guild meeting. And she a newcomer to our little village!

"Please, Mummy!" Abbey was tugging me towards the garden door. Feeling like a nun forsaking the convent, I went with my little girl and boy into a world painted with rainbow colour for a picnic where dock leaves served for luncheon plates. A gull glided overhead, and a thrush peeked down from the branches of the old copper beech to serenade us with the promise that there would soon be bluebells in the wood.

Tomorrow, I vowed while unwinding the string of a faded kite, tomorrow at the very latest I would get down to some serious spring cleaning. And if a distraction should crop up, something totally unavoidable, such as being invited to tea with dear Brigadier Lester-Smith, then I would definitely get back on track the very next day.

# CHAPTER ONE

*When spring cleaning a room, begin
by removing the curtains, all
movable furniture, and the carpet.*

"WHAT'S ALL THIS, MRS. H.?" ROXIE MALLOY, MY PRIZED household helper, stood with hands on her black taffeta hips and looked the kitchen up, down, and sideways. "Had a row with the hubby and gone and got your bits and pieces together for moving out?"

"Ben and I remain blissfully happy. In fact we renewed our wedding vows before he left for work this morning. The reason the place is at sixes and sevens is that I've started spring cleaning," I informed her snappishly while examining my dishpan hands. No cream on earth would ever make them look human again, or regrow my nails, most of which had dissolved after repeated dunkings in a bucket of bleach. "It's a job and a half giving a house this size a full-scale go-through." Tottering over to a chair, I swept off a pile of cookery books so I could sit down. "According to my mother-in-law, only dirty people need to spring clean, but I never seem to get caught up on the hidden muddle."

"My heart breaks," Mrs. Malloy patted her new hairdo. She called the colour auburn sunset, but on a paint chart it would have been labeled as maroon.

"What, have you cleaning for me?" Mrs. Malloy's frown brought her painted eyebrows down over the burnished-gold lids.

"Why not?" A scratching sound caught my ear and I opened the hall door to see my cat, Tobias, looking sufficiently put out to hand in *his* notice.

"You and your ideas, Mrs. H.! Wouldn't do at all, and you know it." Mrs. Malloy assumed a look of withering contempt, partially directed at Tobias, who early in their acquaintance had made it clear he had no intention of treating her as a social equal.

"You're right, it wouldn't be fair," I conceded. "Buzzing through your house with the Hoover and a tin of polish, Mrs. Malloy, would be a walk in the park compared to what it takes to keep Merlin's Court in shape. And"—attempting to speak lightly—"I'm sure you'd be worried I'd break one of your prized china poodles."

"There is that," she agreed. "On the other hand, I'll admit it would tickle me no end to hear Brigadier Lester-Smith that lives two doors down talking about how Mrs. Haskell from Merlin's Court comes to do the rough for yours truly once a fortnight."

"Well, there you are!" Plying her with more tea.

"We all have our pipe dreams, Mrs. H." She emitted a lofty sigh. "But I can't pretend I could live with meself if I was to break the code."

"What code?"

"The one what dictates the ethics of me profession as set out in the bylaws of the C.F.C.W.A."

I was riveted.

"That's the Chitterton Fells Charwomen's Association," Mrs. Malloy explained kindly. "We really didn't need the W, but Mrs. Large, what's our chief bigwig, thought it made the letters flow better. Here." Reaching down for the large black bag she had deposited by her chair, she opened

"I'm not suggesting you don't do the lion's share of the work," I assured her as she sat down across the kitchen table from me and inspected the stiletto heel on one of her shoes. "It's just that I thought life would be easier with the twins going to play school three mornings a week. Instead it seems that by the time I've got them there, come home, made the beds, done the washing up, and got lunch ready, it's time to pick them up." I drank deep from a cup of cold tea left over from breakfast and waited for Mrs. Malloy to administer words of comfort to the effect that if I wanted to rebuild my strength by taking a rest with a good book, she would have everything shipshape in no time.

"Well, I wish I could stay and help you, Mrs. H." She managed to sound regretful as she helped herself to the slice of buttered toast Ben had left on his plate. "It's not like me to desert a sinking ship, but there it is! I've come to hand in me notice."

"What?" I almost went through my chair. Was it something I had done? Forgotten her birthday? Remembered her birthday? Mrs. Malloy had grown more than a little touchy about her age since becoming a grandmother a month before. Her son, George, had married my cousin Vanessa, the beautiful fashion model not known for her heart of gold, unless you counted the one studded with diamonds she sometimes wore on her Chanel suit. Mrs. Malloy hadn't been over the moon about the match. She believed that George, who owned a couple of factories and a chain of exercise-equipment stores, would have been happier with a girl of fewer looks and a little more sweetness and light. The speedy arrival of a bouncing baby girl had aroused mixed feelings on Grandma's part.

Mrs. Malloy was proud to say little Rose was her spitting image. But it isn't easy to cling to the pretense of being twenty-nine and three-quarters when one becomes a granny. The change of hair color dated from Mrs. Malloy's visit to George and Vanessa three weeks ago when Rose was a few days old. So did the burnished-gold eye shadow and the micro-miniskirt. All her own business, I reflected, but there was no denying that the marriage had also complicated my relationship with Mrs. Malloy. I felt awkward about putting my foot down when she spent an hour polishing the TV screen, missing most of the fingerprints but not a word of her favourite soap opera. And the situation had to be equally if not more difficult for her.

"I should have realized you'd have to stop working for me," I said through mounting panic. What on earth would I do without her? Fighting down the urge to attach myself to her legs the way the twins so often did to mine, I got up to empty out the teapot and get the kettle going for a fresh one. "But, Mrs. Malloy, I hate losing you. We've shared so much over the last few years. And the twins adore you."

"Naturally! It's me youthful charm and unbridled vivacity." She plucked a paper serviette from the rack in the middle of the table and wiped toast crumbs from her fingers. "Believe you me, Mrs. H., I'm fully aware life will never be the same without yours truly, but I trust you'll manage to hold your sobs down to a minimum when I walk out that door for the last time. We don't want the kiddies upset."

"They're at play school." I moved aside a floor mop that was propped up against the sink, as if taking a well-earned coffee break. "But Abbey and Tam aren't the only ones we have to worry about. Jonas is also going to miss you. And"—I couldn't resist bringing a teensy bit of pressure to bear—"you know he hasn't been all that well since his bad bout with bronchitis in November. I worry about his doing much in the garden just now."

"You're not doing him no favours." Mrs. Malloy looked around expectantly and I hastily produced another slice of toast. "Most gardeners I know would rather die with their

Wellies on and a hoe in their hands than be brought inside and turned into hothouse plants."

"Jonas isn't most gardeners." I sat down and toyed with the salt and pepper shakers. "I really don't know what [I] would do without him. And it's not as though he's real[ly] old. What's seventy or even eighty these days?"

"You keep thinking along them lines, Mrs. H." Mr[s.] Malloy took the positive approach. "I've heard tell that some of them foreign countries people don't come of a[ge] until they're forty. That makes Jonas middle-aged and y[ou] and me dewy-eyed blossoms."

I had always assumed she was some some thirty ye[ars] older than me, but I was perfectly happy to have her [in]clude me as a contemporary. There were times, I'll [ad]mit, when I found myself yearning to be middle-aged [and] menopausal. Surely by then the twins would have [out]grown the need to unroll the toilet paper in an attemp[t to] see if it was long enough to carpet the stairs and w[ould] have stopped taking bites out of sandwiches laid out [for] Hearthside Guild tea. Better yet, I would have mast[ered] that graceful balance of marriage, motherhood, h[ouse]work, and intermittent forays back into the world of [inte]rior design.

"I do wish you would stay on." My lips quivered as [I got] up to refill Mrs. Malloy's cup.

"Oh, go on, have a good snuffle," she offered kind[ly. "If] you must know the bloody truth, I've shed a few tear[s my]self at the thought of not working here no more. M[erlin's] Court has been like a second home to me, and th[at's a] fact."

"Then couldn't we work something out?" Rea[ching] across the table I squeezed her hand, which as usu[al dis]played more rings than a jeweler's window. "How w[ould it] be if you came to me one week and I did the same [for you] the next?"

it up, then shook her head. "No, I don't have the bylaws with me. I remember now I used them to wedge shut the airing-cupboard door. But it's not like I don't know the Magna Char—as we call it—word for word. Two lines down on page sixteen, it says in big print: 'No member of the C.F.C.W.A., in good standing or otherwise, shall work alongside a person of less than ten years full-time experience or employ such in her own home.' " Mrs. Malloy looked me full in the eye. "There's no getting round it; rules is rules."

"How big is your professional organization?" I leaped at the chance to become sidetracked.

"Give or take"—closing her eyes and pursing her lips— "I'd say there was five of us: Gertrude Large, Winifred Smalley, Betty Nettle, Trina McKinnley, and meself."

"I've only met Mrs. Large," I said apologetically. "If you remember, you introduced her to me once at the bus stop in Market Street. To her and a much smaller woman."

"That would have been Winifred Smalley. Well, I suggest you try to get Gertrude to give you a try." Mrs. Malloy got to her feet and picked up the black bag. "Gertrude is always in demand, but if I was to put in a good word, I think she'd do her best to take you on."

"Oh, Mrs. Malloy." I tried desperately to get a grip on this disaster. "Must it come to this? Isn't there anything I can say to persuade you to stay?"

"Sometimes it don't do to think of ourselves, Mrs. H." Standing up very straight in her spike heels, Mrs. Malloy addressed herself to the greenhouse window above the cluttered sink.

"You're absolutely right." I blinked away tears. "I'm being selfish."

"What I meant is I can't get wrapped up in me own feelings. Not after George ringing up last night and practically begging me to move into the flat and help out with the baby." To my surprise, Mrs. Malloy was doing a heroic job of trying to look cheerful. Even Tobias appeared to give her a sympathetic glance, although he might have been sizing up her legs as potential scratching posts. "But I don't suppose," she continued, with only the faintest wobble of her chin, "that it will be all work and no play. There has to be things to do in London. Although I don't see as how it can seem much of a place after living in Chitterton Fells."

"I didn't understand that's why you have to leave." I felt a surge of hope. "But surely your stay with George and Vanessa won't be permanent."

"George said he wants me until Rose is done with school. But here's looking on the bright side." Mrs. Malloy's hand hovered in the air as if hoping a glass of gin would magically appear. "Rose could turn into a right naughty little so-and-so and get herself expelled. Horrid for a grandma to think about, but there it is! Nothing for it then, Mrs. H., but to ship her off to one of them convent schools in France where they don't let no one but the mum and dad see the child. And then only through one of them peepholes."

Mrs. Malloy often displayed her penchant for romance novels. But something else shone through as I looked at her. Were there tears in her eyes? I'd never seen her cry before. Oh, the occasional dab of her eyes with a lace-edged hanky to heighten the pathos of picturing herself as a misunderstood woman, but this appeared the real thing.

"What is it, Roxie?" (I rarely used her Christian name.) "You can't fool me. I know you adore little Rose. Your handbag's gained twenty pounds with all those photos you carry around. If she were sent packing off to France you'd be on her trail in a shot."

"If I could get a passport." Mrs. Malloy was still deep in the doldrums. "I've heard tell they've started cracking down and I'd need two forms to list all them husbands of mine. There's no good talking, Mrs. H." She wadded up her hanky and returned it to her bag. "I've got to do me duty, even though I hate moving in with George and that Vanessa of his. No disrespect to you, her being your cousin, although I can't say I go along with the idea that people don't get to pick their relatives. Vanessa's never been my cup of tea. Not since I first met her in this house and she treated me like the hired help."

It was impossible not to identify with this outburst. My cousin had treated me like an underling from the time we were both three years old. She was the family beauty, a successful model, the sort of woman who would have made Sir Walter Raleigh forget his cloak and lay himself down in the gutter.

"Motherhood changes women," I said. "On Vanessa's last visit here she even gave me some helpful hints on how I could improve my appearance without surgery. And . . ."—I was determined to think positively—"even if she should backslide and get snippy once in a while, you're not the sort, Mrs. Malloy, to let anyone walk all over you."

"That's true enough." She brightened momentarily. "But even if my daughter-in-law was to welcome me with open arms and bring me tea in bed every morning, I don't like the idea of giving up me home and career. Between you and me and that refrigerator, Mrs. H., I wouldn't agree to do it if every now and then I didn't get to thinking I've not always made enough time for George. The lad's stood on his own two feet since he was six weeks old. Done wonders getting into business for himself. And now here he is for the first time asking his mum to help out."

"But couldn't they get a nanny for Rose and have you pitch in occasionally? I asked.

Mrs. Malloy shook her head. "George was definite about wanting me full-time. Said my room's already fixed up a treat. I suppose it should have warmed the cockles of me heart. And I did do me bloomin' best, Mrs. H., to sound like I was bubbling over with enthusiasm. Like"—pointing a finger at the Aga cooker—"that there kettle's doing."

"Bother!" Leaping across the kitchen, I collided with the stepladder, to the annoyance of Tobias, who had been dozing on the top rung. I'd forgotten I'd put the kettle on for another pot of tea. Peering at Mrs. Malloy through a cloud of steam, I asked why she had to live with George and Vanessa. "Wouldn't it work just as well if you were to have your own little place close by?"

"You think I didn't suggest that?" She sat back down and closed her eyes. "Me own telly and bits and bobs? And who knows, perhaps some fellow I'd meet at the fish-and-chip shop who'd come along of an evening to help me hang curtains and fill up one of the easy chairs. But it's no good dwelling on all that!" She heaved a broken sigh. "Why George wants me under his roof is a bit of a puzzle. But there it is."

"I'm sure he's devoted to you," I proffered. "But, all the same, he and Vanessa are newly married."

"Well, I can't stay rooted to this chair," Mrs. Malloy recovered sufficiently to eye me severely as she got to her feet. "You'll need to get going on your spring cleaning, and I'd best be off to have a word with Trina McKinnley. She's offered to keep an eye on me house till I decide if it's best to sell up or let it to someone who'll keep up the garden."

"You will come again before you leave to say good-bye to the twins?"

"If I can face it. I did bring you something to remember me by." So saying, she reached into her bottomless bag and brought forth one of her cherished china poodles. "This is one of me favourites. It's a money box, as you can see if you look close. Won it I did, off a hoopla stand on the front at Margate years ago."

"Thank you!" I took the garish thing in my hands.

"I can tell from the expression on your face you're overwhelmed, Mrs. H., but there's no need to feel overly beholden. I don't know of no one as would take better care of Fifi."

"I'll treasure it always." My eyes misted and it took me a moment to see that Mrs. Malloy was in an even worse state. Tears were pouring down her face, eroding the makeup that seemed to be the only glue holding her together. I knew she didn't want me to hug her, so I simply touched her arm before she turned and walked to the door.

"I'll do like I said about having a word with Mrs. Large about taking you on, Mrs. H. And now ta ta!" My incomparable Mrs. Malloy walked with the barest totter and not a backwards glance out the door and down the steps into the pale sunshine. Her heels clicked away down the path. The sun shone. Birds sang. And I was left with a china poodle in my hands and more memories than there were jobs waiting to be done in this season of new beginnings.

# Chapter Two

"I WISH YOU'D FORGET ABOUT SPRING CLEANING, ELLIE. It's not as though we live in squalour."

Ben looked impossibly handsome, his dark hair rumpled and the morning sunlight bringing out flecks of gold in his blue-green eyes. We were in our bedroom getting dressed and, silly as it sounds, I still had occasional flashes of shyness with him. Something—a word or a glance—would sweep me back to the first time we met. Then I had wished fervently that a fairy godmother would appear to turn me into the sort of woman who would make this gorgeous man's heart pound the way mine was doing.

Now he cupped my face in his hands and gave me a lingering kiss before reaching into the wardrobe for a navy-blue sweater. "You've got enough on your plate," he said, "with the children constantly on the go and Jonas not up to snuff."

"But there's something primal about spring cleaning," I explained, "the urge to spruce up the nest every once in a while. To throw out the old twigs and bring in the new."

"And do some redecorating?" Ben's voice was muffled by the sweater he was pulling over his head.

"The urge has come upon me," I admitted. While buttoning my floral dress and bundling my hair into a loose knot, I glanced about the bedroom with its wallpaper of pheasants strutting about a silver-grey background. I was tired of the heavy mahogany furniture and the burgundy-velvet curtains and irritated that neither showed signs of wear. But like most men, Ben needed to be led gently by the hand when it came to making household changes.

"Wouldn't you like a new desk for your study?" I asked.

"No."

"But the drawer sticks."

"That's its best feature. I go to write a letter, can't get to the paper, and have to give the whole thing up. And now, my darling"—he moved towards the door—"I have to be going."

Restraining a sigh, I trailed after him. "Ben, you always run off to work when I talk about spending money."

"Do I?"

The forced attempt at lightness in his voice made me quicken my steps. "Is something wrong at the restaurant? You haven't told me much lately. Even Freddy has been unusually closemouthed." My cousin continued to dream of life as a rock star while working for Ben at Abigail's Restaurant and living in what had been the caretaker's cottage at our front gates.

"Business has been down." Ben leaned against the banister railing overlooking the hall. "The dreaded mad cow disease put a lot of people off eating beef ever again. And of course vegetarianism has practically become a national epidemic."

"Don't people bend the rules when eating out?"

"Not so as you would notice at Abigail's. Just when we

learn eggs aren't as bad for us as we've been told all these years, I can't give away an omelet. Never mind." He flashed me a convincing smile. "Things will turn around."

"Absolutely," I agreed. "I remember a couple of years ago having to wait ages to be served in Mrs. Dovedale's corner shop–cum–post-office. A whole queue of people had boxed up their mink coats and beaver jackets and were sending them off to the headquarters of some anti-fur group for a ritual burning. And that fad passed. One of the women guests at the wedding, when Mrs. Dovedale married Sir Robert Pomeroy, was wearing a rabbit jacket. What's important to remember is that Abigail's is a wonderful restaurant. People have always raved about the food, the service, the ambience, everything. I have complete faith you will be back in high gear in next to no time. Still"—I hesitated, afraid of wounding his pride—"perhaps I should try and economize. No redecorating for a while. And I can tell Mrs. Large we won't be needing her. She was meant to come for the first time today, but I'll try to catch her in time to put her off."

Ben moved away from the banisters. "Sweetheart, you need someone to replace Mrs. Malloy, and we can afford it."

"She can't be replaced."

"Perhaps not, but you can give this Mrs. Large a try."

"I suppose." I gave him the smile I knew he wanted to see.

"And you won't worry about Abigail's?"

"Not if you promise to tell me the absolute truth about how things are going." I took my husband's hand and we went along to the room where our children were building a tower with wooden blocks on the rug between their little white beds. So far I hadn't experienced a burning desire to update the nursery. I still loved its daffodil-yellow curtains, the cow jumping over the moon on the ceiling, and Mother Goose painted on the toy chest Jonas had made for the twins before they were born. But as Abbey scrambled up, oversetting the tower in her enthusiasm to climb into Daddy's arms, and Tam raced across the room to get his colouring book to show us his latest masterpiece, I knew I had to accept the fact that the twins were getting too big to be sharing a room. But no new furniture. There were plenty of offerings from the past to be found in the attic.

Tam and Abbey and I stood at the front door and watched Ben climb into the car and drive off. It was a glorious day, with the sun shining gold in a robin's-egg-blue sky and a breeze blowing in from the sea. The trees showed that first lovely haze of green, like young girls standing around in gossamer slips, waiting for their mothers to iron their summer frocks. A sparrow stopped pecking around the base of a rosebush to flit onto the path and peek cheekily up at Tam, who had ventured out onto the stone step.

"Look, Mummy"—my son's eyes widened—"he's wearing a black bib."

I was tempted to say that our feathered friend was clearly on his way to a funeral, where he would be a pallbearer in company with a couple of robins, a chaffinch, and a woodpecker—all close friends of the deceased. But my children were still at that impressionable age, so I settled for telling Tam that little boy sparrows tended to slop their morning cereal, which was why the mummy sparrows had them wear the little black bibs.

Tam bounded back through the front door and looked me squarely in the eye. "Actually, I already knew that."

Abbey's lip quivered. She hated being left out, but as she reached for my hand, the sparkle returned to her eyes and her elfin curls shone in the sun. "We saw a fairy in the garden the other day, didn't we, Mummy?"

"Didn't!" Her brother banged the front door shut, making the two suits of armour by the stairs jump, before he stomped behind us down the flagstoned hall.

"Yes, we did." Abbey added a couple of skips to her walk. "It was a real fairy and her was sitting on a frog stool."

"Toadstool," I corrected automatically, pushing open the kitchen door to find Jonas already seated at the table. The room was still in a state of disorder, with the stepladder blocking the pantry door, the mop resting by the sink, and the china and glassware I had removed from the cupboards for their annual bath taking up every inch of working surface. I should have been ashamed at how little progress I had made, but it was Jonas who occupied my thoughts. I felt a twinge of alarm, realizing how much he had aged over the course of the winter. Today the impression was heightened by a tall, gaunt figure who strongly resembled the Grim Reaper looming over his shoulder.

"Hi, Ellie." My cousin Freddy's cheerful grin broke through his scraggily beard, which along with his lank ponytail and skull-and-crossbones earring bespoke the free spirit. "I'm being a boy scout, cheering up my old mate here." He patted Jonas's balding head and received a growl for his trouble.

"You came looking for breakfast, Freddy," I retorted as the twins raced across the floor whooping with delight.

"How you do wrong me, dear coz." He swooped up both children and tousled their hair. "Thoughts of mooching a plate of bacon and eggs never crossed my mind. I merely ambled over to see how you all were. And lucky I did, because what do I find but dear old Jonas sunk in gloom at the prospect of some woman by the name of Mrs. Large having the cheek to think she can come here and fill the hallowed void left by our beloved Mrs. Malloy."

"We must adjust to change." Feeling righteous, I heated water for boiled eggs and popped bread in the toaster. "We're going to love having Mrs. Large here." I bustled the twins into their seats at the table. "Isn't that so, my darlings?"

"Aren't Mrs. Malloy never coming back?" Abbey dug her knuckles into her eyes, whereupon Tam piped up knowledgeably: "I s'pect she's dead."

"Of course she isn't," I said. "She's up in London looking after her baby granddaughter. Most people don't die until they are really, really old."

"Is you very old, Jonas?" Abbey scrambled off her chair to climb on his lap, putting her arms around his neck and pressing her rosy cheek to his lined one.

"I've seen a good many springs, my fairy." His moustache twitched and his gnarled hand trembled as he stroked her bright hair. He was looking towards the kitchen window, through which it was possible to catch a glimpse of the copper beech. Our favorite tree in the garden was also beginning to show its age; Ben had begun to talk regretfully of having it cut down.

"Jonas, I don't want you to go to that place where the dead people live." Tam scowled fiercely, his way of trying to hide that he was close to tears. " 'Least not till you're two hundred. You've got to show me more stuff that Mummy"—a condescending glance at me as I took the top off his egg and set his plate in front of him—"and even Daddy don't know. Like how to put the wheels back on my train when it gets broke."

"Sounds to me, Jonas, as though some toys of your own might help you feel young again." Freddy lounged over to the table and flopped onto a chair. "How about getting one of those exercise bikes manufactured by Mrs. Malloy's son?

Do you a world of good. And George, poor blighter, is bound to need every penny coming his way. Marriage to Vanessa has to mean bills mounting like the Empire State Building."

"Exercise!" Jonas sucked in his already-hollow cheeks. "Next thing, young fellow, you'll be after me to become one of them bloomin' daft vegetarians!"

"I don't think so." Freddy caught my eye and it occurred to me that perhaps he hadn't forced himself into a two-minute trudge from the cottage motivated only by the hope of cadging breakfast. Did he want to discuss the drop-off in business at Abigail's? Feckless though he might be in many ways, Freddy was sincerely appreciative of all Ben had done for him.

This, however, was not an opportune moment for discussing the fate of the restaurant. The twins' ears were flapping like sheets on a line and the clock on the wall indicated that Mrs. Large was due to arrive at any moment.

I passed Jonas a boiled egg and several slices of buttered toast. "I want you to eat every morsel. Freddy will show you how it's done."

"Ellie, you do spoil us." My cousin gave his egg a mighty whack with the back of his spoon and began chipping away at the shell.

"Reckon as I should keep my strength up," Jonas growled. "A woman by the name of Large is n'owt to tackle on an empty stomach."

"She'll be lovely, and I'm sure very professional, as befits a leading light of the C.F.C.W.A." I wiped Abbey's eggy face, poured the orange juice, and while making a pot of tea, provided what little information I knew of the elite organization.

"I hope the rules don't prohibit gossip," said Freddy.

"Probably."

"But not strictly enforced perhaps." He topped off his juice glass. "After all, you say Mrs. Malloy was a member, and she was never backwards in coming forward with a juicy tidbit about this person or that."

"I'm not bothered about other folks' lives." Jonas was nibbling the edge of a piece of toast.

"What! You don't want the scoop on those two women with the dogs who moved into Tall Chimneys? Something dodgy about them." Freddy shook his head. "One looks as though her parents tried to drown her at birth and other is too hearty by half. Vienna and Madrid Miller. Supposedly sisters. Although my guess is they're bank robbers on the lam."

"Perfectly respectable women," I asserted. "They're having the next meeting of the Hearthside Guild."

"And then there's that woman who looks as though she just left the nunnery and is afraid to cross the road without getting permission from Rome." Freddy was in full flood. "You know the one I mean, Ellie. She bought that cottage on Hawthorn Lane, just around the corner from the vicarage."

"Clarice Whitcombe, and she's doing wonderful things with the garden. Some flowers but mostly vegetables. All very organic."

"Wonder what she uses for fertilizer?" Freddy smirked. "The body of the bishop who refused her request to be allowed to hitch her habit above her knees while weeding? And what about that odd little man? The one who bought the house a couple of miles down The Cliff Road toward Bellkiek?"

"Tom Tingle," I said, "recently retired from the family shipping firm in London."

"Probably a pirate." Freddy helped himself to more toast.

"He looks more like a gnome."

"A real one, Mummy?" Abbey bounced in her seat.

"No, dear, just an ordinary man with a big head on a small body."

"It strikes me"—my cousin settled back in his chair—"that there is something decidedly sinister about this influx of newcomers. Could they be members of some gang? I ask myself. Bent on setting up bingo halls or ice-cream parlours as a cover for their illicit operations."

"Why not make them white slavers?" I suggested, putting a cup of tea in front of Jonas, who blinked his eyes and looked abashed at having nodded off. "Please, Freddy, do not hound Mrs. Large for information. She may not work for any of the new people. Mrs. Malloy told me the Misses Miller had hired Trina McKinnley. Anyway, Mrs. Large is going to have her hands full helping to get me organized, without feeding your fantasies."

Unwilling to be ignored any longer, Tam turned his eggshell upside down in its cup, stuck out his chin, and said, "I wefuse to eat my egg." This was a favourite game, and having invented it, I knew my lines.

"Oh, you naughty boy!" I scolded, face solemn, hands on hips. "Whatever would Daddy say if he knew I had gone to all the trouble of making you a nice breakfast and you haven't taken a tiny bite? Well, no mid-morning snack for you. Only good little boys get a chocolate biscuit."

"Tricked you, Mummy!" Tam triumphantly turned the eggshell back over to display the empty inside. "I fool you every time, don't I?"

Assuring him he was a master trickster, I gave him a hug, which he returned along with a smacking kiss on my cheek before bounding off to join his sister, who was busily engaged in emptying the toy box. Again my eyes went to the clock. It was now almost ten past nine. Mrs. Large was late. Something surely against the rules of the Magna Char. I was just pouring myself a cup of tea when there was a knock at the garden door and in she walked.

"Morning, all." Her voice was deep and gruff and—as

might be expected—she was definitely a big woman. A good six feet tall, with a long, lugubrious face and a plodding walk. Abbey and Tam scampered behind the rocking chair as if she were a member of the household police, Jonas vouchsafed a mumbled greeting before burying his face in his cup, and Freddy was trying not to laugh.

"Mrs. Large!" The twins had now attached themselves to my legs so that I was able to take only minuscule steps, in the manner of someone auditioning for a part in *The Mikado*. "I'm so pleased you're here."

"Sorry to be late." Her deep-set eyes took in the chaotic kitchen without batting a lash. "Had one of my bad nights." She set her bag of supplies down on the floor with a thump. I distinctly heard the clink of bottles, and obviously she did, too. "No, it wasn't drink that done it, Mrs. Haskell. I'm not one for booze, never have been. I just come down with one of my bad heads. Suffer with them cruel at times. Doctor calls them tension headaches."

"Oh, dear!" I was about to suggest that she go home to bed and come another day. But it became clear she was a woman made of sterner stuff. Peeling off her grey flannel coat as if it were a banana skin, she hung it on a peg in the alcove by the garden door and rolled up her sleeves before I could clear my throat.

"How about a cup of tea?" I offered.

"Thank you kindly, Mrs. Haskell." The words rumbled off her tongue, causing Abbey to leap for safety in Freddy's arms. "But I've not come here on my holidays. 'Hard work keeps a body strong' has always been my motto." Appearing to wrap her arms around the length and breadth of the kitchen table, she gathered up the breakfast dishes in one mighty swoop. A couple of cups chattered in alarm, but the whole was safely transported over to the sink.

"The woman's a human forklift." Freddy may have

thought he was whispering, but his voice came at me like a ball, bouncing against my head.

"A bloody marvel, but I don't want n'owt in my room touched," Jonas growled, every hair of his moustache twitching.

"Did you hear that, Mrs. Large?" I caroled cheerily. "There's no need for you to bother with Mr. Phipps's room. He likes to do it himself."

"He's afraid you'll find his girlie pictures," Freddy piped up again.

"You get to see a lot of stuff likely to make your eyeballs pop in my line of work," Mrs. Large pronounced mournfully over the water running into the sink. "And most of the time it's easy enough to keep your mouth shut."

"Oh, but you're here among friends." Freddy handed Abbey over to me and stationed himself at the woman's elbow, the better to dazzle her with his ingratiating smile. "Pour your heart out, fill us in on what happens in Chitterton Fells behind closed doors."

There came a sharp crack. But unfortunately it did not result from Mrs. Large bashing my cousin over the head with a breakfast dish. She had trodden on the base of the floor mop, sending it staggering backwards before hitting the turf.

"Freddy's a terrible tease. Please ignore him," I begged.

"That's all right, Mrs. Haskell, takes all sorts to make a world is what I say. Now don't you go feeling you have to show me the ropes." The mournful voice droned on. "I can work me way round any house blindfold. So on you go about your business. I'm sure you don't have much time for standing looking out the window with them little ones to keep you hopping." She gave Abbey and Tam what passed for a smile, and after apologizing half a dozen times for the chaos, I accepted Freddy's offer to take the children down to his cottage until lunchtime. Jonas put on a jacket and cap and shuffled out into the garden, which left me to get out from under Mrs. Large's feet.

Heading into the hall, I felt a little bereft. There was plenty for me to do, but in all likelihood as soon as I got settled into a job Mrs. Large would want to get started on the room I was occupying. Luckily I remembered my decision to look for bedroom furniture for the twins' new rooms.

"If I'm not back in a hour, send someone to find me," I instructed one of the suits of armour as I mounted the stairs to the attic. I was always halfway afraid that a faceless form would sidle out of the darkness and smother my cries of alarm with its clammy paws. A second staircase, far narrower than the main one, led from an alcove beside the bathroom to a round-topped door. This opened with a creaking sound verging on a wail as I turned the big iron knob. As I hesitated, something soft brushed against my leg.

"Thanks a lot." I picked Tobias up and in return for a discouraging meow kissed his nose before stepping through the black rectangle of the attic doorway. After floundering for a moment I found the cord dangling from the ceiling. When pulled, it produced a watery light that did little more than illuminate the spot on which I was standing. Tobias clearly found the effect delightful. Scratching at my dress front in his impatience to be down, he leaped from my arms and darted behind a stack of boxes and trunks.

I wasn't sure what was in the attic, other than a couple of boxes of my maternity clothes. It would have been sensible, as well as kind, to have given these to a thrift shop. But I remembered my friend Frizzy Taffer. The week after she had worked up the courage to give away the outfits amassed during three pregnancies, she discovered the stork was planning another delivery. At the time, I hadn't known whether to feel sorry for her or envious.

Sometimes I really longed for another child. Edging around the boxes behind which Tobias had disappeared, I now made out the shadowy shapes of the twins' high chairs, wedged between an old wardrobe and a chest of drawers. Suddenly I ached to hold a baby against my heart, to feel again that soft, sweet warmth and breath in that wonderful newborn smell. Perhaps it was this spring business. All that stuff about green things growing and buds a'budding. And mother birds fitting out their nests. Whatever, I told myself sternly, this was not the time to start picturing myself as the great Earth Mother.

Not only were Tam and Abbey little more than babies themselves, there was Jonas needing special attention and the restaurant perhaps in trouble. Far better for me to stop dabbling and get serious about reestablishing myself as an interior designer. One of the newcomers, Clarice Whitcombe, had intimated at the last Hearthside Guild meeting that she would like some help with decorating when she got fully settled. And several other people had made interested noises as well. Of course, the real coup would be a commission to redo Pomeroy Hall to the taste of its new mistress. The former Mrs. Dovedale, who had been in love with Sir Robert since her schoolgirl days working in her father's corner shop, was now his bride.

The attic drew me to its centre. Tugging on a dust sheet at random, I uncovered a cradle, a beautiful thing made of walnut, with carved cherubs forming a broad edge around the hooded top. An antiques dealer friend of mine had sent it to me when I was pregnant. Kneeling down, I tipped that cradle with my finger so that it rocked gently as if lulling a phantom infant to sleep. When two babies had arrived, Ben and I couldn't let only one of our delightful offspring rock in royal splendour. So we'd purchased two white bassinets from the local departmental store, and stowed the cradle in the attic.

Perhaps one day, I thought, covering it back up. For now I would satisfy my nesting instincts by doing what I had come up here to do. Look for bedroom furniture for Abbey and Tam. I had taken only a couple of steps when I froze. Someone was standing behind me. I could feel his shadow imprinted on my back. Heart thudding, knees knocking, I made a half turn and was almost felled by a dressmaker's form, which landed alongside me with the force of an oak tree. Inventing a few new swear words, I backed up against a decrepit armchair and sat down with a wallop that proved I was not as well upholstered as I thought. An uncoiled spring punctured my behind. I pushed my hands down under the seat cushion, struggling for leverage. And when I staggered to my feet, I was holding something. A green clothbound book.

Forget pain! A journal? "Abigail Grantham" was written on the flyleaf. She who had been mistress of this house during the first decade or two of this century. At first I was disappointed to discover I wasn't in possession of her diary. The baize-covered book seemed to contain Abigail's collection of housecleaning formulas. But any contact with the woman whose memory I held in such high esteem and for whom Ben had named his restaurant was welcome. I stationed myself under the feeble lightbulb, flipping through the pages with the feverish curiosity more commonly manifested by pubescent boys ogling naughty pictures.

"Listen, Tobias—here's a fascinating tip: 'Clean cutlery with wood or coal ash. If the knives have ivory handles that have yellowed from being allowed to sit in washing-up water, rub them with sandpaper till white.' " This was marvelous. It made me wish I'd been born a woman living in the good old days before shop-bought cleaning products took all the fun out of a slog around the house. " 'To clean marble slabs, use four ounces of Sal soda, two ounces powdered pumice stone, and two ounces prepared chalk. Mix well, add sufficient water, rub well on the marble, and then wash with soap and water.' "

Turning another couple of pages, I exclaimed in delight. "Here's a recipe for an exceptional furniture polish. 'One pint of alcohol, one pint of spirits of turpentine, one half pint of raw linseed oil, one ounce balsam fir, one ounce ether. Cut the balsam with the alcohol, which will take about twelve hours. Mix the oil with the turpentine in a separate vessel and add the alcohol, and lastly the ether.'

"This is even better: 'To remove bloodstains, make a thin paste of starch and water. Spread over the problem area. When dry, brush the starch off. Two or three applications will remove the worst stains.' " Tobias did not hang about to hear more. I was about to turn another page when I heard a thud, followed by the smashing of china or glass. My heart pounded like a battering ram. I raced downstairs and along the gallery in the direction of the sound. To stop short at Jonas's bedroom. There the door stood open to reveal Mrs. Large, hands on her hips, surveying the remnants of a mirror that had hung on the wall. And I had to bite my lip to prevent an exclamation of dismay.

I knew how much that little mirror had meant to Jonas. His mother had given it to him when he was nine years old. Perhaps realizing she wasn't to be with him much longer, she had told him that whenever he felt lonely or sad, he need only look into it to find her there. Jonas the man understood she was speaking about his physical resemblance to her. But shortly afterwards, that nine-year-old boy had stood at an upstairs window watching his mother's coffin being lifted into a hearse. And in the painful days following he had discovered that if he stood at just the right angle and squinted through half-closed lids he could catch glimpses of her. Sometimes she would be in their kitchen, wrapped around in a big white apron, making pots of ruby-red jam. But mostly Jonas would see her in the garden, unreeling a kite that would flutter for an uncertain moment before straining towards the sun.

"This isn't like me." Mrs. Large turned towards me. "Any member of the C.F.C.W.A. will give it to you in writing, Mrs. Haskell, that I'm not by rule clumsy. Never a cup chipped in the twenty-two years I've worked up at Pomeroy Hall. The late Lady Kitty, that wasn't easy to please, called me a dream char. And I'm sure Sir Robert's new bride—Maureen Dovedale, that was—would say the same. Although, as you could point out"—Mrs. Large squared her massive shoulders—"that can't be said to hold the same clout, seeing as she and I was friends from kiddy days." Mrs. Large's voice petered out.

"You mustn't be upset, accidents happen, don't they?" I tried to sound bracing.

"That's kind of you to say." She stepped away from the shards of broken glass and reached for a dustpan and brush half buried under a heap of dusters on a chair. "And looking on the practical side, Mrs. Haskell, that mirror had seen better days. Wouldn't have fetched fifty pence at a jumble sale. The silvering gone. And when all is said and done, it was a silly size. Not big enough to see your eyes and nose in at the same time." I knew Mrs. Large was talking to make herself feel better but even so I felt a spurt of irritation, especially when she added, "I'd have felt bad if it had been something of any value."

Tears blurred my eyes as I watched her sweeping up the broken glass. Small comfort, but at least the frame could be salvaged. "I'll get it fixed." I had just placed the mirror on top of the dresser when the telephone rang. Glad of the opportunity to escape, I hurried out into the gallery and picked up the receiver.

"Oh, it's you," said Mrs. Malloy as if she'd expected the Pope to answer. "All choked up, from the sound of you, Mrs. H., at losing me. Well, you're going to have to pull yourself together for the sake of them children and that hubby of yours. Look"—her voice softened—"take my photo to bed nights if you think it'll help."

"I'm so glad you rang," I told her. "I've been a little worried at not hearing from you. How are things going with George and Vanessa and dear little Rose?"

"Let's save all that for when they bring out the movie of my life." My former right hand sounded decidedly surly. "It'll be a tearjerker all right, though who they'll get with enough charm and looks to play the main part, I don't know. But why should I worry? What with one thing and another, I'm no longer counting on getting that telegram from her majesty on my hundredth birthday."

This was morbid in the extreme. Could I be talking to the Mrs. Malloy who had long ago made a pact with the Grim Reaper that they would each ignore the other's existence? Knowing my cousin Vanessa, it would not at all have surprised me had she threatened to kill her mother-in-law if she so much as touched one of her designer lipsticks. But Mrs. M. had always been made of stern stuff—the sort to send a firing squad scampering off, their rifles between their legs. So what was happening in that London flat?

"Tell me what's going on!" I begged.

"You've got things round the wrong way," Mrs. Malloy returned austerely. "The only reason I took time out of me busy day to give you a tinkle was Gertrude Large said she'd be at Merlin's Court today. And I wanted to find out what's got her all shook up ready to pop her cork. Phoned me last night, she did. As near to tears as I've ever heard her. But what with all the noise from the bloody traffic that goes past here morning, noon, and night, I only caught bits and pieces of what she was saying. Something about making a nasty discovery and not knowing what to do under the circumstances. And what did I think about calling an emergency meeting of the C.F.C.W.A.?"

"Didn't you ask Mrs. Large to fill in the blanks?" I didn't mean to sound impatient, but I had sat down on a bench where one of the twins had left some small building blocks with very sharp points.

"Naturally I was about to ask for details," Mrs. Malloy explained patiently, "but then little Rose started crying and I had to hang up all of a hurry. And by the time I'd got her off to beddy-bye land I conked out meself."

"Never mind, you can have a word with Mrs. Large now," I assured her. "She's just down the hall in Jonas's bedroom."

"I wouldn't want to interrupt nothing important."

"You won't," I replied. "Hold on a tick while I fetch her to the phone."

"I haven't got all day, Mrs. H.!"

Thus admonished, I speedily informed Mrs. Large that Mrs. Malloy was waiting to speak to her, and for a fraction of a second the woman's gloomy face brightened. I had a moment in which to feel certain that some monumental anxiety had caused her fingers to fumble and drop Jonas's beloved mirror. And then she shook her head. It was against the rules of the C.F.C.W.A., she informed me, to accept personal phone calls, except in direst emergency, while on the job.

"But I don't mind in the least," I protested. "And Mrs. Malloy says this is very important."

It was fruitless. Mrs. Large stood, dustpan in hand, as

unbudgeable as the oak tree she resembled, and I thought I heard her murmur the words "Death before dishonor!" as I trailed off to report to Mrs. Malloy, only to find that she had hung up. Or we had been disconnected? Another of life's glitched moments, which hardly seem fraught with immense importance at the time.

# CHAPTER THREE

*Go over the floor again, removing
the dust that has fallen from
the ceiling and walls.*

ON THE FOLLOWING SUNDAY, SKIES HUNG LOW, LIKE soggy woolen blankets abandoned on a clothesline. The wind gurgled and moaned and rain drizzled drearily down the windowpanes. Spring seemed as much a matter of wishful thinking as the hope that Mrs. Malloy would ever return to Merlin's Court. Perhaps if I had gone to church that morning I would have been blessed with a better perspective on life in general. But I had woken up feeling sluggish and out of sorts, and after I lost my handbag, found it, and misplaced it again, Ben had suggested that I stay at home and enjoy a little peace and quiet without him and the children. That's the trouble with husbands. They know when we are dragging our heels and they help butter the stairs to hell by being nice about it.

Fortunately I did have something to feel holy about. I had finally finished reorganizing the kitchen cupboards. The shelves were freshly lined; every piece of china and glass was polished so that the Wicked Queen could have seen Snow White's face in their mirror gloss. Speaking of which, Jonas had been every bit as upset over Mrs. Large's accident as I had expected. I hadn't told him about it until after she had left, which was wise, because he grumbled and growled so loudly that she would in all likelihood have never returned. That would have been a pity because she had done an excellent job. On and on he'd gone about seven years of bad luck (which would include violent death and a plague of locusts), and how he never wanted that woman setting her boat-sized feet in his room again. What he didn't mention was that the mirror had been a gift from his mother. That was the sad part.

Ben had taken Jonas an early morning cup of tea, and after pottering down to the kitchen and admiring the freshly ironed curtains at the windows, I now buttered some toast and spooned honey into a small dish. Jonas was very fond of honey. His mother had kept bees. I pictured him as a small boy with a cow lick and freckles while I added a cup of tea and small glass of orange juice to the wooden tray before carrying it up to his room.

After knocking with my elbow a couple of times and getting no reply, I nudged the door open and trod across the wooden floor onto the Turkish-red carpet that some-how managed to look all right with the dusky-pink roses on the wallpaper, probably because not a lot of either was showing. Jonas had so much stuff in his room it looked like a rescue mission for homeless furniture. There was a huge old-fashioned wardrobe, several turn-of-the-century tallboys, at least four bookcases crammed with well-thumbed volumes, and an assortment of chairs stacked with additional books, newspapers, and shoe boxes over-flowing with odds and ends.

I crossed slowly to the massive mahogany bed where Jonas slept, gripping the breakfast tray as if it were a bal-ance pole and I a tightrope walker. There was something about the curve of his back under the huddle of blankets and the way his hand rested on the fold of the sheet that made me think for one terrible moment that he was dead. But then Jonas made a sound, something between a sigh and a grunt, which let me know he was still among the living.

Setting the tray on a chair, I eased myself down on the edge of the bed. I had a wonderful husband and two precious children, but the heart has many nooks and crannies, each of which can only be filled by certain people. If I hadn't felt the tickle of an oncoming sneeze, I would probably have sat there for another five minutes, like a cross-legged cherub on a tombstone. But to blast Jonas awake would not have enhanced his life expectancy. Edging off the bed, I picked up the tray and tiptoed back to the kitchen as Ben came in through the garden door. He looked like an advert for *Outdoor Living* in his handsome new raincoat.

"There's nothing like a good old-fashioned wife," he said, looking at the tray.

My smile met his. "Sorry, this was breakfast for Jonas, but he was asleep when I went up. And I didn't want him thinking I had gone to any trouble for nothing. How about a cup of lukewarm tea and a piece of toast?"

"Thanks, sweetheart, but I had coffee and biscuits in the church hall after the service."

"That's nice," I said. "Where are Abbey and Tam?"

"Oh, them!" Ben unbuttoned the raincoat, which was very damp, especially around the shoulders. "I put them in the collection plate. Not only was it a particularly moving service, Tam was making the most frightful nuisance of himself crawling under the pew and looking up the skirts of the women in front."

"What have you really done with my children?" I picked up the bread knife as I spoke, simply to wipe it off, but he feigned alarm, backing away into an open cupboard door.

"That nice woman, Clarice Whitcombe, who recently

moved into Crabapple Tree Cottage, made a big fuss over the twins. They really took to her. So when she asked if she could take them home, feed them lunch, and keep them for part of the afternoon, they were delighted. I didn't think you would mind. It will give you a little time to yourself, as I have to go in to work"—glancing at his watch—"in half an hour or so."

I stared at him. "But, Ben, we don't really know anything about Miss Whitcombe."

"I thought you'd talked to her several times and that she wanted you to help her redecorate the cottage."

"That's true, and as you say, she seems very nice, but she could still be an ax murderer or deeply into witchcraft or any number of other beastly things."

"As could be said of almost anyone else here in Chitterton Fells. Ellie, I agree we have to be protective of the children, but I don't think there is anything wrong with them being babysat for an afternoon by a kindly middle-aged lady. But if you're really worried"—Ben kissed me before rebuttoning his raincoat—"I'll go and fetch them now."

"Don't do that." I smiled. "I'll get them after you go to work. My nerves are on edge, that's all. Perhaps it's Jonas. I was afraid when I went up to his room just now that he'd died. I don't think I'm superstitious, but that broken mirror has rather haunted me."

"You're overtired," came the husbandly response. "You've done yourself in with this orgy of spring cleaning. And you're down about Mrs. Malloy leaving. Why don't you phone her and cheer both of you with a nice long chat?"

"I'll do that, though every time I manage to get hold of her it's impossible to keep her on the line for more than a couple of minutes. She always has to go and see to the baby. I told you how she hung up before I could tell her Mrs. Large wouldn't come to the phone the other day. And when I rang back she almost bit my head off—she accused me of almost causing her to drop little Rose."

Ben shook his head. "I thought she was making a big mistake moving in with George and Vanessa, but we both know Mrs. Malloy. There's no budging her when she sets her mind to something."

I sighed. "I'm sure there's something wrong—something even worse than having to live with my cousin Vanessa. Curiosity is Roxie Malloy's middle name. Under any normal circumstances nothing short of electrocution would have kept her from staying on the phone that day to find out what had Mrs. Large's knickers in a twist."

"Mrs. Malloy probably phoned her at home that same day," Ben said lightly, "and I'm sure they had a good chinwag about the whole thing."

"I expect you're right." I managed a smile. "Let's hope that whatever upset Mrs. Large was a tempest in a teacup and that when she comes back she'll not be all fingers and thumbs. Although I do have to say I wouldn't mind terribly if she broke one or two of the things I unearthed in cleaning out all those cupboards."

Delving into dark corners where no hand had gone since time began, I had come across some of those horrors—the ones received as wedding presents and painstakingly lost as soon as the thank-you card is sent. Or worse yet, the ones you buy your very own self on a day that you are out shopping and have left your brain at home. So that not only do you think the size 3 dress in the window might come in your size, you decide a whole herd of fake ivory elephants with beaded and fringed black-satin saddles would look lovely on the mantelpiece.

"What are you thinking about?" Ben asked.

"That from now on I'm going to be frugal to a fault." I wallowed for a moment in virtue. " 'Waste not, want not' shall be my motto. In fact, I may even start making my own housecleaning products. Remember that book I found in the attic the other day, the one that belonged to Abigail? Well, I think I'll curl up with it this afternoon and see which of her formulas I think I can concoct without taking a course in chemistry."

"You're not doing this because you're worried about the restaurant, are you?" A crease appeared on Ben's forehead to match the one in the collar of his raincoat. "Has Freddy been scaring you half to death in his hunger and thirst melodrama? Have you been picturing us out on the street trying to sell clothes-pegs for a living?"

"How worried *are* you? That's what I need to know, darling." I looked at him anxiously, then became alarmed when I saw his stricken face. If ever a man looked as though he were trying to come to grips with life at its worst, it was my husband at that moment.

"This isn't my raincoat," he muttered, patting the front and poking his hands into the pockets.

"What on earth are you talking about?"

"I took mine off during the service because the church was stuffy and laid it over the back of the pew. Come to think of it, so did Brigadier Lester-Smith, who was sitting next to me. His raincoat was beige, too. Damn! I must have picked up the wrong one." Ben's blue-green eyes met mine in what wasn't entirely mock horror. The brigadier was an exceptionally fastidious man who would be bound to find a crease where there hadn't been one.

"Are you sure you've got the wrong coat?" I was determined not to laugh. "This looks like yours."

"The cuffs." Ben extended his arms. "I suddenly noticed these each have an extra button. And look." He flapped open the front. "The lining is different. This is brown. Mine is a green-and-navy plaid."

I smoothed my hands over his damp shoulders. "Dar-

ling, there's no need to panic. I don't suppose Brigadier Lester-Smith is meeting with the police as we speak and insisting they arrest you. It's quite possible, you know, that he was the one who took *your* raincoat. Clearly he didn't realize the mistake either, or he would have said something before you both left the pew."

"That's odd, isn't it?" Ben now looked more puzzled than concerned. "The brigadier is such a persnickety fellow, I can't imagine him not realizing it instantly. But this is his coat, all right. See." Again he turned back the front flap. "Those are his initials—W.L.S."

"It does seem out of character," I agreed. "But perhaps the brigadier had something on his mind today. Would you like me to ring him up and arrange for you to switch back?"

Ben looked thrilled at my offer, adding—with a glance at the kitchen clock—that he really must get to work, even though Freddy was there to make sure no one tried to make off with the building. He enfolded me in his arms, kissed me with the fervour of a man being rescued from a shipwreck, and was already heading outdoors when he turned on his heel and exchanged the brigadier's raincoat for a worn navy-blue one hanging in the alcove.

Men are peculiar creatures. They can dismantle and reassemble entire governments, remap the world, and organize a war as though it were a golfing outing—all in a single afternoon. But when it comes to such things as returning an aerosol can of shaving cream that will neither fizz nor spit or, as in this case, making a phone call to straighten out a simple mistake, they go weak at the knees.

I knew Brigadier Lester-Smith's number by heart. Not only was he a fellow member of the Library League and regular attendee of the Hearthside Guild, I had help him redecorate his house on Herring Street, just two d down from Mrs. Malloy's. The brigadier—who lived b

watch—always lunched at noon on Sundays. But it wasn't until the fourth or fifth ring was drowned out by the first boom of the grandfather clock in the hall that I realized how inconsiderate I was being. Then before I could put the phone down, he was speaking into my ear.

"Walter Lester-Smith speaking." He sounded somewhat agitated.

"Brigadier, this is Ellie Haskell." I was forced to shout over the clock's bonging. "Please forgive my bad timing—"

"Not at all." I could hear his deep breathing. "I wasn't doing anything important."

"It was thoughtless to interrupt your lunch."

"Lunch?" He exclaimed as if pronouncing an unfamiliar foreign word. "No, no, Ellie, I haven't started to get a meal on the table, let alone sat down to eat. Believe me, your apology is unnecessary. You haven't interrupted a thing."

This was said with an emphasis that rang hollow, making me curious as to what had the brigadier in a tizzy. But I wasn't about to pry. He was in many ways an intensely private man, one whose friendship I valued. So I launched into how Ben had come home in the wrong raincoat—only to be interrupted within half a sentence. Highly uncharacteristic! Brigadier Lester-Smith was always punctilious in letting a woman have her say, even if she went on for a week.

"I suppose that means I have Ben's coat, Ellie. I can't say I had noticed." And this from the man some people said was married to his clothes! "Not to worry. I'll get his back to you. Perhaps later this afternoon or whenever suits." Here the brigadier interrupted himself with a gasp. "My goodness!" he exclaimed in a voice of utmost alarm. "It's been more than ten minutes. I'll have to talk to you another time, Ellie!" With that he hung up, leaving me at a loss. What was he talking about?

I didn't get to dwell on the matter. Glancing up, I be-

held Jonas stumping down the stairs. He looked very cross. His moustache and eyebrows bristled and he gripped the banister rail as if it were an arm he enjoyed pinching.

"What's with you, Ellie girl?" he huffed on reaching the bottom step. "You left me to sleep away the best part of the day. Time enough for a lie-in when I'm underground, that's always been my motto, and well you know it."

"It's Sunday," I reminded him. "Everyone except perhaps the vicar is entitled to an occasional late snooze. Come along and I'll fix us lunch. Ben's gone to work and the children are with Miss Whitcombe down the road."

"And who's she?" Jonas followed me across the flagstones into the kitchen. "Some retired nanny that's never happy without little feet scampering about the place?"

"I don't know what she did before moving here," I replied. If I sounded tart it was because I was back to wondering if Ben had done a wise thing in letting Miss Whitcombe take Abbey and Tam home with her.

"You know, I think I'll go and fetch them," I said after handing Jonas a cup of tea and a cheese sandwich. "She's probably ready for them to go home by now. And Tam really wants to watch a program that comes on in an hour, the one about lions in Africa."

"I reckon he'll make me put on that safari hat, like he done last week, and pretend him and me are game wardens slapping at our mosquito bites." Jonas still sounded cross, but I could see from the way his eyebrows twitched that he was coming out of the grumps.

Planting a kiss on his cheek, I grabbed up an old jacket from one of the pegs in the alcove by the garden door and hurried out to the courtyard towards the old stables, where we now garaged the cars. Ben had taken the more reliable of our two vehicles, leaving behind his ancient convertible whose hinges had long ago rusted, making it always topless. It also had an unbecoming tendency to stop without warning to admire the scenery, usually with a couple of lorries honking from behind.

It wasn't raining now, although the sky looked as though it could turn weepy given the least encouragement. I decided to walk to Miss Whitcombe's house. Once out on The Cliff Road, I turned right and within a couple of minutes was passing St. Anselm's church with its Norman tower and graveyard of sagging, moss-covered tombstones. From there it was only a few steps to Hawthorn Lane, where Crabapple Tree Cottage stood on the corner. It was a charming place, one of only two or three cottages with thatched roofs in Chitterton Fells. Purple and yellow pansies bordered the path to the front door and a bird feeder was strung from a tree branch near a latticed window.

There was no bell, just a brass knocker shaped like a little Welsh girl. It produced a dainty tap, which I repeated after a full minute of standing on the steps. A shabby grey cat appeared around the side of the house to mew at me plaintively, but there was silence from within for several more moments before footsteps approached and I heard the creak of a bolt being drawn.

"Mrs. Haskell! Come in!" Miss Whitcombe stood bathed in light from the hall ceiling fixture, which was rather too big for the narrow space, as were the Victorian table standing against the staircase wall and the two Windsor chairs facing each other from either side of the open kitchen door. But Miss Whitcombe herself fitted the cottage perfectly. She was trim and neat, with carefully set hair and the look of a woman who always wore sensible shoes and colours that didn't run in the wash. The most attractive thing about her was her smile. It brightened her Victorian face—in fact, the entire hall—as she beckoned me inside.

"I've so enjoyed having the children. What little darlings they both are. Tam all boy and Abbey a fairy child. We were in the dining room when I heard the door. We've had roast beef and Yorkshire pudding with two vege and I left them tucking into big plates of spotted Dick and custard. You will stay, Mrs. Haskell?" She bent to scoop up the grey cat, which had sneaked in behind me. "Being new to the area, I don't have a lot of visitors, just Mrs. Grey here from two houses down who likes to pop in for a square meal now and then"—she stroked the cat's head with a ringless hand—"and occasionally, very occasionally, Walter Lester-Smith drops by to discuss the Hearthside Guild, which as you know I recently joined."

"I had heard you'd become a member," I agreed. "I haven't managed the last few meetings. But I do promise to be at the one on Tuesday morning, since it's at Vienna and Madrid Miller's house. I'd like them to get a nice turnout." My feeling that Miss Whitcombe wasn't listening was confirmed when she allowed the cat to jump out of her arms and looked at me without meeting my eyes, speaking in a voice not quite as sensible as her shoes.

"I never call him Walter to his face, Mrs. Haskell. Believe me, I didn't mean to represent that we are on those kind of terms. He's always Brigadier Lester-Smith in our dealings, and being the gentleman he is, I know he would be mortified"—a blush mounted Miss Whitcombe's cheeks—"completely mortified were he to think for one moment that I was creating the impression hither and yon that he and I are on first-name terms. So if you would very kindly not mention my little slip . . ."

"I won't say a word," I promised.

"Thank you, my dear." Miss Whitcombe clasped my hand in a heartfelt way. "Rumours get started so easily, and when a man is single and as distinguished and handsome as the brigadier—well, you understand me." Her blush was deepening by the moment. "I would hate him to think I presumed on our very brief acquaintance, or thought there was the least chance of it blossoming into . . . friendship."

"I'm sure you're concerned unnecessarily," I said. Her worried eyes were reflected in the oak-framed mirror on the wall, which like the rest of the furnishings looked as though it had been purchased in the hope that the hall would grow a couple of sizes in the near future. But when Clarice Whitcombe again looked at me her smile was back in place.

"The trouble with living alone is you tend to babble the moment you get the chance to talk to someone. My mother was always a chatterbox, so I've probably got some of that from her. Although I didn't get much chance to practice while she and Daddy were alive. Mummy had always hated housework and cooking, so when I left school I took over running the house. But my parents might as well have been on their own desert island. They were everything to each other. Two turtledoves right till the very end."

"They died recently?" I asked.

"Six months ago." Miss Whitcombe stood stock-still, her hands flat at her sides. "Mummy hadn't been feeling well and she wasn't good with pain. One night she and Daddy took an overdose of sleeping tablets after celebrating with a candlelight supper. Much the best way out for both of them, because he couldn't have lived without her."

"You found them?"

"The next morning."

"What an awful shock!"

"Oh, yes!" she said, moving her hands. "But life goes on. I felt disloyal at first—if you can understand, Mrs. Haskell—selling off the big old house and most of the furniture, but I knew if I didn't make a new start at once, I never would. That before very long I'd be one of those eccentric old women living for her cats."

"I'm sure you were a very good daughter," I said lamely.

Again Clarice Whitcombe glanced towards the mirror. "Well, it wasn't," she continued wistfully, "as though I was much good at anything else. Not brainy or artistic like some."

"I see you have a piano," I had caught sight of the grand through the open sitting-room door. "Did you bring that from your parents' home?"

"Oh, yes, my mother was a great one for banging out a tune."

"Do you play?"

"I always wanted to . . ."—her cheeks were again faintly flushed—"to have . . . more time to practice. But unfortunately I haven't been able to do so recently." She wrapped one hand around her other wrist. "A bout of tendinitis, not all that painful, but the doctor says that any strain could make it worse." Once more her eyes didn't quite meet mine; but why would she lie about such a thing? "The children," she said suddenly, "we'd better get back to them."

"I never trust them long on their own," I agreed, following her down the hall. "Tam in particular is such a mischief. And I would hate to find them having a sword fight with the knives and forks."

"You'll have something to eat? One thing I can do is cook." Clarice Whitcombe was pushing open the dining-room door as she spoke. "There's so much I'd like to ask you about decorating this house. As I said, I'm not artistic, but I want the place to look welcoming. And even I can tell that my furniture isn't quite right here—" She broke off. But not because Abbey and Tam were up to tricks.

My little girl was seated at the table spooning steamed pudding and custard neatly into her mouth. Her brother was nowhere in sight, although his plate had been cleaned down to the china pattern.

"Hello, Mummy." Abbey beamed at me. "Tam's gone

home." She turned so that she was kneeling on her chair, waving a sticky spoon at the open French windows that lead to a path along the side of the house. "It was bad of him not to tell Miss Welcome bye-bye, wasn't it? I hope he don't fall into the sea." She now sounded anxious.

What I was felt bordered on hysteria. How could he have just gone? He was only three.

"I should have taken them with me to answer the door." Miss Whitcombe was clearly struggling to become a tower of strength. "I'm so sorry for keeping you talking. But it doesn't do to go on about that, does it? You go after your little boy, Mrs. Haskell, and I'll keep Abbey till you find him."

She took my daughter in her arms as I raced outside, to stand like a tree swaying in the wind for a moment. Which way to go? Would Tam have cut around the back of the house, through that dark, wooded area? Or would he have taken the longer but straighter route home, along The Cliff Road? Deciding the latter course was the more probable, I somehow managed to uproot my legs, which felt as though they had been planted deep in the soil for decades.

"Tam, darling!" I called as I ran. "Can you hear me? Please answer Mummy!" Lurching around the corner of Hawthorn Lane, I experienced the conflicting emotions that every mother knows at one time or other. The vow to God that if He would but restore my son, I would smother Tam with kisses and never let him out of my arms until he was forty. Coupled with the urge to kill my own child. I was also torn between wishing I'd asked Clarice Whitcombe to phone Ben at the restaurant and being glad he was spared the panic gripping me.

It started to rain lightly, and I shivered in my thin cardigan. Thank heavens there wasn't any thunder to drown out my voice as I continued to shout Tam's name. A seagull answered with a wild screech that set my heart pounding, but as I blundered on down the road I fastened on the hope that somehow, miraculously, Tam was already safely home waiting for me. Please let the only thing seriously wrong be my lurid imagination!

But what if Tam had wandered too close to the cliff edge? His fall might have been broken by one of the jutting rocks. I could picture his small battered body trapped in a crevice. Even more agonizing was the thought that he might have gone tumbling straight down onto the narrow strip of pebbled beach that separated the cliffs from the sea. I was moving at what seemed like a snail's pace along the road; but surely if Tam were ahead of me I should have caught sight of him by now. He couldn't have left Crabapple Tree Cottage more than a few minutes before me; he wasn't usually an enthusiastic walker. In fact, he, far more often than Abbey, demanded to be carried.

I was a hundred yards or so beyond the church and hoarse from shouting when I heard someone come up behind me—but not my son. It was Madrid Miller, who with her sister had recently moved into Tall Chimneys.

"Mrs. Haskell! I was on my way to your house to ask if your gardener would come along some time to take a look at one of the trees in our garden. It needs pruning, but I'm afraid to start lopping willy-nilly." She was now trotting alongside me. Seemingly unaware of my preoccupation, she reminded me that she and her sister were hosting the Hearthside Guild meeting on the following Tuesday morning. And she suggested that I might like to bring Jonas along with me that day in the car, as she'd heard he was getting up in years.

I barely slowed to give her a glance. On first meeting Madrid Miller some six weeks earlier, I had thought unkindly that she resembled an aging wood nymph. Her brown hair hung almost waist-length from a middle parting, and she had watery green eyes that peered uncertainly out at the world from behind granny glasses. The free spirit was abundantly evident in her long sack-coloured frock, ropes of dried rosebud necklace, and thonged sandals. I sputtered a high-pitched explanation of why I couldn't stop to talk, the only semi-coherent words of which were Tam's name and "lost."

"You must be out of mind with fright." Madrid Miller managed to keep pace with me despite her flip-flopping sandals. "Poor you! I remember being sick with worry one day when the postman left the front gate open and my darling Jessica got out on the road. She was only quite tiny at the time and the thought of her being abducted or run over or—"

"But you found her?" I stopped walking, forcing myself to peer over the cliff edge.

"A neighbour saw her and brought her back."

"That's good!" I took a small measure of comfort in Jessica's safe return. I needed to be reminded and wanted most desperately to believe that most often there is the sort of happy ending that leaves a mother saying years later with a roll of the eyes and a mock sigh: "How well I remember the time you scared me half to death . . ."

"Yes, we were lucky that time." Madrid Miller flapped after me as I turned away from the cliff.

"That time?" Suddenly I couldn't move; it was as though I had been visited by Doom in human guise.

"We lost our darling when she was only three."

"Lost?"

"She died."

"Oh, I'm so sorry!" Numbly I watched the rain, or it might have been tears, drip down her face.

"It's been thirteen years." She adjusted the granny glasses. "Yet it seems like yesterday. It was so sudden and she was so young, darling Jessica! My sister was my only comfort! Vienna was always the strong one. She tried to make me see it was God's will. But if it was"—Madrid Miller's face contorted and she twisted her ropes of rose-bud necklace into a noose—"he must be a wicked god to let my angel die like that in childbirth."

"Childbirth?" I was shocked into momentarily failing to focus on Tam.

"Technically, complications from." Her hands now fell limp at her sides. "Jessica developed eclampsia—milk fever is another name for it."

"But I thought you said she was only three!"

"So she was."

I could only gape at her.

"She actually died on her birthday. Such a dear little doggie."

"Jessica was a dog?"

"The dearest, sweetest, kindest little Norfolk terrier that ever blessed this earth. What breed is your boy, Mrs. Haskell?"

"He's a boy . . . boy," I cried, hurrying forward again. "I'm looking for my son, Miss Miller."

"Please call me Madrid!" She flung back her hair, which seemed to stretch even longer in the rain, and panted a lit-tle, trying to keep up with me. "I must have heard wrong, I thought I heard you shouting *Tam*, but I suppose it was *Tom*."

"His name *is* Tam. It's short for Grantham, a family name."

"Really? I thought it would be short for Tam o' Shan-ter. We once showed against a dog of that name. His grandfather was a champion, but it hadn't rubbed off. He was once very rude to one of the judges. Cocked his leg at him."

My heart was back in my throat as I dodged through the iron gates of Merlin's Court, past Freddy's cottage, and down the drive to the house, which had never looked more like a fairy-tale castle, wreathed as it was in a rainbow so vivid Tam might have painted it. Please, please let him be safely indoors!

"If your little boy had been a dog," Madrid said breathlessly, "you could have eased your mind about his running off and getting lost with an identification microchip inserted by your vet. It's a simple procedure, done by injection and no more painful than the ones he would get for his usual inoculations. Perhaps they can do something similar for children. You should check into it, Mrs. Haskell."

We had crossed the courtyard and I was now running ahead of Madrid Miller over the moat bridge. It would have been quicker to have gone in by the front door, had I brought my key. But knowing Jonas might be at the other end of the house and not hear the bell at the first ring, I was about to enter by the garden door when it opened to reveal Freddy and—joy turned me faint—Tam, about to step outside.

All was quickly explained. Freddy had been driving his motorcycle home from the restaurant when he had spotted Tam trotting along The Cliff Road and had brought him home.

"On the bike?"

"I knew better than that." Freddy's grin took in Madrid Miller standing at my shoulder. "You'd have had a fit, Ellie, if I'd popped him on my knee and roared on home. I left the bike inside the church gates and piggybacked Tam back here. We made good time, let me tell you."

"I had to go pee-pee," explained my son as I scooped him into my arms. "I'm sorry I didn't wait for you, Mummy, at that lady's house. Was you scared?"

"Very." I hugged him tight. "We're going to have to have a long talk about this after I phone Miss Whitcombe and let her know you're home. What you did, Tam, upset her as well as Mummy."

"I didn't like to tell the lady about having to go pee-pee. So now can I go and watch the lions and tigers on TV with Jonas? Please!"

It wasn't hard to imagine what Madrid Miller was thinking. Give her a nice puppy any day. She was a character, all right. And I decided that getting to know her and her sister Vienna would be interesting. In a neighbourly sort of way. The beginning would be something as cosily well-intentioned as a coffee morning.

# Chapter Four

*If the woodwork is varnished,
wipe with a cloth dipped
in milk-warm water. If
it is unvarnished, wipe
first and oil well.*

JONAS WASN'T EXACTLY CHUFFED WHEN I HAD SUG-
gested he come with me to the Miller sisters' house on the
morning of the Hearthside Guild meeting. He grumbled
that he didn't even know the women and didn't we have
trees enough of our own that needed tending. But I per-
sisted, asking if he didn't want to add a few more jewels to
his heavenly crown. Words I instantly regretted when he
looked thoughtful and agreed he was at that time of life
when he needed to be a sight more conscientious about
loving his neighbour.

The Millers didn't live bang next door to Merlin's Court,
but it wasn't far to their house, only a couple of turnings
past Hawthorne Lane, where Clarice Whitcombe lived. I
could easily have walked had not Jonas been with me. We
took the old convertible, which for once behaved itself and
got us to Tall Chimneys without dragging its wheels.

I had visited the house only once before, when an elderly eccentric known as the Lady in Black had been in
residence. At that time the garden had been unkempt and
a tangle of creeper had overhung the door, from which

most of the varnish was gone. Now the bushes were clipped, the lawn was mowed, and tulips and daffodils added a splash of colour to the flower beds. But as I lifted the heavy iron knocker, I shifted closer to Jonas. It was silly, but Tall Chimneys somehow reminded me of someone newly turned out in smart new clothes and flashing a freshly painted smile while still the same creepy person underneath.

When the knocker landed with more of a thud than I had intended, what sounded like a hundred and one dogs started barking. The Miller sisters had built kennels at the back of the house, where there was at least an acre of lawn and woodland. Those kennels had, according to Mrs. Malloy, cost the earth.

"What sort of dogs?" Jonas did not sound enthusiastic.

"Norfolk terriers," I reminded him. He had refused to come out and meet Madrid Miller on her Sunday-afternoon visit; otherwise he would have known pretty much all there was to know about the breed. Over several cups of tea Madrid had taken Freddy and me step-by-step through the physical and personality traits that made for a good Norfolk. Interspersed with this scintillating lecture were anecdotes about the late much-lamented Jessica, who liked to wear pink bows on her hair during the week and lilac ones on Sundays and had a passion for liver à la something or other, which she insisted on having spoon-fed to her sitting up at the table wearing an embroidered bib.

"I never did take to doggy women," sniped Jonas, his head sunk into the neck of his coat.

"That's because you're a cat man." It was taking someone an awfully long time to answer the door, despite that thunderous knock. "I'm sure the Millers are very nice women," I said firmly. "And I doubt they lured you over here under the pretext of having you look at that tree in the hopes that you'd marry one of them."

"Don't be so sure." Jonas perked up a little. "I be a prime catch at my age, with one foot in the grave and my life savings tucked under the mattress."

"You don't have anything under the mattress except those schoolboy whodunits you're afraid someone will catch you reading." I smiled at him and he gave one of his rusty chuckles before sobering.

"Aye, and that's where I should've put that mirror afore Mrs. Large went plowing through my room in her seven-league boots."

"I'll get it fixed for you," I promised. "Now, Jonas," I began, "all you're to do is look at the tree and advise them on what needs doing. Leave the pruning to someone else. I'm sure the sisters can afford to hire a man to do it."

"You'd best knock again, Ellie girl," he offered. "I don't suppose God himself could hear n'owt first time around over the racket those dogs was making."

I had my hand on knocker when the door was opened by Vienna Miller. Apologizing in a deep voice for keeping us waiting, she ushered us inside. There was nothing of the middle-aged nymph about this woman. Short and heavyset, with closely cropped hair and rather nice hazel eyes, she was completely different from her sister. No trace of the Bohemian in her dress, either. Slacks and a jumper, both of which were faded and fuzzy in places. Definitely a doggy sort of woman, I thought, trying not to look at Jonas.

"Ellie Haskell and Mr. Phipps! How good of you to come!" She bore us a little way down the narrow hall to a hat rack and clothes tree. "If you like to hang up your things, I'll take you into the sitting room. I expect you'd like a cup of tea and biscuit, Mr. Phipps, before going outside to look at the apple tree?"

"Thank ye kindly, missus." Jonas scuffed at his moustache with a finger, hiding part of his glower. "But I don't take no pleasure out of sitting along a bunch of church people, all blithering about what hymns to sing of a Sunday. I'd sooner be outside talking stuff as makes sense with old Mother Nature. When I'm done looking at the tree, I'll take a sit in your kitchen until Mrs. Haskell here is ready to go."

"I prefer kitchens to sitting rooms myself," Vienna Miller told him. She struck me, as she had on the few previous times I'd met her, as a pleasant, straightforward sort of person, but one who wouldn't stand for much nonsense. The sort there would be no getting two biscuits out of if she had decided it would be one per cup of tea.

Madrid appeared suddenly in the hall. I didn't see which door she'd come out of, but she looked harried. Her granny glasses were askew and her mouth was turned down, somehow emphasizing the jowls that didn't go with the flowing brown hair.

"Vienna, there's a problem." Madrid paid no attention to Jonas or me. "You have to come at once."

"Of course, dear, no need to panic. You know there's nothing we can't fix between us." Vienna's face softened and she spoke as one might to a child. "I'll just show Mrs. Haskell into the sitting room and be right with you." She opened a door, and taking my cue, I stepped inside. Clearly the scones were burning in the oven or possibly one of the Norfolk terrier bitches was in the process of giving birth. Watching Jonas stump down the hall after the sisters, I wondered if something about this house set the stage for melodrama.

The sitting room looked different from when the Lady in Black had lived at Tall Chimneys. The once-dark walls were now painted an off-white. The dingy net curtains were gone from the windows, letting in a view of the front garden. There was new furniture: a red carpet and a comfortable-looking sofa and chairs; a secretary desk and several sets of nesting tables. But what really caught my eye was the life-size portrait in an ornate gilt frame above the mantelpiece. It was of a Norfolk terrier with lilac bows in her hair and a shilling-sized red stone flashing on her left paw. Jessica, I presumed.

I was so busy looking at it that for a few seconds I rudely ignored the fact that several members of the Hearthside Guild were grouped in front of the fireplace like a bunch of candlesticks. Sir Robert Pomeroy, who was inclined to hold forth if given half a chance, was talking about the flower fund and how, if he were not very much mistaken, there had been a misappropriation of money. His wife—the former Maureen Dovedale being a new bride—was naturally paying close attention to his every syllable. Brigadier Lester-Smith appeared to be studying the design on the hearth rug. The fourth member of the group was Tom Tingle, who had moved to the village a couple of months previously. He was a gnomelike man with a large forehead accentuated by a receding hairline. He looked crabby. But being stuck with a name that made one sound like a storybook character who was three inches tall and lived among the hollyhocks could not be easy.

Finally Sir Robert drew breath and looked my way. He was a man well into his fifties, red-faced and bulldoggish in his country tweeds with a mustard-and-maroon cravat tucked into the neck of his shirt. "Come along, Ellie." He waved a pudgy paw in my direction. "Doesn't do to stand around like a lamppost, you know! We need your opinion on what should be done about the church secretary's behaviour."

"But Miss Hardaway is in charge of the flower fund." I looked from one face to another. "Isn't she *supposed* to send a plant or a bunch of daffs when someone is ill?"

"Only when that someone is a faithful St. Anselm's

parishioner." Sir Robert wagged a remonstrating finger. "She sent flowers to her cousin. A Mrs. Rogers who only comes to services at Christmas and Easter."

"But, dear, the poor woman almost bled to death after a hysterectomy." It was the baronet's wife speaking. I had always liked her. A pleasant-looking woman with softly waving grey hair, blue eyes, and a strawberries-and-cream complexion, she looked as comfortable in her elegant lady-of-the-manor outfit as she had done standing behind the counter of her grocery shop on Market Street.

Brigadier Lester-Smith turned pink all the way to his forehead. His crinkly hair, perhaps because of the bright sunlight breaking through the windows, already looked redder than usual. Clearly he was afraid her ladyship might elaborate on Mrs. Rogers's gynecological problems. There had always been something sweetly innocent about the man, making me wonder if even at age sixty he understood exactly where babies came from. He was now staring down at his shoes. Both were polished to their usual mirror gloss, but I was stunned to see that they weren't a matched pair.

"The point is"—Sir Robert's face puffed out like a blowfish—"Miss Hardaway had no business dipping into the flower fund to send that plant. You may all"—his eyes swept the group—"think me harsh, but I have never been able to abide anything that is sneaky, underhanded, or devious!" His voice was lost in a harsh buzzing sound coming from outside the house, commingled with a frenzied barking. After a minute or two the dogs quietened down, but the other noise continued.

"Are the Millers drilling for oil in their back garden?" Tom Tingle cocked a gnome's ear.

"It's like having all my teeth drilled at once." Lady Pomeroy attempted a smile.

"Someone's using a chain saw," supplied the brigadier.

"It's Jonas," I snapped. "They've got him pruning that tree." I was angry enough to have stormed from the room, demanding that the Miller sisters explain why they had put Jonas to work when all they had supposedly wanted was advice on what branches to lop off. But suddenly there was silence. The room stopped vibrating. The brigadier wondered aloud without raising his voice what could be keeping the Misses Miller from joining us.

"I expect they're busy in the kitchen," said Lady Pomeroy. "You know how it is when you have people in for the first time. You want everything perfect, even down to the cherries on the cakes. Why don't I go and see if I can lend a hand?" She had always struck me as a kindhearted woman, but I now wondered if Sir Robert's spiel had upset her. Was she grasping at the chance to get out of the room and sort out her feelings?

For several minutes after Lady Pomeroy had left the room the remaining four of us chitchatted about Hearthside Guild matters. Sir Robert, restored to amiability—perhaps because he no longer felt the need to flex his masterful-man muscles for his wife's benefit—expressed regret at the morning's small turnout. We usually had twice today's number present. He voiced the hope the Millers would not feel that they had opened up their home for no good purpose. Brigadier Lester-Smith put in the odd word now and then about holding youth-club meetings on the second rather than the third Thursday of the month, but he was clearly distracted. His eyes kept straying to the windows, with their view of the front garden and the path leading out to the wooded lane. Every time the dogs barked, which they did with unpleasant regularity, he would stiffen as if being told to hold his breath for a chest X-ray, and afterwards exhale slowly. Tom Tingle also appeared on edge, but this was explained when he announced with considerable urgency that he needed to "pay a visit." I told him that if I remembered correctly, there was a bathroom directly at the top of the stairs.

"I had two cups of coffee before leaving home"—he scowled as if this were my fault—"so if you will excuse me." The door clicked shut behind him.

"Odd little chap." Sir Robert caught my eye and cleared his throat. "Mean that as a compliment, of course. Understand Tingle's retired, from the family firm. Came down here for the peace and quiet, I suppose. Funny how people think nothing ever happens to rock the boat in a place like Chitterton Fells."

The brigadier wasn't listening, but I knew Sir Robert had to be reliving the day, not so very long ago, when his first wife was murdered. I'd heard it suggested he'd married Maureen Dovedale on the rebound. I hoped not, because she had been in love with him for years; she deserved some happiness after struggling to make a go of things following her late husband's death. It pleased me, therefore, when Sir Robert checked the clock on the mantelpiece and pondered aloud whether his wife had got lost looking for the kitchen.

"No sense of direction, most women!" He was back to flexing those masculine muscles. Giving his cravat a tug, he ambled over to the door. "Better go and see what's keeping the old girl. Definitely beginning to seem peculiar, our being left kicking our heels this long. Don't suppose the Millers are trying to put out a grease fire? Or chasing down burglars? What! What!"

Left to ourselves, the brigadier and I settled into a couple of arm chairs. I remembered I hadn't brought his raincoat, and uncharacteristically, he said that it didn't matter. He had also left Ben's behind. He returned to looking out of the window, while I fixed my eyes once again on the portrait of the Norfolk terrier. The expression in the eyes was soulful, almost saintly. Had it been painted after her untimely death, if indeed this was Jessica? I was wondering how her orphan puppies had fared when the door opened and Vienna came bustling into the room wheeling a wooden trolley crammed with a coffeepot, cups and saucers, and a couple of platefuls of scones and fruitcake. Behind her came Madrid, hands clasped and wearing the otherworldly look of a nun taking her morning constitutional in the convent grounds.

She flinched when Brigadier Lester-Smith got to his feet, as if shocked to find the room occupied. Her sister apologized for the delay without offering any explanation, and I wondered if the two of them had been having words about the problem Madrid had mentioned on my arrival. It most likely had been something extremely trivial, but Vienna had lost her temper. That strong jaw and firm mouth suggested a woman who didn't mince words. And I could readily imagine her sister getting unhinged and having to be soothed back to coherence with a thimbleful of brandy.

"What happened to the others?" Vienna demanded in her deep voice, which tended to vibrate around the edges as if run on a motor implanted in her throat. She glanced from me to the brigadier. "Hope they didn't give up and scoot off home? I've made enough scones for an army and we don't want to be left with too many, do we, Madrid? Not when we're both trying hard to watch our diets." She smiled at her sister, a bracing smile, filled with an affection that lit up her no-frills face. I decided it was unlikely they had quarreled. Vienna handed Madrid her cup of coffee without first serving either me or the brigadier. She even stirred in the cream and sugar and afterwards plumped up a chair cushion before Madrid sat down.

"Comfy, dear?" Vienna asked before turning and explaining to me and Brigadier Lester-Smith that her sister had been feeling a little under the weather.

"Oh, dear!" The brigadier sounded alarmed. "Not that I ever catch anything myself, but we can't know who will yet turn up; members of the Hearthside Guild sometimes arrive after the refreshment stage." He again stared, this time in mingled hope and anxiety, towards the windows. "And some people are susceptible to the least thing going around."

"It's nothing physical." Madrid shifted the curtain of hair that had fallen forward over her granny glasses. "It's just that I am"—her voice faltered—"of a melancholy nature and . . ."

"And the scones not turning out as well as she had hoped upset her." Vienna supplied this information along with a cup of coffee for me and another for the brigadier. I took a couple of tentative sips of the brew; it was only lukewarm and tasted as if it had been stewed for a week. Sir Robert and his wife returned, followed shortly afterwards by Tom Tingle. No sooner were they seated with cups and saucers and plates of scones on their laps when the sitting-room door inched open and Clarice Whitcombe poked an inquiring face into the room.

Suddenly the brigadier glowed like a schoolboy as he sprang to his feet, his plate leaping off the arm of his chair. So it was Clarice he had been watching for, I thought happily.

"The front door was ajar, so I just came in," she apologized, stepping further into the room, her eyes riveted to the brigadier's, the flush on her cheeks matching his as she fiddled with her cardigan buttons. She was wearing lipstick inexpertly applied in a shade that was a little too bright, and she had obviously taken great pains with her hair, although one side was curled a little more tightly than the other. "I suppose I should have knocked. But I thought"—tearing her eyes away from the brigadier and addressing Vienna—"that you might not want people setting the dogs barking. I could hear them woofing as I came up the path."

"I must have left the door open," Lady Pomeroy confessed. "I stepped outside to . . ."—she was clearly racking her brains to come up with a reason—"to . . . see what changes you'd made in the garden." She smiled at the sisters, a wasted effort where Madrid was concerned. That lady was staring fixedly at the portrait of the dog on the wall.

"We're glad you're here, Miss Whitcombe." Vienna bustled forward to shake hands. "As you can see, we're a small group, but the welcome is large."

"Yes, delighted, my dear lady." Sir Robert extended a well-bred hand to the latest arrival, and even Tom Tingle bestirred himself to do likewise.

"It would really make me feel at home if you'd all call me Clarice." The lady was trying extremely hard not to look at Brigadier Lester-Smith, who was rooted to the spot, incapable of speech.

"What a pretty name," Lady Pomeroy said. "I don't think I've heard of anyone else being called that."

"My father's name was Clarence and my mother was Doris, so they just put them together."

"That's interesting," I said. "And how did your parents come to name you Vienna and Madrid?" I asked the sisters.

"They were very fond of both cities." Vienna sounded slightly irritated, but that might have been because she had started to pour Clarice a cup of coffee and discovered that the coffeepot was empty. "I'll have to go and refill it," she began, but the brigadier rushed forward, sending a couple of occasional tables wobbling in the process and offered to do the honours.

"I may be a bachelor," he said, only half looking at Clarice, "but I do know my way around a kitchen." I wouldn't have been surprised had he added the information that he didn't drink or smoke, possessed a healthy bank account, had been good to his mother, didn't object to pets, and enjoyed entertaining in moderation. But he left the room without another word, after bumping into only one chair. Clarice took a seat on the sofa.

"I'm sorry I was late." She accepted a scone from Vienna and moved it around her plate. "My clock must have been wrong." She wasn't even close to being a good liar. I could guess what had kept her from getting to the meeting on time. She had rifled through her wardrobe, emptied out half her bedroom drawers, and spent half an hour sitting among the rubble on the bed regretting the fact that she had nothing to wear—nothing at any rate that would make her look ten years younger and five times more attractive than her mirror bluntly informed her was the case. I thought she looked very nice in her paisley wool frock, but I doubted she had any idea that she had knocked the socks off the brigadier.

He seemed to be an age coming back with that coffeepot. Had it taken him five minutes to steady his hands sufficiently to fit the plug in the socket to brew up another batch? Or was he even now primping in front of a mirror, smoothing down his crinkly auburn hair, sucking in his tummy and straightening his tie? The dogs started barking again and Lady Pomeroy asked if they spent most of their time in the kennels.

"Damn fine chaps, dogs," her husband put in. "But I prefer the working sort m'self. Got a black lab, Daisy— going on fourteen, she is, and still the best bird dog I've ever had." He thrust his face round to eye Tom Tingle. "Do you shoot? I'm also master of hounds, don't you know, and could provide you a decent horse. Or are you one of those bleeding hearts who'd like to see fox hunting banned?"

Tom Tingle drew himself up so that his head reached the top of the mantelpiece. "I dislike all sports. I know it's un-English, but there you are."

Silence settled heavily on the group. Was I wallowing in melodrama? Or was there really something unsettling about this house? Something dark and depressing, despite the freshly painted white walls? I shivered even though there wasn't a hint of a draft, only half listening as Lady Pomeroy tried to get the conversation back to Hearthside Guild business, with the suggestion that we hold a bring-and-buy sale in August. I moved closer to the fireplace, pretending to pay attention, but really looking at the portrait of the Norfolk terrier.

"There will never be another like Jessica." Madrid touched my sleeve and I almost jumped out of my cardigan. "So good! So beautiful! We had absolutely no trouble finding a suitor for her paw in marriage. We held an engagement party for her and the Baron Von Woofer. He was best of breed at Crufts two years in a row, but even so"—Madrid's voice cracked—"he wasn't good enough for her. There wasn't a dog alive who would have been. Madrid and I had to provide the ring. It was a ruby, our angel's birthstone. We had the artist paint it on her paw, but she wore it on a little chain around her neck."

"Did they have a wedding?" I focused on Brigadier Lester-Smith, who was back at last with the coffeepot.

Madrid parted her flowing hair to peer at me through her rimless glasses. "We had it in the garden of our old house, under the rose arbour. Vienna had made Jessica the sweetest little veil with an orange blossom wreath and she woofed in all the right places when the clergyman—who specialized in pet ceremonies—read the service. The Baron wasn't nearly so cooperative. 'Uncouth' is the word I would use, which just goes to show the best pedigree in the world doesn't always make for a gentleman. He kept sniffing around Jessica's dear little rear and even tried to climb on top of her when she was woofing 'I do!' He couldn't wait to get down to the honeymoon suite."

"Which was?" I had to chew on a smile.

"A precious little silk canopy, with a Persian rug inside and tapestry cushions with 'His' and 'Hers' embroidered on them. I'll always remember"—Madrid shifted the granny glasses to dab at her eyes—"how frightened Jessica was when the moment came, wrapping her sweet paws around my neck so that Vienna had to pry her out of my arms. Just like any other poor little virgin."

I wasn't so sure about the universality of such moments, but was saved from having to reply by Vienna's approach. She gave Madrid, who was gulping down sobs, a concerned look and squeezed her shoulder. "Why don't you go and see about more scones," she suggested as gently as her deep voice would allow, "and in the meantime I'll have a word with Mrs. Haskell."

She sat purposefully down beside me. "Ellie, I've been hoping for the opportunity to get to know you better. We're quite close neighbours, after all, and Madrid rallies a little when she's around people. She's always been sensitive and inclined to brood. A job was out of the question. Madrid couldn't have sat in an office pounding a typewriter with phones ringing right and left. So I came up with idea of breeding Norfolks. Jessica was our first." Vienna lifted her eyes to the portrait. "Sadly we lost her because we didn't know enough at the time to recognize the symptoms of eclampsia. It came on so suddenly and I'm afraid I talked Madrid out of calling in the vet. I thought it was normal for Jessica to be a little poorly after giving birth." Vienna shook her closely cropped head and squared her broad shoulders. "Luckily we did manage to raise three of the puppies. Madrid could never bring herself to hold any of them, but *one* of us had to be practical! We'd invested in a house with enough land to build the kennels and I finally convinced her we must continue as planned, although I did agree that no other dog would ever live in the house."

This sounded sad to me, but maybe most breeders housed their dogs in outside quarters and didn't attempt to make pets of them. Tom Tingle must have overheard at least part of our conversation because I heard him say he wouldn't have a dog or cat if they offered to pay half the household expenses.

"Really?" Clarice gently observed. "And I've always longed for a pet, but it just wasn't in the cards. My mother was afraid of animals, even goldfish. I remember bringing one home from school, and Mummy almost went into convulsions and Daddy had to ring the doctor. But now"—her voice brightened—"I'm free to start up a zoo if I like. A cat from down the lane comes round for afternoon tea most days and . . ."

"How fortunate that you have your piano for company, Miss Whitcombe." Brigadier Lester-Smith had to clear his throat several times between words. "I was something of a loner growing up, and I often think that if I had been taught an instrument I'd have had a happier time of it."

"The only thing I ever learned to play," Vienna said briskly into the resulting silence, "was the record player, and I can't say I was very good at that." The group acknowledged this sally with a round of chuckles.

Madrid returned with a plate of scones, moved over to Vienna, and gave her a wan smile. "How lucky I am to have you for an older sister. I feel sorry for people who have to manage life alone, especially in times of tragedy."

Sir Robert again took center stage on the hearth rug, thumbs tucked into his waistcoat pockets. "I say we're lucky, damned lucky, if you ladies will pardon the forceful language, to discover that Clarice plays the piano. You'll have to give us a couple of solos at the summer pageant, m'dear, and delight us with carols at Christmas." He was at his most expansive. "Have a word with the vicar. Our current organist, Mrs. Barrow, is hopeless. She gallops through the hymns, keeping the choir always at least one verse behind, and if the sermon goes on too long she bunks off without doing her final number, to go picketing— which seems to be her thing."

"Oh, I don't think . . . Really, I'm not all that good." Clarice sounded more flustered by the word. "I'm sure there are people far more musically gifted than I—"

"Mustn't hide your light under a bushel, m'dear." Sir Robert puffed out his chest. "One of the seven deadly sins, false modesty." Another awkward silence followed this indictment, with Maureen Dovedale looking especially embarrassed. Rallying, she asked Clarice what sort of music she particularly liked to play.

"Not much of anything at the moment, because I've got tendinitis and I'm not to strain my wrist. Well, so the doctor says."

The remainder of what Clarice had to say on the subject got lost as Vienna's deep voice boomed directly into my ear. "I understand, Ellie, you are an interior designer."

"That was my job before I married," I told her, "and I am getting back to it, a little at a time on a part-time basis."

"Then if you wouldn't think it imposing"—she was eyeing Madrid, not me, apparently gauging her reaction—"I'd like to show you the study and hear your suggestions on making it more inviting. I know you'll want to leave with the others and not keep Mr. Phipps waiting, so perhaps we could slip down the hall now, just for a couple of minutes?"

So saying, she ushered me out into the hall and I told

her how much better it looked, now that the walls were painted white and the stairs brightened with that red carpet.

"You're right, it was rather grim—like living inside a trunk until we tore out the old wainscotting." She trotted ahead of me past the dining-room door. "But the poor old girl who lived here was past looking after the place—if she'd ever done any decorating in forty years. It is important to me to make changes quickly, Ellie, because as you might guess, Madrid is tremendously susceptible to atmosphere. We moved from our former home because our neighbours let their garden go to rack and ruin and it depressed Madrid to the point where she couldn't get out of bed."

"What a shame," I answered ineptly, catching a glimpse of Jonas seated at the kitchen table through the open door. He appeared to be asleep, and I became annoyed all over again about the chain saw.

Obviously reading my mind, Vienna explained. "Mr. Phipps looked at the apple tree and, in addition to providing general advice on pruning, pointed out a dead branch that he said could break at any time. When he saw how worried Madrid was, because that tree overhangs one of the kennels, he asked if we had a saw and insisted on doing the job at once. I gave him five pounds. Such a nice old man."

"He's the world's best."

"And here's the study." Vienna turned to our right. "Even though it has French doors it never seems to get much sun—it's always such a cheerless room." She pushed open the door. Standing behind her, looking in, I was overwhelmed by the urge to agree with her. The words, however, stuck in my throat. It wasn't the dark brown paint or poorly constructed bookshelves that depressed me. It wasn't the dustpan and the scattering of fireplace ashes left on the floor or even the overturned stepladder that made my spirits sink. The focal point of unpleasantness was Mrs. Large, who was lying dead on the floor with a feather duster still cupped in her limp hand.

# CHAPTER FIVE

*The windows (sash and all) must be washed. A little soda dissolved in the water will improve appearance.*

DRIVING DOWN THE CLIFF ROAD THAT AFTERNOON, ON my way to tell Ben what had happened, I relived every shiver of that ghastly moment. Unlike me, Vienna hadn't stood rooted to the spot; she'd bent down to feel for a pulse. A ritual gesture, for it was brutally apparent from Mrs. Large's staring eyes and slack jaw that all hope was flown. Yet however badly I felt, Vienna must have felt even worse. Mrs. Large had died in her house, not mine, after all.

Now as I drove along, scenes from the last few hours kept replaying themselves inside my head: Vienna saying she didn't know how to break the news to Madrid, while looking like a woman who could cope with flood, famine, and pestilence at a go if duty called. Madrid going into hysterics. The shocked faces of the other members of the Hearthside Guild. Paramedics charging down the narrow hall. My talking with a kindly policewoman.

Somewhere in the middle of all this I phoned my friend Frizzy Taffer. One of her children went to the same play school as the twins. I hastily explained what had happened and asked Frizzy if to take the twins to her house, to which she just as hastily agreed.

As soon as I was able to leave Tall Chimneys, I took Jonas home and made him lunch before setting off for Abigail's. I didn't plan to fall sobbing into Ben's arms, but I needed to be with him. Perhaps if I had known Mrs. Large was at Tall Chimneys, doing her half day or whatever it was, the shock wouldn't have been quite so great. But of course it wasn't to be expected that either sister would have mentioned her presence. Probably they had told Mrs. Large company was expected and to leave the hall and rooms at the front of the house until everyone left.

It was now early afternoon, and a glorious one at that. The pink and white loveliness of blossom was just appearing on the trees and a lazy-hazy drift of clouds tinged with gold drifted in a pale blue sky. There was not a hint of the rain that had seemed likely earlier in the day. No sharpness in the air to suggest Mother Nature had taken Mrs. Large's passing to heart. Turning onto Market Street, I looked for a parking place. If I'd been thinking sensibly I would have realized that the one I found wasn't big enough to accommodate a child's tricycle.

I had the nose of the car against the curb and the back end jutting out into traffic, much to the annoyance of a passing Jeep, who gave me a distinctly four-letter honk. That's the trouble with driving a convertible, it's very easy to make a public spectacle of oneself. Worse was to come. Just as I was attempting to go into reverse and bounced forward instead, who should appear alongside but my dear cousin Freddy!

"Don't gloat," I told him.

"I never make cracks about women drivers," he responded smugly. "Do you want to get out and let me straighten up for you?"

"Thanks, but no. Just tell me when I hit something."

Being Freddy, he had to play traffic cop, jerking his thumb this way and that, looking as though at any moment he would give a blast of a whistle. After but one harrowing moment—when I thought I was about to collide with a lorry—I turned off the engine and dropped my hands from the wheel. Safely double-parked.

"This is just fine," Freddy informed me blithely, "because if you're thinking of crossing the street and going around the corner to Abigail's you might want to change your mind. Ben's got a lot going on at the moment."

"Is business picking up?"

"We've got people knee-deep at the door."

"That's wonderful," I said as my heart sank. The news about Mrs. Large would have to wait. If I barged into Abigail's now with my tale of woe, the distraction might be sufficient to cause Ben to curdle the hollandaise sauce and oversteam the asparagus, thus ruining his chances of winning back his customers' hearts.

"Yes, it's all very exciting." Freddy didn't sound as jubilant as might have been expected. But I didn't pay much attention. Neither did I consider telling him about Mrs. Large— Ben mustn't get the news at second hand. Surely—I was wavering—there wouldn't be any harm in looking in at Abigail's, just in case he had a few minutes free. Even to catch a glimpse of my husband's reassuring back would be something. "I really do have to see Ben." I started to open the car door, but my cousin poked his head through the opening.

"Ellie, don't you have to pick up Abbey and Tam from play school?"

"Frizzy Taffer's getting them."

"Then why don't you go off and have a day to yourself, coz?" Freddy gave the car bonnet a pat. "Think of all that lovely spring cleaning waiting to be done. Or better yet, you could take a drive along the coast and commune with old Mum Nature."

"You're being awfully thoughtful, Freddy."

"I know." He tossed his ponytail. "When I looked out the window and recognized the car, I came at the run to save you from putting any more dents in this dustbin on wheels."

"Well, thanks," I said.

Had I not been so preoccupied by the nightmare of finding Mrs. Large's body, as well as weakened by hunger—having skipped breakfast and eaten only one scone at Tall Chimneys—I would have realized that my cousin was up to something. I'm not usually quite as dense as he thinks I am.

"If you really think my timing is bad," I said, deciding I was being immature and selfish, "I'll wait to talk to Ben until he gets home."

"That's the ticket," Freddy didn't actually give the car a push, but close. Turning my head at the traffic light, I saw him cross the road, dodging nimbly between cars, ponytail flying, and turn the corner of Market Street and Spittle Lane. But since I was heading in the opposite direction I didn't get to see the march of customers entering and exiting Abigail's.

Still in a woolly state of mind, I thought about picking up the twins from Frizzy's, but decided to wait. I needed to get myself together. I hadn't driven more than a few yards past the traffic light when I spotted a parking place directly outside Bellingham's, Chitterton Fells's attempt at Harrods. Usually one had to park one's car on top of at least two others to get anywhere close to the entrance. So I decided the gods were telling me something and my insides rumbled in agreement. Bellingham's has a cafeteria on the second floor where they dish up good old British cooking in large quantities at reasonable prices.

As I came level with the perfume and cosmetics counter on my way to the escalator, a saleswoman caught my eye and I returned her smile. Unfair! I probably set her heart racing at the prospect of selling me a lipstick. Passing the home furnishings department I slowed and found myself holding a fringed velvet cushion. Given the fact that the study at Tall Chimneys had been a gloomy room to begin with, would the Miller sisters ever be able to cheer it up with enough cushions and lap rugs to banish Mrs. Large's ghost? Would any amount of redecorating enable Vienna to plaster over the memory of the dead woman's look of bulgy-eyed, slack-jawed surprise? Or rid herself of the feeling that somewhere inside that still body was a mind frantically trying to blink itself back to life, so Mrs. Large could sit up and explain how she had come to fall off that stepladder?

I realized, getting my feet moving again, that I was projecting my thoughts onto Vienna. And the last one was rubbish. Because why would it be important for Mrs. Large to have a final say? Unless . . . —I came to a halt in Bellingham's aisle—unless she hadn't misjudged her step or turned suddenly dizzy while dusting the bookcases. Unless (feeling wobbly myself) the reason she had taken a fatal tumble was that someone had given the stepladder a shove. A saleswoman stopped folding bath towels to inquire whether I needed assistance, and I found myself buying a couple of facecloths while trying to figure out what had got into me. People have accidents. They keel over all the time from heart attacks. Mrs. Large's abrupt passing was sad, but there was nothing sinister about it. Was there?

What I needed was lunch, but after gathering up cutlery and pushing my brown plastic tray along the chrome railing of the cafeteria counter, I couldn't decide between the Cornish pasties or the turkey with sage and onion dressing. The server stood trying to look patient while swinging her giant serving spoon like a clock pendulum between the metal pans.

Then someone tapped me on the shoulder. "Mrs. Haskell?"

"Yes," I turned to face a tiny elderly woman clutching a very large handbag with both hands.

"I've just heard the awful news." Her face was pinched with distress. "I mean about poor Gertrude Large."

"Oh," was all I could get out. The cafeteria server huffed in the background.

"You see, I clean for Mrs. Taffer, and I was there when you rang. Me and Gertrude was friends." The tiny woman dropped her handbag and wiped at her eyes as I picked it up for her. "So naturally Mrs. Taffer told me what you'd told her, and I fair broke down. Just couldn't help it. And now here I am talking away without saying my name." She reached into the bag for a hanky and blew her reddened nose. "You did meet me once at a bus stop when I was with Roxie Malloy, but you wouldn't remember that."

"But I do," I said, the light finally dawning. "You're Mrs. Smalley."

"And a member of the C.F.C.W.A." A tinge of pride crept into her voice even as she continued to dab away at the hanky. "We're a close-knit little group, but Gertrude was always closer to Roxie than the rest of us, which has me thinking she might have spilled the beans to her."

"About what?" I asked, finally sliding my tray down the counter to the sandwiches and salads covered in plastic wrap, where I could help myself.

"That's just it." Mrs. Smalley squeezed up close to me and lowered her voice to a whisper. "She wouldn't open up to me, nor Betty and Trina. Not one to pour out her troubles, was Gertrude. Kept a lot inside. But it was clear she was worried about something—she was almost sick about it. I did think she might have mentioned something to Roxie."

"But Mrs. Malloy is in London," I said stupidly, adding a bag of crisps to the tomato and cheese sandwich on my plate.

"Gertrude could've gone and seen her," suggested Mrs. Smalley helpfully, "and there's always the phone."

Of course there was, and instantly the foggy feeling of unease underlying the shock of Mrs. Large's death crystallized. Now I knew why the thought had entered my mind that she might have been pushed off that stepladder. It was that phone call from Mrs. Malloy the other morning. As I added a cup of tea to my tray and the girl at the cash register rang up my bill, I tried to remember exactly what Mrs. Malloy had said. But what I recalled most was how upset I'd been at Mrs. Large's breaking Jonas's mirror.

"Why don't we find a table and talk?" I suggested and Mrs. Smalley gratefully agreed. We were soon settled in a corner by the window overlooking Market Street.

"It's kind of you to talk to me, Mrs. Haskell." Mrs. Smalley took a birdlike sip of her tea and set the cup back in its saucer with a rattle. "You see, it's been playing on my mind ever since I got the news. About Gertrude's being that worried and upset, I mean. She was never what you could call jolly-like, but this was different. All fingers and thumbs she got to be, which she never was. Told me she broke a teapot washing up at Brigadier Lester-Smith's, one that belonged to his mother, an ugly old thing Gertrude called it, but all the same . . ."

"Mrs. Large broke a mirror at my house." I hastened to add that I wasn't saying this to tell tales. "And I remember she arrived late that morning, which says something, I suppose, seeing that it was her first time working for me. She mentioned having had a bad night. But she did a wonderfully thorough job. And while she was still there, Mrs. Malloy phoned." I was about to repeat what I remembered of the conversation relating to Mrs. Large, but stopped myself in time. It was up to Mrs. Malloy to do the talking, or not, as she chose.

"Roxie knew Gertrude would be at your house that day?" Mrs. Smalley nodded to herself. "That tells you something, doesn't it, about how close they was?"

"Mrs. Malloy was the one who put in a good word for me with Mrs. Large. So it's only natural that they may have discussed days." I took a bite of my sandwich and a swallow of tea, waiting for my companion to sort out her thoughts.

"Mrs. Taffer said that Lady Pomeroy—Maureen Dovedale that used to be—was one of them there at Tall Chimneys when it happened. I'll bet she took the news bad," Mrs. Smalley had to resort to the handkerchief again.

"Everyone was shocked, but yes, I think Lady Pomeroy seemed the most upset," I said.

"Save for Roxie there wasn't nobody closer to Gertrude than Maureen. Grew up together, they did, went to the same school and Saturday morning pictures together. And they stayed friends, which isn't always easy when you've got homes to run, besides helping out the hubby by putting money on the table. Well, there's one good thing." Mrs. Smalley stowed away the hanky and I waited for her to put a positive spin on the situation. "Gertrude's Frank has been dead this good many years, so there's no need to worry about him having to rush out and buy a black suit. There's the children, two daughters, both of them married and living not too far from here, but they was never what you could call chums with their mum. She wasn't, if you get me, Mrs. Haskell, the cuddly sort. But truer heart there never was—decent and honest. Gert wouldn't have picked up a penny in the street without taking it down to the police station." Mrs. Smalley's voice cracked. "You'll have to excuse me, Mrs. Haskell, I suppose it's the shock that's got me rattling away like this, and after all you've been through, finding the body and all."

"Vienna Miller was there, too." I put down my barely nibbled sandwich.

"A nice lady, from what Gertrude said, and wonderful good to her sister, the one that suffered a terrible tragedy some years ago. Leastways, that's the word going around."

"There was a little dog that died."

Mrs. Smalley had been blowing her nose as I spoke and now looked up at me. "A little boy, did you say?"

"No, a dog. Her name was Jessica."

"Well," digesting this information, "there's heartbreak everywhere you look, isn't there? I suppose the vicar would tell me to be glad Gertrude's in a better place, and maybe I could think that way if she'd gone peaceful in her bed. But I don't think she was peaceful. And if she went with something on her mind, who's to say she'll ever rest proper in her grave, Mrs. Haskell?"

"I think you need to talk to Mrs. Malloy," I said, "and see if she can shed any light on what was worrying Mrs. Large. And what about Lady Pomeroy? Perhaps Mrs. Large confided in her."

"Oh, I wouldn't think so." Mrs. Smalley shook her head. "Gertrude told me things had to be different after Maureen married. Said it wouldn't have done for them to go on being pals, not in the old way. They had to think of Sir Robert. A man in his position and all wouldn't want his wife in thick with the woman who cleaned his house. Gertrude counted herself lucky she got to stay on at Pomeroy Hall, even after working there thirteen years. She was careful as can be to draw a line between the past and the present."

We sat in silence for a few moments, after which I asked Mrs. Smalley if she had Mrs. Malloy's phone number in London. She said she was almost sure she had written it down in her address book, but just to be on the safe side, I said I'd give it to her again.

"There isn't something you haven't told me?" Mrs. Smalley leaned forward. "You're not keeping anything back?"

"What sort of thing?" I dropped my pen and watched it roll across the laminated tabletop.

"Well, about how Gertrude died." The small elderly face was more pinched than ever. "For instance, did the people that looked at her—the doctors and police and such—say if she went quick?"

"I'm sorry, no one said very much to me at all." I picked up the pen as it was about to roll off the table. "There was very little information I could provide. And they talked to the Miller sisters in private."

Mrs. Smalley wrapped work-worn hands around her teacup. "You're sure no one said nothing about how maybe it wasn't no accident that killed Gertrude?"

"Not to me. What are you thinking?"

"Well, what has had me scared is thinking that . . ."

"Yes?" I leaned forward and Mrs. Smalley did the same, until our faces were only inches apart.

"That . . . it was done on purpose."

My nose almost collided with hers. "You mean, someone pushed her off that ladder?"

"Well, now." She straightened up. "I wasn't thinking nothing like that. People don't really get murdered, do they? Leastways not people we know. What I meant, Mrs. Haskell, was that what with the nasty minds some people have, it might be said Gertrude did it on purpose. Jumped off that ladder, I mean, because she was in a depressed state of mind and wanted to end it all. 'Course anyone that knew her well wouldn't believe that for a minute. Not of a God-fearing woman like Gertrude, but—"

"Oh, Mrs. Smalley!" I covered her shaking hands with mine. "You're worrying for nothing. It was a stepladder. A tall one, but not the kind used for cleaning second-floor windows. No one jumping off a stepladder would have a hope of killing themselves. If Mrs. Large didn't fall because she was taken ill, she must have lost her footing and come down at the wrong angle or hit her head just that bit too hard."

Mrs. Smalley gave me a watery smile. "It must be the shock, making me think silly."

Which made two of us, I thought, sucking in a relieved breath, because what held true for suicide did the same for murder. If someone had wanted Mrs. Large dead, surely they would have come up with a method that had a strong possibility of success? No murderer would want his intended victim hopping up, not dead and eager to point an accusing finger. But what if it were a case of something in between? What if someone had entered the study at Tall Chimneys while Mrs. Large was on the stepladder? Mrs. Large, who, according to my brief phone conversation with Mrs. Malloy, was worried because she had discovered something about someone and wanted advice. And what if that someone with a secret to keep confronted Mrs. Large in the study and, losing all control, gave that ladder a shove?

"You've been so kind." Mrs. Smalley's voice snapped me back into the present. "If I didn't already have all my days filled, I'd be glad to come and work for you. But if you are looking for someone now that Gertrude's gone, I could talk to Trina McKinnley when she gets back from her holidays. That should be the day after tomorrow, if I remember rightly. A couple of her ladies have moved away and Trina told me she'd wait till she got back to take on anyone new. Poor girl!" Mrs. Smalley sighed. "Trina's going to be more shocked than any of us when she hears the news."

"Why?"

"Because it could have been her on that stepladder this morning. It was only because Trina was on holiday that Gertrude went to clean for the Millers. Gertrude was good that way, always kept a half day free so she could fill in if one of our little group needed her to."

"How kind of her," I said. "And I really would appreciate your asking your friend about coming to work for me."

"She's not just a friend, is Trina. More like the daughter I never had." Mrs. Smalley's pale face creased into a smile. "Confides in me, she does, all about her boyfriend. Not much, he isn't. And I worry about him knocking her about, even though Trina's a girl who knows how to look after herself. But there I go rattling on again, when I expect you need to be going, love. Oh, I do beg your pardon—Mrs. Haskell."

I smiled back at her. "I'm glad we met, despite the sad circumstances." Getting to my feet and gathering up my bag, I hesitated, wondering if she was also ready to leave. But she explained she had to wait for her colleague, Betty Nettle. They had arranged to meet for a quick bite to eat and some shopping.

"She must have got held up," said Mrs. Smalley. "But she'll be here. She knows I'll wait. Telling her about Gertrude isn't going to be easy."

Feeling rather as though I were leaving a baby on a doorstep, I said good-bye. I was almost out the door when I heard a peevish female voice at close range; she wasn't talking to me, but to someone named Edward. Even so, I turned around and looked to where a couple were standing at the cafeteria counter.

"But you know I've been wanting to go to Abigail's, Edward, ever since your mother told us what a wonderful meal she had there a few months back." The woman had one of those expensively simple haircuts and wore a silk scarf in spring tones draped around the shoulders of a pink mohair coat. "I can't tell you how disappointed I am." She was now begrudgingly placing a napkin-rolled set of cutlery onto a tray.

"Yes, my dear," responded the man with the practiced patience of one who began a lot of sentences this way. "But what would you have me do? I didn't put those picketers outside that restaurant, now did I, dear? And if you had insisted on going in, I would have been right behind you."

"I'll say! Cowering under my skirts!" The woman gave a derisive snort and slapped away the man's hand as he reached for a roll and butter, which in all fairness, from the looks of him, he may not have needed.

"Of course I was frightened," he protested after sucking on his knuckles. "Any reasonable person would have been, getting shouted at like that. Being called a blood-sucking, gristle-chewing cow murderer isn't my idea of a day's outing; but if you had been prepared to risk your life to . . ."

I didn't stay to hear more. Now I knew why Freddy had overcome his aversion to exerting himself in order to cross the street and dissuade me from going to Abigail's. His heart hadn't been touched because I was having trouble parking. He had been bent on preventing me from seeing those picketers. People standing knee-deep at the door, he had said! Talk about skirting the letter of the truth. Undoubtedly Ben had been fully occupied making sure none of the waiters or waitresses stood too close to the windows, just in case one of those opposed to the spilling of animal blood tossed a brick at the window.

The escalator brought me down by the Estée Lauder cosmetics counter. From there it was only a few yards to the Market Street exit. I saw no point in driving and having to re-park outside Abigail's. It was a short walk and I needed time to simmer down. I couldn't be cross with

Freddy, who'd undoubtedly had my interests at heart. But I was both angry and alarmed. I was tempted to charge into the thick of the picketers and start hitting them with my handbag. I needed to squash those feelings. Ben didn't need me making things worse by getting myself arrested.

Sunlight sprinkled the pavement with fairy dust. Unfair, I thought. Where was rotten weather when you needed it? It should be pouring down rain, drenching the picketers to the bone. So that they could enjoy suffering for the cause.

Turning the corner onto Spittle Lane, I saw them. A straggling group of people was standing outside Abigail's, all holding their placards aloft—although not as high, I hoped, as before their arms started to cramp up. Most of the signs read: "Stop the Slaughter. Don't Eat Veal." A couple brandished the words "Thou Shalt Not Murder." And some were splattered with brownish-red paint—at least I hoped it was paint.

One face stood out in the crowd. It belonged to Mrs. Barrow, the church organist, a woman known to be militant on a number of issues, including sending missionaries to Mars to convert the aliens. It was she who had organized the anti-fur drive a couple of years back, as well instigating a writing campaign to Queen Elizabeth demanding that the Tower of London be torn down because it glorified the nation's bloody, barbaric past. Ignoring her pitying look, I marched forward to the chant of "Old Mac-Donald Had a Farm," with a lot of "Eeh aye, eeh aye, oh's" (presumably from the poor little calves who had just discovered they weren't just pasture decorations), and almost collided with a teenage girl. It was Frizzy Taffer's daughter, Dawn, someone hard to miss at any time. Her long, once-brown hair was streaked flamingo pink and lime green. And she wore more eyeliner than Cleopatra. Her placard read: "People Who Kill Baby Calves Should Be Eaten Themselves."

"Hello, Dawn," I said. "Shouldn't you be in school?"

"Oh, hello, Mrs. Haskell." Her expression became one of mingled embarrassment and defiance as she slung her sign over her shoulder, almost knocking out the eyes of the man standing behind her. "I took the afternoon off; anyway, it was only boring old geography." She shrugged. "Who needs to learn that stuff when we've got travel agents to tell us the really important stuff—like don't go to Rome in the winter because you won't get a tan. And places to really party in Spain." Her confidence was mounting. "I don't care if you tell Mummy you saw me; she and Daddy can lock me in my room for a week and feed me only bread and water. Sometimes you have to stand up for what you believe in, whatever the consequences."

There was no point in arguing with her. Dawn had already made up her mind what she wanted to be when she grew up—a martyr. But she was only a child and I was rather fond of her. So I couldn't see myself carrying tales to Frizzy, who was even now watching my children. I urged Dawn to own up before someone, as was bound to happen, spilled the beans that he had seen her sporting a picket sign. Then, sidestepping the rest of the bunch, I ran up the steps shaded by the dark green awning.

Abigail's entryway looked as it always did, dignified but inviting. I loved the narrow hall, with its Regency-striped wallpaper and the eighteenth-century rent table serving as a reception desk. I loved the way the walnut banister looped at the bottom like the satin-smooth coil of a young girl's hair. I loved the long case clock that stood at the foot of the stairs. And most of all I loved the man now walking towards me.

"I thought Freddy persuaded you to go home." Ben

stood with his hands deep in his pockets, a rueful smile on
his lips.

"No one and nothing can keep me away from you for
long," I said, dropping my shoulder bag on the floor and
tossing down my cardigan in an impetuous heap.

"What is this?" He raised a bemused eyebrow. "Have
you come to take advantage of me in this, my most desperate hour?"

"Don't be silly. I'm a wife, so naturally I throw my
things on the floor and expect you to pick them up." I
put my arms around his neck and drew his face down to
mine in a long, deep kiss, making for one of the most
thrilling embraces we had shared in a long time. It was as
though something was dredged up from deep inside me,
some emotion that I had experienced only once before—
when the twins were born. The blossoming of that primi-
tive protective instinct, the one that enables women to
scale buildings in a single bound or lift up lorries with one
hand while directing traffic with the other in order to
rescue their children from danger. Women can wear coats
of shining armour too, the only difference being that his-
torically we have always worn them under our everyday
clothes.

"Who cares if the staff is watching?" I whispered, coming up for air and twining my fingers through the dark
curls at the nape of my husband's neck.

He held me tighter and traced another kiss across my
lips. "I sent them home, even Freddy."

"So it's just you and me and all this lovely empty space,"
I said, promptly bringing us both back to reality.

"Unless we count the picketers at the gates."

"Darling, I'm so sorry."

"I wish you hadn't had to see them." Ben stepped back
but did not let go of my hands.

"Rubbish!" I tried to speak briskly. "You can't help it if those people out there are a bunch of crackpots."

"Not all of them, Ellie." He smiled wryly. "Some of my best friends are vegetarians."

"Well, Mrs. Barrow is a fruitcake if ever there was one."

My staunch protest was once again silenced with a kiss, and then he asked the inevitable question. "What did you want to talk to me about, sweetheart? Freddy said you seemed all on edge."

"It was about the Hearthside Guild meeting, or rather what happened at the meeting." My lips quivered but I looked steadily at him. "Vienna Miller was showing me the study and we walked in on an overturned stepladder and Mrs. Large lying dead on the floor."

"My God, Ellie!" Ben drew me to him and stroked my hair. "What a shock! What happened?"

"I don't know." I lifted my face, drawing immense comfort from the look in his eyes. "There'll be a postmortem and I suppose an inquest if it turns out that she did die from the fall, rather than some medical problem like a thrombosis or something similarly quick."

"Didn't anyone hear the crash?" Ben raised a questioning eyebrow. "Tall Chimneys isn't all that big a house."

"The Millers' dogs barked quite a lot," I told him, "or it could have happened, I suppose, when Jonas was using the electric saw. He had gone with me, you see, to take a look at a tree that needed pruning and ended up taking off a dead branch or two. We couldn't hear ourselves talk, let alone anything else when that was going on."

"But the thinking is that it happened during the Hearthside Guild meeting?"

"Well, that's what I've been assuming," I said, "although I suppose it could have been before. But not much, because Mrs. Large's starting time was nine o'clock. Someone—a policeman or one of the paramedics—did ask Jonas if he had seen anything, since he was out in the garden a good part of the time and the study has French windows. But he said he never went near them."

"I think what you need"—Ben cupped my face in his hands—"is something to eat and drink in peaceful surroundings. You don't have to rush home, do you?"

"No, Abbey and Tam are with Frizzy."

"Good." Ben propelled me down the hall. "You go and freshen up while I prepare a meal fit even for you, my Greek goddess. Lamb and rice deliciously seasoned with anise and turmeric, wrapped into little grape-leaf bundles and sautéed in a delectable persimmon sauce."

How, I wondered, looking after him as he disappeared into the kitchen, did I get so lucky? He was quite right, I *was* hungry, having barely nibbled my sandwich at Bellingham's. Even the thought of a meal revived me. While in the pretty powder room off the hall, I pondered what suggestions I could make about restoring Abigail's reputation. But when I went into the elegant dining room and saw the white linen-clad table Ben had prepared for us—one small inhabited island among a sea of deserted ones—I decided to bide my time. There would be plenty of opportunities to talk about all that when we got home. Now I sensed that both of us needed to let the unpleasantness of the day float beyond the horizon.

Ben had prepared a truly superb meal in what to me seemed an impossibly short time. We allowed ourselves just one glass of champagne, because we would both be driving. The stuffed grape leaves were preceded by a fresh fruit salad and followed by a dark, dense, and delicious chocolate torte. And neither of us allowed grim thoughts to intrude.

My mother had told me something about love. She'd said that it was like a river and that sometimes after you have been married for a while it settles into a gentle flow, very pleasant and safe. And lovely in its way. But suddenly, just when it is least expected, the river makes a sharp bend and there is a new sense of wonder, so that the middle becomes the beginning again—only better, because now there is a shared past to buoy the husband and wife up when they go over the rapids.

# CHAPTER SIX

*After being washed, the windows should be dried with crumbled newspapers. Polish wood floors to a rich gloss by attaching buffing cloths to the feet.*

MRS. LARGE'S FUNERAL TOOK PLACE ON AN AFTERNOON turned grey and rainy after a sunny morning. That was spring, I thought. Like a young girl on the brink of womanhood, bursting with smiles one minute and all teary the next.

Ben came with me and it was nice to see that the front pews of St. Anselm's were full. A good number of Hearthside Guild members had turned out, including all who had been at the fateful coffee morning. Sir Robert and Lady Pomeroy, Brigadier Lester-Smith, Tom Tingle, and Clarice Whitcombe were all seated two rows in front of us. The Miller sisters sat directly in front of them. The one person conspicuous by her absence was Mrs. Malloy.

I had telephoned the London flat as soon as Ben and I returned home that night, but got only George, who explained in an agitated voice that his mother was busy with the baby. So I asked that Mrs. Malloy ring me back. Not having heard from her by the next morning, I tried again. I thought George might have forgotten to relay the message. My cousin Vanessa answered this time and demanded to

know, in a voice verging on hysteria, what I could be thinking to call at such an ungodly hour. (It was eleven o'clock.)
Didn't I realize how little sleep new mothers got, lying
awake half the night worrying if they would ever get their
figures back and whether the baby would ever learn to give
itself a bottle? Or maybe—voice spiraling into a yell—I
wouldn't know, never having been a sex symbol and seeming to enjoy the grind of being a mother. By the time
Vanessa wound down, I was wrung out, but I still managed
to stress that a friend of Mrs. Malloy's had died and would
she please phone me back. Unfortunately, as so often happens, when Mrs. Malloy finally rang I was out—picking up
the twins from play school. But Jonas, who begrudgingly
took the call (not holding with telephones), reported that
he had given her the time and date of the funeral, and she
had assured him she'd be there.

So why, I thought, turning my head to peer at the empty
pews behind me, hadn't she come? Was she having such a
grand old time in London that she couldn't tear herself
away even for a few hours? Or had Vanessa gone into a
major snit? Saying she shouldn't be expected to look after
baby Rose all by herself and that if Mrs. Malloy were any
kind of grandmother at all she would know where her duty
lay. Very probably. I knew just how ruthless my cousin
could be in pursuit of getting her way, but I also knew Mrs.
Malloy. Making it hard to picture her lightly setting aside
loyalty to an old friend.

The vicar—a visiting one, because our regular was away
on holiday—concluded the eulogy, the usual sort of thing
when not knowing the deceased from Adam or Eve. He
praised Mrs. Large as a good Christian woman and wished
her good speed and all the best, rather as if she were tod-
dling off for a fortnight at the seaside. Mrs. Barrow played
the final hymn at full gallop; probably, I thought nastily,

because she couldn't wait to rush off and picket to her heart's content. Her troops hadn't paraded outside Abigail's for the past several days. Ben thought they would be back after enjoying a change of scene in front of the Odeon, currently showing *Jane Eyre*—which Mrs. Barrow staunchly believed should have included a caption warning against the dangers of living in antiquated houses not equipped with smoke detectors.

The coffin was borne from the church, followed at a stately remove by the clergyman and, a few steps behind, by two women whom I concluded to be Mrs. Large's daughters. They were both six-footers and solidly built. As they drew level with my pew, I heard one complain that the hymns had given her a headache. And the other said she hoped they would not have to stand too long at the grave.

It was still drizzling when Ben and I fell in line behind Brigadier Lester-Smith. He was wearing a bottle-green raincoat, which reminded me that I still had to return the one Ben had taken home by mistake. We made our way along the moss-grown path to the graveside to huddle with the other mourners under a gnarled old tree that looked as though it had been ordered to stand there indefinitely as penance for a lifetime of sin. While the vicar fumbled in his vestment pockets for his prayer book and produced everything but (including a couple of dog biscuits, a set of keys, and a black sock), I looked around for the Miller sisters.

They stood only a few feet to my left, sandwiched in between Tom Tingle and the brigadier. Vienna looked composed and tweedy in an old-fashioned suit and a felt hat with a wisp of feather tucked in the side. It could have been there by design or the result of a molting pigeon flying overhead. Madrid wore one of her trailing Flower

Child outfits, but I couldn't see her face. Her head was bowed, her long hair falling forward, so she looked rather like a weeping willow, shivering a little in the wind. I had thought about the Millers a good deal, wondering how they were doing. Would it have been easier for them had it turned out that Mrs. Large had succumbed to some dire ailment? Rather than dying as a result of the fall—as had proven the case? Did Vienna and Madrid lie awake at night questioning whether the stepladder had been sufficiently sturdy, or the floor uneven?

The vicar had now found his little book and was rustling through its pages for the appropriate passage while the little black marker ribbon flapped in the breeze. My thoughts returned to Mrs. Malloy. How could she have failed to attend? Surely her fellow members of the C.F.C.W.A. would feel she had let them and the organization down.

My gaze shifted to where Mrs. Smalley stood, looking more than ever like a workhouse waif in a black coat that was clearly borrowed, being three or four sizes too big for her. Her nose was reddened either from crying or the cold. Alongside her stood a stringy woman with heavy eyebrows, a beaky nose, and dark hair liberally streaked with grey, bound around her head in a double row of tightly woven plaits. Mrs. Nettle, I wondered? She certainly looked prickly enough to fit the name. Standing just behind her was a curly-haired youngish woman, arm in arm with a man of similar age in a black leather jacket. From the scowl on his face and the restless shifting of his feet, I suspected he thought only dead people should go to funerals. Trina McKinnley, I presumed? I drew back so she wouldn't catch me staring.

Ben squeezed my hand. I shifted closer within the circle of his arm as the vicar recited the burial prayers in a voice almost as brisk as the wind. His cassock flapped against his legs and his hair fell forward in a monk's fringe. Mrs. Large's daughters stepped forward to toss handfuls of earth onto the coffin and others straggled forward to do likewise. I tried to read the faces as they went by. Brigadier Lester-Smith leaped forward, at the risk of getting mud on his shoes, to offer a steadying hand when Clarice Whitcombe moved within a few feet of the grave's edge. The man in the black leather jacket wore the pained expression of someone having several body parts pierced at once. Mrs. Smalley was sobbing hard and being lectured on being dignified by the woman I took to be Mrs. Nettle. Lady Pomeroy looked truly grief-stricken as she bent to lay a small posy of flowers on the sod-strewn grass. But mostly people looked more moved by the cold and damp than anything else.

It was time to go. And as we wended our way between the tombstones, many of them dating back to the seventeenth century, I caught the eye of one of Mrs. Large's daughters and stopped to introduce myself and Ben before offering our condolences.

"Haskell!" She chewed on the name with a good-sized set of dentures, while looking more at Ben than at me. "Oh, I get it! You're one of the ladies that found Mum. Must have been a nasty shock. Life pulls some funny tricks, don't it! But it's good she went quick. She wouldn't have wanted to linger and be a burden to me and Roberta." She jerked a gigantic thumb in her sister's direction. "And I doubt Mum would have been an easy patient, tending as she did to look on the dark side at the best of times. Not what you could call a cheerful Charlie, if you get me."

"Well, I'm sure you'll miss her" was all I could think to say, and Ben added a few words about it always being hard to lose a parent.

"I guess it'll take some getting used to," the woman

agreed without much conviction, "not hearing Mum's voice on the phone every few months or bumping into her in the high street of a now and then. But as they say"— looking around and beckoning to her sister—"life goes on, and right now me and Rob need to be getting down to see Mr. Wiseman, the solicitor, about the will. Doesn't do to be late for that sort of appointment, does it."

A few moments after she strode away, I heard a mocking voice say, "She's in for a surprise, her and that oaf of a sister. Gertrude won't have left them a tea towel apiece. Selfish, rotten cows!"

The speaker was the curly-haired woman. I saw Mrs. Smalley give her arm a squeeze before guiding her towards us, while the man in the black leather jacket slouched along behind.

"Trina, love," said the elderly waif, "I want you to meet Mrs. Haskell, that I was talking to you about, and this must be her hubby." She peeked at Ben. "Glad to meet you, sir, I'm sure. Ever such nice things I've heard about you from Roxie Malloy. Can't think why she hasn't turned up, it's not like her one bit."

Standing within the shadow of a very large monument to the deceased members of the Pomeroy family, Ben murmured polite somethings to Mrs. Smalley while Trina said she understood I needed someone to come in and clean.

"I realize, Mrs. Haskell, that Roxie gave you a full day once a week, but I can't manage but four hours of a morning every other week, and it'll have to be a Monday." She had snapping black eyes and a determined chin, along with a crisp way of talking that had me feeling beholden before I had agreed to anything. "You see, Tuesdays I go to Tall Chimneys. Perhaps you know Gertrude was only filling in for me because I was on my holidays, and . . ." She rattled off the names of other people she worked for, including all of Mrs. Large's former clients, whom she was taking on.

"You couldn't possibly give me a full day on alternate Mondays?" I asked hesitantly, aware that I was being scrutinized from head to toe without winning much favour by the man in the black leather jacket.

"Can't do." Trina shook her curly head. "Monday afternoon's kept for Joe here"—tossing him a glance—"and we don't get near enough time together as it is."

"You know how life goes on." He gave me a man-to-woman wink. "Got a wife at home that keeps me on a short lead."

"Pesky of her," I said.

"So you going to take these Monday mornings?" He reached into the pockets of his tight jeans and pulled out a flattened packet of cigarettes. "You won't find no one better than Trina. A real hard worker and very particular. She's got one of them—what do you call it? Photogenic memories."

"People like to have their little knickknacks and such put back just like they had them arranged. I can clear everything off for dusting, and when I'm done you wouldn't know nothing was ever moved." Trina was too self-assured to preen. "It helps that I know a lot about china and glass and stuff from being brought up by my granny that was housekeeper to an earl."

"Could you start this coming Monday?" I hoped I didn't sound too deferential.

"Don't see why not. Will nine o'clock suit?"

I said that would be perfect.

It was no longer raining, but the wind was picking up by the minute. Leather Jack or Joe stuck a cigarette in his mouth, flicked a match, and cupped his hand around the flame. He eyed Trina through a smoke ring produced, I was sure, to impress the knickers off any woman watching. "Don't you think that you need to talk to Mrs. Haskell about how you charge more than the others? Well, stands to reason, doesn't it?" He fielded me a thin smile. "You'll get twice the work out of someone Trina's age in half an hour than you'll see out of one of the old bats in a day."

I was spared from replying because Sir Robert Pomeroy, who had moved up to talk to Ben, now turned to include me in the conversation. Trina said we could discuss wages when she came on Monday and off she went with Joe, leaving me glad to see the back of him, hoisting up his jacket collar and stubbing out his cigarette on a gravestone.

"I didn't like the look of that chap," Ben observed as we drove home. I agreed, without elaborating. I was thinking about Mrs. Malloy and feeling very cross with her for not showing up at the funeral. If she had been taken ill, surely she would have had George or Vanessa telephone with the news. We all have a selfish streak, I decided, and remembered Mrs. Malloy once telling me that she wasn't keen on funerals. In fact she wasn't sure that she'd bother turning up for her own. Even so, I thought as I followed Ben into the house, we all need to make sacrifices now and then for the sake of our loved ones.

"Back already?" Freddy stuck his head around the drawing-room door and favoured us with a woeful smile. "I haven't finished teaching the children their psalm for the day."

"Mummy! Daddy!" Tam came bounding out into the hall as if he hadn't seen either of his parents since birth. "Did you have fun at the fun'ral?"

"We missed you," Abbey leaped from the sofa onto a chair and began jumping up and down, the skirt of her pink-and-white-check frock swirling with every bounce.

I stood unbuttoning my coat. "Get down from there. That chair isn't a trampoline." I thought back to the days when we first came to live at Merlin's Court. We'd had a marvelous time redecorating the old house. The drawing room had been the most fun of all. I had been lucky to find swatches of fabric and slips of wallpaper in the attic, along with discarded pieces of furniture and a wonderful Persian rug, all dating from the time when Abigail Grantham lived here. Her portrait, handsomely framed, now hung above the fireplace, and I liked to think she smiled because she was pleased to see the room looking much the way she had known it. But when picking out the ivory damask for the sofas and the Queen Anne chairs, I hadn't foreseen children. And even if I had, it would have been through rose-coloured glasses. Other people's offspring might jump, pounce, and spill things. Not mine.

Now looking down at the turquoise-and-rose carpet, I noticed several spots that had steadfastly refused to respond to the no-fail stain remover I had bought at a shop specializing in products guaranteed to put the merriment back in housework. Maybe I would have more luck using one of the formulas from Abigail's book of handy household hints. But not this minute. I settled on one of the ivory damask chairs, with Abbey and Tam on my lap.

My son burrowed his face into my neck. It was a sticky face because, as Freddy languidly confessed from the sofa, he had fed the twins chocolate and bananas for lunch. As for Abbey's hands, they would have stuck like Velcro to anything she touched. But all I could think at that moment was how much more beautiful the room was with children in it. Looking up at Abigail's portrait, I thought of the one at Tall Chimneys, of little dog Jessica in her lilac bows. I was, I decided, a very lucky woman.

"So," Freddy said, drumming his fingers on his raised knees, fingers which looked every bit as sticky as my son's, "how did old Roxie hold up at the funeral?"

"She wasn't there." Seeing that Abbey had fallen instantly asleep with that wonderful knack possessed by only the very young and the very old, I relinquished her to Ben, who whispered that he would take her up to the nursery.

"That's rum!" Freddy observed. "I thought Roxie and Mrs. Large were great mates. I trust the deceased's family at least showed up?"

"Her two daughters were there." I resettled Tam on my lap and watched his silky dark lashes flicker before his lids drifted shut.

"Did they both take after Mum?" Freddy batted at a yawn with the palm of his hand. "I mean, could you see them living in the giant's castle at the top of the beanstalk and saying 'Fe fie fo fum' every time they stubbed a toe?"

"I can imagine them saying a lot worse than that," I conceded, "if they didn't hear what they hoped to hear at the solicitor's office. They were off to see Lionel Wiseman, my friend Bunty's ex-husband, to talk to him about Mrs. Large's will."

Freddy sat up and scratched at his beard. "I wouldn't have thought that a woman in Mrs. Large's position would have a lot to leave."

"You can never tell about that sort of thing." I stroked Tam's hair. "She might have won the pools or inherited money from a nice old uncle for all we know. But Trina McKinnley thinks her daughters are in for a nasty surprise."

"Interesting!" Freddy was rapidly perking up. "Especially if one of them snuck into the study at Tall Chimneys and pushed dear old mum off that ladder in hope of getting hold of the loot sooner rather than later. And there I was"—shaking his head—"thinking the evil deed was most likely done by one of the Miller sisters, because it happened at their house. What had me stumped was the motive, but that's water under the bridge now the ugly daughters have entered the picture."

"I don't know where you come up with these crazy ideas." I didn't even try to keep the exasperation out of my voice. "Accidents happen; people fall off stepladders all the time. Mrs. Large was unlucky, she hit her head too hard, and she died. It was tragic, but if the medical examiner didn't find anything to puzzle his little grey cells, Freddy, I don't know why you should."

"You're absolutely right," he said, sounding meek. "It's just that Mrs. Large struck me as the kind of woman someone might murder one day. I'm sure Jonas thought about it when she broke that mirror of his." Freddy paused and dropped his jaw in mock horror. "Crikey, coz! What if there is an investigation into her death? The police would be bound to question Jonas because he was on the spot the day she died. They'll wheedle that business of the mirror out of him in no time. Do you think"—glancing around as if afraid the walls had ears—"we should encourage him to flee the country?"

I stood up with Tam in my arms. "Freddy, you are the absolute limit."

"Thanks." He tried to look modest. "But be honest, coz, don't tell me it's never crossed your mind that Mrs. Large was given the heave-ho into the next world."

"Not for a second," I lied. "Now let's get back to Jonas; is he taking his afternoon nap?"

"He went upstairs right after lunch, but don't go skipping off, Ellie." Freddy trailed after me as I crossed the room to the door. "You haven't finished telling me about the funeral. Were there gobs of flowers?"

I didn't get to fulfill his curiosity because Ben came down the stairs two at a time, saying he really did need to get back to Abigail's. Freddy, muttering that he liked to keep in with the boss, took Tam from me and carried him upstairs. Leaving me free to accompany my husband outside, where the skies remained murky and rain dripped off the trees.

"Couldn't you take the rest of the day off?" I urged as we neared the car. "Better yet, couldn't you—"

"Close the restaurant door, put up a 'For Let' sign, and walk away?" He turned and placed his hands on my shoulders, his eyes intent, although his mouth was relaxed, almost smiling. "Ellie, you know I can't do that."

"Why not?" I'd had this conversation before, several times in my mind, and I'd always agreed with everything I said. "We could get by. We've got it better than most people, not having a mortgage on the house. We've savings and Uncle Merlin's legacy, and I'll earn a bit here and there with the decorating. Clarice Whitcombe seems very keen for me to do work for her. And one thing always leads to another. So why shouldn't you take a break? Not to loaf," I said, reading his face, "I'm thinking more of your trying something different."

"Such as?" He still wore that half smile.

"Well, not exactly different, just not the restaurant. I've been thinking ever since I found that notebook of Abigail's in the attic that you might want to do something with it. Try out the formulas to make sure they work and then get them into shape for publication, the way you did with her recipe collection. Remember how excited we both were when we found the one for the unsinkable cheese soufflé?" I tugged on his coat sleeve. "Darling, this could be fun and you might even make us a lot of money."

"Ellie, I can't." He took hold of my hands, drew them to his lips, and kissed the tips of my fingers. "I won't walk away from the restaurant. Not to please the picketers. Not even to please you, my love. And things will turn around, just you wait and see."

"I'm sure they will, but . . ."

"But what?"

"I don't think you're really in love with the business any-more. The excitement's gone, it's become . . . just a job."

"So?" He looked up at the sky. "People don't get to chop and change careers every time they hit a rough patch or begin to find the routine a grind. I'm supposed to be a grown-up. A family man. What worries you most, sweet-heart?" He wrapped an arm around my shoulders. "Is it my being fed up with Abigail's, or that I'm turning into a bit of a bore as a husband?"

I was about to respond fiercely, but studying his somber profile, decided a lighter approach might work better. "Well, now that you bring it up, darling, and if you're sure it won't hurt your feelings, I have to admit that when I meet a man like Joe—Leather Jacket—at the funeral, I do get to thinking that life *could* be a lot more interesting."

Ben was smiling as he got into the car. Before he closed the door I bent down to kiss him.

"You'd better get back into the house," he urged, with that light in his eyes I loved. "It's about to pour."

"I'm sure," I said wistfully, keeping hold of the car door and kissing him again, "that Joe has at least a couple of tattoos and all of his important body parts pierced."

"Ellie, go in before you get soaked" was Ben's husbandly response as he started up the engine.

"You could at least get my name tattooed—"

"It already is, on my heart." With that he drove away and I nipped smartly back into the house because my hair was already wet and my skirt and blouse damp. Jonas and Freddy were at the kitchen table. The former still looked sleepy and the latter announced that he was starving, not having eaten a square meal since lunch. It was now only a little after three, but as it was one of my missions in life to fatten Jonas up and because I really did appreciate

Freddy's willingness to babysit, I got busy grilling sausages and tomatoes, frying a panful of chips, and rounding out the meal with heaping helpings of baked beans.

"An egg or two wouldn't have gone amiss," observed Freddy kindly when I set down the plates and went back for toast, butter, and marmalade, "but I'm glad you didn't go all out, Ellie, when you're in a rush to be off."

"Off where?" I asked, pouring cups of tea and handing the first to Jonas. "I haven't said anything about going out."

"Oh, but I can see it in your eyes." Fred extended a patient hand for his cup. "Always could read you like a book, dear coz. Comes from reading your diaries when we were children. So there's no point in telling me you aren't dying to zip along to Tall Chimneys and see how the Miller sisters survived the funeral."

"The thought never crossed my mind," I replied, not quite truthfully. Actually, I *hadn't* been thinking about Vienna or Madrid right then, but it *had* occurred to me during the service that I ought to pop in and see them.

Freddy sighed soulfully. "I wonder if they'll take down the picture of the dog, the one you said was over the mantelpiece, and put up one of Mrs. Large instead."

"There's no way they could get all of that woman inside a frame," growled Jonas, picking away at his food. "It would have to be one of them murals."

Telling him that was no way to speak of the dead, I ignored his grunted reply that he'd never been a hypocrite and didn't intend to start at his age. I collected an old raincoat from one of the hooks in the alcove and told Freddy that if he wanted me to go, he would have to stay and listen for the twins. Not that they were likely to wake up before I got back. They didn't always take naps, but when they did, they were usually down for the count for a couple of hours.

It was gusty when I set out, but I didn't see any point in driving the short distance to Tall Chimneys, especially in a convertible with a top that wouldn't go up. I pulled a scarf from my raincoat pocket and tied it around my head. With the wind shoving me along, I broke into a trot and soon found myself at the Millers' front door. It opened before I could ring the bell and Vienna ushered me inside, saying that she had just been on her way out to the shops.

"To get something tempting for Madrid's tea," she explained, tapping the woven raffia-type carrier bag strung over her arm. "The poor darling hasn't been eating well since the day of the accident. And she is not what one could call robust at the best of times. Never has been—not since she lost Jessica."

"It's all very sad," I said. Tall Chimneys was incapable of being a happy house. The staircase seemed to slink up the wall, squeezing itself into as narrow a space as possible, so that no one would notice that every one of its dark treads was eavesdropping on our conversation. The newly painted white walls should have helped, along with the strip of red carpet running down the hall, but they provided only a sense of false cheer. Luckily, Vienna did not appear to be a woman susceptible to atmosphere. She was wearing the same comfortable-looking suit she had worn at the funeral, but the hat now hung on the hall tree and I doubted that it would be worn again until somebody else died. Sensible haircut. Sensible shoes. All the dramatics must be left to her sister.

That was unkind of me and I tried to unthink the thought as Vienna shifted the carrier bag higher up her arm. My explanation that I had stopped by to see how things were going made me sound like a busybody, so I hastily added the hope that she and Madrid would come for tea one afternoon soon.

"You might like to talk to Jonas some more about the garden," I added for good measure, "and very likely you would get to meet my cousin Freddy. He's always popping in when he's not at work, and then there are the children, if you don't mind being bounced on by three-year-olds."

"What a dear you are." Vienna's face showed real pleasure. "Madrid has been so worried that we'd find ourselves shunned after what happened. But that's because she's been blaming herself that we didn't get to Mrs. Large sooner. I keep telling her the postmortem revealed the poor woman died instantly. But I can't get Madrid to believe something might not have been done if we hadn't both been so preoccupied. It's no surprise we didn't hear the crash when Mrs. Large and the ladder went down."

"You both had a lot to do," I responded, "getting ready to entertain people you hardly knew. When I'm in that situation a whole herd of elephants could come trumpeting through the house and I wouldn't hear them."

"There was something else." Vienna seemed glad of the chance to talk frankly. "I should not have agreed to have the coffee on that particular morning. Foolishly, I thought it might help Madrid get through what is always an extremely hard day for her—the anniversary of Jessica's death. But all it did was make things harder for her. She tried so bravely to help with the preparations, but she was in tears half the time, and just before you arrived, she had dropped a plate of scones. Which meant that we had to rush and make up another batch. All in all, it was extremely trying for her."

"And you're blaming yourself," I said, understanding because I was very good at doing the same thing. "But you mustn't, Vienna. If not for the accident, the coffee morning might have succeeded in cheering up Madrid just as you hoped."

Vienna shook her head. "If only, and I know this sounds

awful, Mrs. Large had died on any other day of the year, then I really think Madrid could have coped better. As it is, I'm amazed she was able to go to the funeral at all. I tried to discourage her, but she was so afraid people would talk if she didn't show up. But perhaps . . ." Vienna paused and looked at me questioningly.

"Yes?" I said, eager to be of any help.

"Perhaps if you were to go in and have a word with Madrid—she's on the sofa in the sitting room. It would let her know there are people besides her fussy old sister who care how's she doing."

"I'll be glad to."

"I would certainly feel happier going down to the shops, knowing that someone was with her. Of course, I'll hurry back. Do you mind if I just slip away now without even getting you a cup of tea?"

"Off you go." I opened the front door for her. "And don't worry, I'm in no great rush to get home."

"You're sure?" Vienna fumbled in her bag for her key. She unearthed bundles of stuff—tissues, a coin purse, an address book—but no key. She said, as she stuffed everything back, that it didn't matter because there was always the one hidden under a flowerpot by the back door. A fact that I hoped she didn't relate casually to all and sundry. That was the trouble with frank people such as Vienna; they were sometimes too trusting.

I tapped on the sitting-room door before poking my head around the corner and announcing myself. The curtains were drawn against the rain, the lights were on, although turned down low, and a fire burned in the grate. Madrid was stretched out on the sofa, her head supported by a couple of plump cushions, and a large book lay across her middle. Parting her screen of hair and tucking it behind her ears, she squinted up at me through her glasses.

"Hello," she said in a neutral voice, watching me cross

the room to her side. "I thought I heard voices in the hall, but everything gets a bit vague when I'm having one of my low spells. Where's Vienna?"

"She went down to the shops," I explained, "to fetch you something for your tea."

"Yes, I haven't been feeling very well." It's not easy to look wan and piteous when one is moonfaced and has jowls, but Madrid somehow managed it. I even thought I caught a glimpse of the very pretty girl she must have been once upon a time, before sorrow claimed her for its own.

"Vienna told me you haven't been up to snuff." I tried to strike the right note between sympathy and an attempt at raising her spirits. "You've both been through a lot, haven't you?"

"My sister is tremendously strong. Of course she's gone through the change and they say the male hormones kick in at that time. But she's always been a rock." Madrid started to heave herself up, thought better of the idea, and sank back against her cushions. "It's her being the eldest and our parents dying when we were quite young that makes her that way. I'm Vienna's entire life. But I do try not to be a burden. Would you mind"—waving a languid hand—"putting another log on the fire? And could you perhaps fetch my shawl from that chair?" She valiantly lifted her head. "The one over by the door."

"It's very pretty," I said after seeing to the fire and handing her the shawl, which she proceeded to arrange bunchily around her shoulders. It was made out of string and looked like an extremely large dishcloth. "Did Vienna make it for you?"

"No, I did it years ago, when everyone was doing macramé." Madrid rested her hands on the open book lying across her middle. "I was very arty when I was young. That's how I came to know the artist who painted Jessica's portrait." She tilted her head to look above the mantel-piece. "He—Raimondo Genovese—was mostly known for his sculptures." She bit down on her lip and removed her glasses to wipe them with the shawl. "But as you can see he was a gifted painter. Of course Jessica was an artist's dream. She would pose happily for hours, just so long as she could see me out the corner of her eye. Raimondo let us have his sketches of her. They're all over the house. And we have hundreds of photos. I've been looking through this album." She lifted the book and held it out to me. "My darling Jessica had that wonderful affinity with the camera that the great fashion models all seem to have. She knew instinctively how to project her innermost self, with just a tilt of her dear little head. Precious angel!"

Silence settled on the room, relieved only by the faint ticking of the clock and an occasional crackle of the fire. Madrid then asked wistfully if I would like to see the album for myself. So I drew up a chair and settled down to admire Jessica in dozens of poses and myriad settings.

"Here she is the day we took her to Madam Tussaud's." Madrid pointed her finger proudly. "But she wouldn't go in."

"Do they allow dogs?"

"I don't know, but the poor little darling started to shake when Vienna mentioned the Chamber of Horrors, so we took her for an ice cream instead. Strawberry was always her favourite, and after that we took her to have her nails done at a wonderful little doggy spa in Soho."

Madrid continued turning the album pages slowly. There were photos of Jessica at the seaside, photos of her reclining on sofas and chairs draped in a shawl that was smaller, but otherwise identical to the one Madrid was now wearing. There were photos of her being paraded in shows and photos of her sipping from a champagne glass.

And here we had Jessica stepping daintily into a taxi on the way to meet her betrothed, the Baron Von Woofer, for the first time.

"She was so happy. I'm sure for her it was love at first sight." Madrid's voice broke and she snapped the book shut. "But his feelings couldn't have gone that deep, or he would at least have observed a proper mourning period after her death," she continued with great bitterness. "Instead, what did the lusty Baron Von Woofer do but hook up with that rump-twitching minx, Elizabetta Dance-foot. Little slut. Not a decent championship to her name. The sort of bitch who would give herself to any dog for a biscuit."

It was at that moment that it occurred to me that Madrid Miller wasn't just odd, she was completely potty. She couldn't help it, and there are people with far worse fixations, but I found myself eager to get away before I put my foot in my mouth. Unfortunately the tongue is often-times faster than the foot.

"Did any of Jessica's orphan puppies turn into champi-ons?" I asked. Madrid's expression grew even more sullen.

"I don't know. What a question, I can never stand talk-ing about them. It was bad enough that Vienna insisted on keeping a couple of them. Oh, I'm sorry." Her voice mel-lowed and she reached out to squeeze my hand. "I shouldn't have snapped—it's ungrateful when you're being so kind. It's just that my nerves are in such a state. Perhaps if I could have a glass of brandy. I'm sure there's a bottle in the pantry. Would you mind?"

"Not a bit." I was on my feet and at the door before she had finished speaking.

"You know where the kitchen is, and while you're there, you could take a peek in the study—some of the best sketches of Jessica are hanging there."

After agreeing with what I hoped amounted to appropriate enthusiasm I escaped into the hall. I had no desire to see anyone's etchings of the late lamented Jessica. But I did pause to peer around the study door, forcing myself to look inside in hopes of laying Mrs. Large's ghost to rest. What a depressing room it was, even without a body taking up half the floor. I hadn't done myself an ounce of good, because memory had lost none of its brutal clarity. I could see it all again: the overturned ladder, Mrs. Large's look of slack-jawed bewilderment, the feather duster in her hand, the dustpan and ashes on the floor.

I practically fled down the hall as if at least six ghosts were chasing me. After fumbling for the kitchen light switch, I blundered across the room. The pantry was a few feet from the back door, a small square of walk-in space; there was a marble shelf with almost all the polish gone, and rows of yellowed white wooden ones ranged up the walls to the high ceiling. The tiny window six feet above my head was festooned with cobwebs and there was no light. But there was food. Boxes and jars lined all the shelves within reach, and yes, there it was—the brandy bottle. I had my hand around it when the door slammed shut on me.

Darkness dropped like a black cloth over my head, and my heart began to pound. So silly, because all I had to do was find the doorknob and give it a turn. There was only one problem. The knob turned but the door wouldn't budge. Not even when I pounded on it with my fists and kicked at it until my shoes hurt. And by the time I got round to shouting I wondered if it would be any use. If someone or something had locked me in, might not he or she be off somewhere in that horrible house laughing?

# CHAPTER SEVEN

*Every chair and article of furniture
should be carefully checked for
woodworm, then cleaned before
being returned to the room.*

"WOULD YOU LIKE ME TO GO IN WITH YOU?" FREDDY
offered kindly. It was the following Monday morning. Ben
had already left for work and I was about to enter my own
pantry to fetch bread for toast. It's possible I did hesitate
on opening the pantry door and that Freddy was sincere in
his concern for my mental well-being.

"Actually, I think I'm bearing up very well," I told him,
returning with the bread and popping slices into the
toaster. "I wasn't stuck in that awful pitch-dark pantry
for very long, but it *was* harrowing. Another few minutes
and I would have been like poor Jane Eyre when wicked
Aunt Reed locked her in the room where her uncle had
died—seeing ghosts and spooks at every turn."

"Now be reasonable, coz." Freddy stirred himself to
pour his own cup of tea. "There wouldn't have been room
for both you and Mrs. Large in there. You have to learn to
relax in a crisis. Savour the moment, so to speak."

"The only moment I savoured," I told him, buttering
away at the toast, "was when I got out. I suppose it was

like a French farce. Vienna returning to the house because she'd forgotten her shopping list. The back door colliding with the pantry door, shutting me in. Her dashing off to explain to Madrid she wasn't a burglar. Then almost out the front door when she heard my pounding and guessed what had happened. Because that pantry door had a tendency to stick, or jam, or whatever you call it, and Vienna had been meaning to get it fixed."

"It's good for you to talk about it." Freddy was at his most benign, graciously accepting the toast with two poached eggs on top. "I don't mind that I've heard about it seven times already. You need to get the experience out of your system, Ellie, if there's to be any hope of your ever fully functioning in society again. And after what you've told me about Madrid Miller, I really don't think the world needs too many more crackpots."

I sat down across from him at the kitchen table and sipped my tea. "The trouble is, Madrid isn't what I would call a nice crackpot."

"Because she didn't get off her sofa when you were trapped in the pantry?"

"Not that; I'm sure it's always a case of Vienna to the rescue. Madrid's used to letting her sister take care of everything. What really put me off her was seeing the kennels. Vienna told me to take a look at them if I were interested, and the little dogs were so adorable, especially of course the puppies, that it was hard to imagine none of them ever being allowed in the house."

"It does sound harsh." Freddy held out his cup for a refill. "But be fair, Ellie, those women are running a business."

"Oh, knickers!" I snapped. "I thought that. But the reason Madrid won't let those Norfolk terriers set paws in the house is she's punishing them because they're alive. And her darling Jessica is dead and gone. That's spite, under the guise of sensitivity. Also downright creepy, if you ask me." Ignoring Freddy's proffered cup, I took away his eggy plate and slapped it in the sink. "Nice crackpots, otherwise known as lovable eccentrics, aren't like that. They think they're teakettles or decide to live in trees while seeking their inner selves. Very clever, some of them. Take Dr. Johnson." I turned on the tap and squeezed in some washing-up liquid. "Now there was an oddball, though I think he would have been lots of fun, if you could keep him from talking about his dictionary."

"I get the point." Freddy stood up, stretching until his fingertips almost brushed the ceiling and yawning half his scraggy face off. "You don't like Madrid Miller and she isn't coming to your birthday party even if she does promise to bring you a balloon, so there! Nothing wrong with that!"

"You are saying?"

"That the nasty crackpots are the ones to whom we can't relate because they espouse viewpoints that conflict with our own."

"Did you get that out of Dr. Johnson's dictionary?"

"My point," Freddy explained gently, "is that sometimes it's personal. You and I, coz, would put Mrs. Barrow high on the unlovable wackos list, because she went and picketed Abigail's, instead of toting her placard over to that dress shop you told me about on Lost Sixpenny Road, the one where they don't sell anything above a size two."

"Agreed." I wiped my soapy hands on his sweater.

"Could it be, Ellie"—still the avuncular approach—"that you're not being a hundred percent fair to Madrid Miller about this business of the doggies? Because she didn't overtake her sister in a race down the hall to let you out of that pantry?"

I folded my arms and looked him straight in the eye.

"Tell me, Freddy, what's going on in that maggoty brain of yours? Why do you care so much what I think of a woman you've never even met?"

"Okay." Now he was the one looking me straight in the eye. "I'm concerned you'll take the leap from not liking Madrid Miller to deciding it's entirely possible that she pushed Mrs. Large off that ladder. Bother the motive! That can always be figured out later."

"Of all the cheek!" I flared. "I seem to remember your suggesting on the day of the funeral that it might not have been an accident. And that being the case, the Miller sisters were the most likely suspects, because it happened at their house."

"Mea culpa." He pressed a hand to his chest. "I admit I'm the last one to talk. It's fun poking around, playing at Sherlock Holmes, but I just don't think this is the time, Ellie. You've got other things going on. You keep talking about getting all this spring cleaning done, and . . ." Freddy paused to stand scratching at his beard.

"And there's the restaurant." I stopped being cross with him. "Have Mrs. Barrow and her troops returned with their picket signs?"

"No, all's quiet on the western front." He cocked a questioning eyebrow. "Or does Abigail's face east? Never mind. Ben seems quite chipper, so I wouldn't get into a wifely tizzy about him, coz. He's not going to chuck in the towel."

"I told him I thought he should."

"Well, he won't. Your husband's not cut out to be a lovable eccentric whiling away his productive years living in a tree thinking he'd like to be a teakettle. The one I think we should all be worried about is Jonas." Freddy took another scratch at his beard.

"Why do you say that?" I asked, heart starting to thump.

"Ellie, have you taken a good look at the old boy lately?"

"Of course I have."

"And you don't think he's getting awfully frail?" My cousin looked as truly concerned as I'd ever seen him. "Maybe I'm overreacting, but I hate to see him going downhill when maybe something could be done to perk him up."

"You've seen me try to get him to eat," I said. "Still, I'm glad you brought this up, Freddy." I gave him a hug and a tweak of the earring. "I suppose I've been trying to kid myself Jonas was just feeling the effects of winter and would get back to his old self now that spring is here. But I'll talk to Dr. Solomon again. The last time we spoke, he assured me that apart from the bronchitis Jonas is fit as a fiddle for a man his age. And that older people often take a while regaining their energy after a bad bout, like the one Jonas had before Christmas."

"I'm not suggesting you don't take great care of him, and I don't want to come off acting like I'm the old boy's mother." Freddy, who never got embarrassed, looked and sounded flustered. "It's just that he's a great <u>mate</u> in his way, and I suppose I . . . I'm fond of him."

"Actually," I said, sounding like Tam, "you love him, but I promise never to tell. There's no reason to." I gave the earring another tug. "Jonas knows. And he feels just the same. You and Ben are the grandsons he never had. So try not to worry." Advice as much for myself as him. "I'll go and see Dr. Solomon. There's no point in trying to do this over the phone. And I want to have my say before having him come out to give Jonas a thorough going-over."

"You'll do that today?" Freddy was already looking more cheerful.

"Dr. Solomon's not going to be in the surgery for the next couple of days. I found that out when I took Abbey in with that earache on Friday. We had to see one of the other doctors. But with Jonas I really think it's best to wait until Wednesday or Thursday to talk to Dr. Solomon himself."

The man under discussion opened the door and scuffled into the kitchen in a pair of old plaid slippers, which he refused to give up even though he had at least two new pairs. He was wearing an equally ancient dressing gown over striped pajamas. But as is often the way after picturing someone at death's door, he looked livelier than usual. What hair he had was standing up in wisps and his moustache needed a good trim, but there was a sparkle in his eyes. A malevolent sparkle perhaps, but that was our Jonas.

"I thought as how I'd come down and meet this new woman you've got coming in, Ellie. Make her feel at home like." He gave an amused grunt before planting himself at the table.

"Hoping she's your type, mate?" Freddy gave him a man-to-man wink.

"If she is," I said, getting the kettle going for another pot of tea and popping more bread into the toaster, "he's too late. Trina McKinnley already has a boyfriend, one of those mucho macho types, who makes the two of you look like a couple of choirboys. But by all means be as charming to her as you like. We haven't had much luck recently keeping help. And I count myself more than lucky to have her one morning every other week."

"Be warned, Jonas." Freddy was actually buttering the toast for me. "If this Trina doesn't stick the course, you and I will each be given a pinny with our name embroidered on it and told to heave-ho with the Hoover."

"I've got to be getting out in the garden." Jonas eyed the window, although it didn't give much of a view outside, except for the old copper beech tree. "Those lawns be need-ing mowing, and I ain't even started bedding out, nor tidy-ing up the tulips and daffs as they die off."

"You've had other things to do," I told him, scooping a poached egg out of the saucepan with a slotted spoon. "I'm always asking you to keep the twins amused while I'm doing something else." I glanced up at the clock. "Which reminds me, I'd better get them up and dressed so they can be finished with breakfast by eight. That way I'll be able to get them to play school and be back in plenty of time before Trina arrives at nine."

"I'll take them for you," offered Freddy. "Ben's an easy-going boss, but he does like me to toddle into work at least half an hour before I clear off for the day. So I have to leave shortly anyway. But what about the car? Are you go-ing to be left stuck if I keep it for the rest of the morning?"

"Not if you could also bring them home."

"No problem," replied Freddy the Fantastic, "although if you'd only be a sport and let them ride on the back of my motorbike, you wouldn't have to do without the car."

"I don't want the car," I told him firmly. "I want to stay at home and bond with Trina McKinnley. The minute you leave with the twins I'm going to have a race round trying to make the place look halfway presentable so she doesn't take fright and do a bunk before I even take her upstairs."

Luckily it was one of those mornings when my children decided to be reasonably cooperative. Abbey put her frock on backwards, but that was quickly rectified. Tam remem-bered it was show-and-tell that day, so there was a scram-ble to find his Paddington Bear. After hugs for me and Jonas, they went happily off with Freddy a good ten min-utes ahead of schedule. All very promising, I thought, until I turned back from the door to face the kitchen.

Jonas, clearly afraid I would attempt to tidy him up too, abandoned his cup of tea and went off to get dressed. The hall door closed behind him, leaving me trying to outstare the kitchen in hope that it would squirm with embarrassment at having got into such a muddle. And offer—no, beg to be allowed—to clean itself up. Talk about ingratitude, I thought, shoveling crockery into the sink. After all I'd done for this kitchen! Taking down the horrid green wall tiles and replacing them with a wheat sheaf–patterned paper, remodeling the fireplace, installing the greenhouse window above the new sinks, and as a final treat, presenting the kitchen with a lovely Aga cooker.

Rolling up my sleeves I finished clearing off the table and wiping it down. But it was impossible to stay cross. I loved this house too much. It had a way of wrapping its arms around me, making me feel securely tied to the past, the present, and the future. The breakfast china I was now washing up had belonged to Abigail Grantham. Her hands had dried this cup, had put away this plate. One day perhaps it would be Abbey's or Tam's wife's turn to stand here, looking out the window to see the sun rise and listen to the birds singing, as if it were all happening for the first time.

When putting away the last cup, I noticed Mrs. Malloy's china poodle staring out at me from the cupboard shelf. It was more than time I put it on display, yet for a moment or two I stood doing battle with my baser self. The temptation to put that poodle on the toilet tank in the downstairs loo was almost overwhelming, but I did not succumb. Marching into the drawing room I set Fifi on the mantelpiece next to one of a pair of Chinese vases on either side of the Buehl clock. There was no denying poor Fifi destroyed the artistic integrity of my entire decorating scheme. Everything else had been selected with an eye for harmony and good taste—*my* taste.

I slumped down on the sofa. But it only took a couple of glances around the room to make me realize I was kidding myself. True, I loved the furniture, but I hadn't selected it.

All I'd done was rescue it from the attic. Yes, I'd bought those Chinese vases and a couple of table lamps. But in the years since my marriage various other items had pretty much made their own way into this room. There was the misshapen bowl that my aunt Lulu had made at a pottery class. A picture painted by Freddy when he thought he wanted to be an artist. And cushions embroidered industriously, if inexpertly, by an old friend.

In fact, I spotted quite a few other knickknacks that would never have won my heart on a shopping spree. At one time I must have regarded them as eyesores, just as I now did Mrs. Malloy's Fifi. But over time they had settled in, had become those touches that make a house a home. Picking up one of the cushions to give it a fluff, I noticed the small dots of dried blood that were the result of repeated jabs with the embroidery needle and thought about Abigail's book of household hints. What had she said to do about blood? And would it work if the blood was already dry? It came to me as I returned to the kitchen—starch and water mixed into a thin paste. Simple, and definitely worth a try. I would have to pick up a box of starch, because all I had in the house was the spray kind. And there was something else I needed to do. Get the glass replaced in Jonas's mirror.

There was a knock at the garden door. For a foolish moment I was swept back to the days when it would have been Mrs. Malloy standing outside wearing one of her fur coats whatever the season, and not the least affected by the disapproval of those such as Mrs. Barrow. As Freddy had once kindly informed Mrs. M., it wasn't as though any of her furs came from animals likely to be categorized as an endangered species. In fact the National Society of Exterminators probably felt extremely beholden to her.

My eyes were misty as I opened the door to Trina McKinnley.

"Well, here I am," she said, unbuttoning her jacket and hanging it with speedy efficiency on a peg in the alcove. "It's not bad getting here. The Cliff Road bus stops just around the corner from where I live." Setting her bag down on the table, she looked the kitchen over, her snapping dark eyes missing nothing, neither the crumbs by the toaster nor the cobweb that had defiantly grown back in the corner since I began spring cleaning. I found myself comparing Trina McKinnley's professional-looking white uniform with Mrs. Malloy's work outfits, which had run the gamut from cocktail frocks to the miniskirts she had taken to wearing after she became a grandmother.

"I've got a bit behind," I apologized, spotting a place where one of the twins had scribbled on the wallpaper.

"I can see that, Ellie. Makes it easer using first names, doesn't it?" She was now prowling the room, to the obvious annoyance of Tobias, who hissed at her from the rocking chair before leaping from the table to the edge of the sink and up onto the window ledge.

"Oh, yes," I said, "much easier."

"Well, I'm sure you don't want to be calling me Miss McKinnley, and we're not living in the Dark Ages, are we?" She was now trailing a finger through the dust on the Welsh dresser and eyeing the double row of plates. "Poole pottery, right?" She gave a jerk of her curly head before turning back to face me. "My granny collected it, and that juice jug by the sink is Edinburgh crystal." She pointed a knowing finger. For the first time I noticed she was wearing a small black bow in her curly hair, just above her right ear.

Fingering it, she explained: "This is for Gertrude Large. Betty Nettle wanted us—her, Winifred Smalley, and me—to wear black armbands. I ask you! In this day and age. But when Winifred suggested the bows, I gave in. The only reason I'm in the organization is because of her." Trina flashed me one of her black-eyed looks. "I expect you've heard all about the C.F.C.W.A. from Roxie Malloy."

"Not a lot," I replied cautiously. "I understand it's all highly confidential."

"Downright silly is what it is." She shrugged her white-uniformed shoulders. "But Winifred's always been very into it, and as I said, I go along because she's a good old egg. Like a mum to me in lots of ways, although I hope she won't . . ." Trina didn't finish the sentence. She had picked up the teapot and was looking it over from handle to spout.

I took the hint. "How about a cup of tea?"

"Don't mind if I do, but just this once." She stood watching me as I filled the kettle, noting, I'm sure, that I dribbled water from sink to cooker. "After today I'll want to get straight to work. I believe in giving my money's worth. I start punctual, but I also leave on the dot. Especially of a Monday, because it's my afternoon with Joe. By the way, we still have to discuss money." She proceeded to quote me an hourly rate that was a little higher than Mrs. Malloy and Mrs. Large had charged. It was still reasonable, but I couldn't help wondering if Trina was in violation of the wage code agreed upon by the C.F.C.W.A. and duly recorded in the Magna Char.

"That's fine." I handed Trina her cup of tea. "Please be sure and let me know what I can do to make things go smoothly."

"Don't worry, Ellie, you'll always know where you stand with me." Blithely spoken. With a practiced gesture, she set the cup down, removed the saucer, and turned it over to inspect the maker's name. "Just as I thought. Very nice."

"A wedding present." It was silly to feel so defensive, but Trina McKinnley was quickly getting under my skin. "This *is* rather a big house," I said, wondering if Mrs. Large had reported to her colleagues that Merlin's Court was in an awful state when she came.

"Depends what you're used to." Trina opened the hall door and stood, hands on hips, doing a tour with her eyes. "I don't think it's as big as it looks from the outside. Roxie Malloy was always going on about Merlin's Court. But I'm not easily wowed."

Before I could reply, Jonas, still unshaven, came down the stairs, wearing his deplorable dressing gown. Trina's eyes took in every missing button as he scuffed towards us on his slippered feet.

"And who's this?" she asked.

"I'm her son." Jonas jerked a thumb in my direction. "Who else would I be? The other two kiddies are at school, but I got to stay home so I could play with my trains." He shuffled off towards the kitchen.

"Senile?"

"Oh, no!" I fought down annoyance. "Jonas has every one of his marbles. He just isn't much of a one for new faces. So you might want to give him a wide berth and not bother doing his bedroom."

"You'll have to show me where it is," she replied, reasonably enough. So we began our tour of the house. She asked a few sensible questions, but it was clear she was just doing so to let me know she was the consummate professional. After showing her where to find buckets, cloths, and other cleaning supplies, I warned her that the Hoover occasionally made threatening noises, but not to panic, because it didn't mean them.

"I'm not the panicky sort, Ellie." She flashed me one of those looks that somehow managed to vacuum the confidence out of me. I headed for the kitchen.

"I don't like that woman," Jonas spoke without turning around from the cooker, where he was heating up some porridge.

"You don't have to," I replied, bundling him over to a chair and tucking a serviette into the neck of his dressing

122 • Dorothy Cannell

gown. "She isn't a mail-order bride I found for you. Trina McKinnley is here so that I will have more time for you and Ben and the twins. So don't let me hear any more grumbling."

"You're a good girl." He reached for my hand and I sat with him at the table, neither of us speaking, just relishing the peace of being together until the porridge began making burping sounds, kindly letting me know it was about to boil over.

I had just placed a steaming bowl in front of Jonas and advised him to let it cool a little when Trina McKinnley's voice floated down the hall, and I went scurrying in response.

"Ellie?" She was standing in front of the trestle table, drawing a finger along the top. "What furniture polish have you been using?"

"One of the lemon-scented ones."

"The spray kind?"

"Yes, isn't that all right?"

"I suppose, if you don't mind a waxy buildup." Trina gave one of her shrugs. "Though I'm surprised at Roxie Malloy not sticking to the rules of the Magna Char about using good old elbow grease. Didn't Gertrude Large say anything?"

I experienced a belated wave of fondness for Mrs. L. "No, but it so happens I have been thinking about making my own furniture polish, from an old family formula." I escaped to the kitchen again, leaving Trina looking unimpressed.

"Problems?" Jonas roused himself from a doze that had him half out of his chair.

"Not really." Resettling him, I sat with him while he sipped at his porridge. I was trying to convince myself it was putting a little colour into his sunken cheeks when another summons brought me leaping up from my chair.

This time Trina was standing in the drawing room, tapping her toes.

"Ellie?"

"Yes?" I was beginning to dislike my name.

"You've got an awful lot of ornaments."

"Don't most people?"

"Not like this." She swept out an arm that seemed to grow in breadth of sweep. "You've got them everywhere, haven't you? Not just on the tables, but down close to the floor and up near the ceiling."

"I like to vary the focus."

"And I'm sure it's all lovely. You've got some nice things, Ellie. Wouldn't mind buying some of them off you. But I've got a rule, you see. No more than three ornaments to a single surface. Any more and there's an extra charge."

"Is that in the Magna Char?" I couldn't help asking.

"Can't say it is." Her black eyes sparked. "Doesn't do to be a total conformist, does it?"

"I suppose not." After agreeing to cough up a couple more pounds I headed back to the kitchen. Somehow I felt sure Trina had made up her little rule on the spur of the moment. The question was, Why? Little did I know I was shortly to be provided with a clue.

Jonas had just gone upstairs, having voiced the intention of getting dressed. I was congratulating myself on having chivied him into finishing most of his porridge when someone tapped on the garden door.

Bunty Wiseman could have auditioned for the role of gorgeous dumb blonde any day of the week. She had eyes so blue they should have been the result of tinted contact lenses, but weren't. She had a figure to cry for, great legs, and what Freddy described as the lushest lips going. The only thing missing was the dumb part. Bunty hadn't been lucky in love: her marriage to Chitterton Fells's urbane, silver-haired solicitor Lionel Wiseman had folded. As had her several business ventures—due to what might be called acts of God. But these misfortunes weren't due to any lack of brains. And she took her lumps with a perky perseverance that left me both baffled and awed.

Bunty never stood on ceremony. Had I not been home she would probably have made herself lunch and then proceeded to scour the place from sink to ceiling. Instead she twirled around for me to admire her black minidress. Told me she had made it at sewing classes and demanded to know what I had been doing with myself these last weeks, because she hadn't seen me—not even the tip of my head in church.

"When were you in church?" I asked.

"Last Sunday. Or maybe I only dreamed it." Bunty perched on a corner of the table, swinging her legs like a child. "I was getting married to Lionel again and the place was packed—standing room only. I remember being very hurt, Ellie, that you didn't show up."

"I must not have received my invitation." I was about to put on the kettle, but looking at the clock saw the morning was getting on, and suggested sherry instead. "Cheers!" I said, handing Bunty her glass. "And is there really cause for celebration? Are you and Lionel a couple again?"

"Not really," she sighed, looking no less cheerful. "I've been letting him take me out to dinner. A girl has to eat, and you know how stingy he was with the divorce settlement. Not that I really blame him for that." She wrinkled her pretty nose as she sipped her sherry. "He knew he'd made an idiot of himself over that ghastly woman he thought he was in love with. Poor old Lionel! He hoped that if he cut me off with a shilling, I'd have to come crawling back to him. And he can hardly stand it that I've managed to stay afloat. Just as I'm about to find myself out of a job for one reason or another, something else always turns up. Did I tell you, Ellie, that I'm working for Ward and Gantry, the estate agents on Seascape Road?"

"I haven't seen you in ages." I returned from the pantry with a box of crackers and set these out on plate with some cheese. "But it was nice of you to come by and tell me."

"Oh, that's not why I'm here." Bunty slid off the table without spilling a drop of sherry and shushed Tobias cat off the chair where he had just settled so she could take his seat. "I came racing over on my lunch hour because I have some gossip for you. I shouldn't be telling you, because of course Lionel shouldn't have told me . . ." She paused to eye the plate of cheese and crackers and asked if I had some Branston pickle.

"What shouldn't Lionel have told you?" I unscrewed the jar for her and even dabbed a spoonful of pickle onto her plate so she could keep all her energy for blabbing.

"About the will." Bunty began to eat with relish.

"What will?"

She reached for another piece of cheese. "The one he's been handling for the late Mrs. Large. Oh, I knew you'd be interested, Ellie! It's written all over your face. You're dying to know the scoop, but perhaps"—attempting to look soulful—"it would be wrong of me to repeat what Lionel told me in the strictest of confidence."

"Care to drown your conscience in another sherry?" I inquired.

"Oh, all right." Bunty held out her glass. "It's not likely the bus driver will drop dead at the wheel and I'll be forced to take over. Although it does happen, doesn't it? Mrs. Large being the classic example—here yesterday, gone today. And you were there when she had the accident, weren't you, Ellie? That must have been awful." She shuddered, but her eyes looked anxious. "I'm being insensitive, aren't I? Did you know the woman?"

"She took over for Mrs. Malloy, but she only came

once." I managed to sound brisk. "And I can talk about her quite comfortably, so there's no reason for you to hold back, unless you really think it might be better not to tell me about her will."

"Fiddle sticks!" Bunty sat up straight in her chair and attempted without marked success to assume a righteous expression. "You've an absolute right to know, considering all you went through. Practically stumbling over the body. Clarice Whitcombe came into Ward and Gantry—she had some questions about the purchase of her house—and she told me about being at Tall Chimneys the day Mrs. Large died. She said she felt so sorry for you and Vienna Miller being the ones . . ."

"It was nasty," I agreed. "Now about that will?"

"Knowing Lionel," Bunty mused, "he told me because he thought it would soften me up. I'm sure he'd like us to get married again. And you can bet he knows I've been seeing Joe."

I let the name blow over my head, so eager was I for Bunty to spill the beans. Luckily she glanced up at the clock, saw that she was running out of lunch hour, and told me what Lionel Wiseman had told her. Mrs. Large had left her two daughters a hundred pounds each. The rest of her estate, a considerable one for a woman in her position, had been left to Trina McKinnley. By way of a trust to be administered by Winifred Smalley.

# Chapter Eight

*When unable to remove*
*stains on white tablecloths*
*by regular washing, sprinkle*
*spots with lemon juice while*
*cloth is still damp and spread*
*out on lawn in full sun.*

"LIONEL SAID THE DAUGHTERS WERE LIVID." BUNTY munched contentedly on a mouthful of cheese while giving the clock another glance. "Oh, to hell with it," she said. "I'll just be late back to work. And if old Mr. Ward says anything, I'll mention how he's always looking at my chest. Poor old thing, he can't help it, being so bent over he couldn't look up to save his life. He's also practically blind. But it's so easy to induce male guilt in these days of sexual harassment." She fluttered her eyelashes.

"I'm sure you're right." I was uneasily aware that at any moment there could be another snippy summons from Trina McKinnley. Although to be fair, I thought charitably, one couldn't blame her for being uppity. Becoming an heiress might make one somewhat disenchanted with cleaning other people's houses. Obviously it occurred to me to tell Bunty that Trina was in the house. But, given the fact that my friend shouldn't have been repeating a word of what Lionel shouldn't have told her, I didn't want to risk the possibility that she might clam up. Vulgar curiosity had me by the throat.

"Did Mrs. Large leave a lot?" I fetched more cheese and began opening another packet of crackers.

"Depends on the point of view, Ellie darling. You and Ben don't exactly live from one bite to the next." Bunty chose Stilton this time instead of cheddar and slathered it with Branston pickle. "Whereas in my straitened circumstances a hundred quid wouldn't go amiss. 'Take what you can get' has always struck me as a pretty good motto. But apparently Mrs. Large's daughters don't share that view. Those ungrateful women told Lionel where he could stuff what they got from Mummy! Poor Lionel! From the sound of it, he was scared silly that one or both of those very large women would punch the daylights out of him."

"You already told me Mrs. Large only left her daughters a hundred pounds apiece," I said as patiently as I could, "and I do appreciate your trying to build up the moment by prolonging my curiosity. But before I hit you over the head with the kettle, you'd better tell me what Mrs. Large left Trina McKinnley."

Bunty mumbled that it was rude to talk with one's mouth full, but swallowed hastily when I reached for the kettle.

"Lionel said about fifty thousand pounds."

"What?"

"And that's before her house is sold."

"My goodness!" I had to sit down.

"The house isn't much from the sound of it, but every little bit helps." Bunty looked well pleased with the success of her revelations. "Ellie, you should see your face. It is a shocker, isn't it? There's Mrs. Large trudging out to do the rough five days a week for the so-called well-to-do, and all the time she's got this nice little nest egg."

"How?"

"An insurance settlement. Apparently her late hubby was injured in an accident at work. Lost the use of his legs or something." Bunty became a little vague. "Anyway, he was permanently disabled. A nurse had to come in every day for several years until he finally croaked."

"That's sad," I said. "For him and for Mrs. Large."

"But not for Trina McKinnley. Talk about landing in the gravy! Her only problem will be if this Winifred Smalley woman refuses to dish out the money with a large spoon."

"I wonder why Mrs. Large set things up that way?" I mused. "Why the need for a trustee?"

"She didn't explain that to Lionel." Bunty wandered over to the sink and returned with a glass of water. "But I happen to have a pretty shrewd idea what was in Mrs. Large's noggin, because you see I'm in the know about Joe."

"Trina's boyfriend. She introduced me to him at the funeral. What exactly do you know about him?"

"Only that he's married and"—Bunty looked just a little guilty—"he's also seeing me on the side. Now don't look at me like that, Ellie! As it is, I have whole minutes when I'm thoroughly disgusted with myself. But honestly, I only started with Joe to make Lionel jealous, and you know how much he deserves to suffer after what he put me through."

"And Joe's wife?"

"Ellie, I hate it when you turn all Victorian." Bunty pouted adorably, which is not hard to do when one is blonde and cute.

"Joe is a thug."

"Only on the outside."

"Right! On the inside he's merely a creep. Bunty, you need to have your noggin examined!" I removed the plate of cheese and crackers—the only punishment I could come up with on the spur of the moment. Then I put the kettle on so I wouldn't be the only thing steaming. "Men like Joe are only out for one thing."

"Not true," came the equable reply. "In Trina's case, Joe's also after the money. Why else didn't he ditch her when I came along? I know it sounds vain, Ellie, but she doesn't have half my sizzle."

"But Mrs. Large might have lived for years."

"Perhaps. Perhaps not."

"What's that supposed to mean?" I stood, teapot in hand, eyes locked on Bunty's face.

"Only that there are no guarantees in life. Why? What did you think I meant?" Her eyes widened. "Oh, I get it! You're wondering if Joe decided to hurry things along. But he wasn't at Tall Chimneys that day, was he?"

"Not that I know of," I conceded.

"But you're thinking maybe he got into the house when nobody was looking and gave Mrs. Large a shove into eternity." Bunty sat thinking this over for a few moments before saying, "Ellie, you're such a spoilsport. Can't I have a fling without you suggesting I've hooked up with a murderer?"

Before I could reassure Bunty that I didn't seriously think anything of the sort, a thump came at the garden door and I yanked the steaming kettle off the cooker before crossing the kitchen to see who was out there. Freddy wouldn't have knocked. Or would he? It might be a game he was playing to amuse Abbey and Tam. Pretending that they were Jehovah's Witnesses or a band of lost explorers needing directions to the North Pole. It was almost an hour early for him to have brought the children home from play school. But my cousin did tend to make his own schedule.

Another thump made the door shake, and when I yanked it open, I found myself nose to nose with Trina McKinnley's and Bunty Wiseman's . . . Joe. Speak of letches and leeches! I was so taken back I blinked twice before realizing he was in a foul temper—if he had any other kind.

"Trina here?" He elbowed past me.

"Yes, she's upstairs, I believe. She's not due to leave for another half hour." This response didn't appear to go down well with Joe Cool, and Bunty didn't look happy.

"Ellie! Why didn't you tell me?"

A good question.

"What the bloody hell are you doing here, Bunty?" Joe snarled. If looks could kill, she would have keeled over on the spot. "Trying to muck things up between me and Trina, is that your game? Better get it through your dumb skull, girl, you and me is through. I ain't about to risk Trina giving me the shove, not now when everything's coming up right for a bloody change."

"I didn't know your other girlfriend was here," responded Bunty with commendable dignity. "But don't sweat it, Joey boy. I was going to tell you to get lost. I noticed the last time we were out"—giving him a lush-lipped smile—"that your hair's getting thin on top."

Joe, whatever his other shortcomings, had a fine head of well-greased black hair, but Bunty obviously knew just where to stick the knife. Clutching at his temples, he swung around in search of a mirror. Of course, there being no mirror in the kitchen, he was reduced to the materials at hand. He grabbed up a metal spatula lying by the cooker, shifting it this way and that in a frantic attempt to get an overhead view. The faces he made were not pretty, even before Bunty suggested he also check out the bags under his eyes. I almost felt sorry for him when Trina came into the room.

"Joe?" She stood, a model of efficient household help in her crisp white uniform—curls vibrant, black eyes snapping. "Just what's going on here?"

"Doesn't he always hop about looking at himself in pretend mirrors?" Bunty asked kindly.

"You shut your bloody mouth!" Joe rounded on her.

"Why, you rude man! Call me a nosey parker, Ellie"—turning sweetly to me—"but I feel you should discourage Miss McKinnley from having him pick her up here in future."

"Hey, Trina don't work no place without my say-so! And I've decided I don't want her coming here no more." Joe was working himself back up into a comfortable state of belligerence. "Besides, she don't need to. So we're outta here. Right, Trine?" Casting the spatula into the sink, he thumbed for his woman to come to heel. To my surprise Trina nodded and followed him to the door.

"But I haven't paid you," I protested.

"Forget it." She turned around and shrugged. "You don't seem to be having much luck keeping help, do you, Mrs. Haskell?" She was looking at Bunty as Joe jerked on her hand and dragged her out the door.

"Here, hit me with this if you like." My friend picked up the discarded spatula. "I've properly mucked things up for you, Ellie, and I am sorry. What are you going to do?"

"Find someone else, I suppose."

"Will that be easy?"

"Oh, I expect so." Actually, I did have someone in mind. Me.

"You have to be wondering what I ever saw in Joe," Bunty smoothed out a crease in her tight skirt. "I suppose I was off my loaf. But what does that make Trina?"

"She didn't strike me as a woman who could be ordered about," I said, "but life is full of surprises, isn't it?" Lending substance to this vacuous statement, the garden door opened and in came Ben with the children. He said he'd decided to take the afternoon off so we could go for a picnic.

"Come on, Mummy!" Tam pleaded as Abbey tugged on my hand. "We got food in the car. A whole basket. Daddy made sangriches"—my son always had trouble with this word—"and there's cake and biscuits and everything."

"It was a fairly slow morning at the restaurant," Ben said. "Tam's right. There's plenty to eat, as well as a bottle of wine on ice. Why don't you join us, Bunty?" He'd always liked her.

"Thanks, but no thanks," Bunty tiptoed up on her high heels to kiss his cheek. "I have to get back to work, and anyway I'm in disgrace. No treats for bad girls like me for at least a week."

"What's that about?" Ben asked as the door closed behind her. "Or would you rather"—eyeing the twins—"tell me later?"

I picked up Abbey, who blew fairy kisses into my neck. "The gist is that Trina McKinnley threw in the tea towel without even finishing her half day."

"Are we under a curse, Ellie? She and that bloke were heading out onto The Cliff Road as I pulled into the driveway. It sounded to me as though Trina and her boyfriend were having a blazing row."

So Trina hadn't gone meekly down the garden path. But would she make a complete break with Joe? I wondered. All depended, I supposed, on just how dotty she was about the creep.

"Where's Jonas?" Abbey peered around the room as if suspecting he was hiding under the table or behind the pantry door. "He's got to come, too, Mummy."

" 'Course he has." Tam scampered out into the hall, the rest of us following more sedately at his heels. "Daddy made egg sangriches 'cause he knows Jonas likes them best. And a chocolate cake, with lots of icing. But I think that's for me."

"No, it's not." Abbey poked him in the back. "It's got my name wroted on it."

"I put both your names on it." Ben separated the children, who had gone nose to nose and were growling like an angry pair of puppies. "But I can always scrape them off if you don't behave." The threat instantly brought them to heel, although both still looked cross until they heard footsteps overhead and raced across the hall to wait for Jonas to come stomping down the stairs. It made my heart ache to see him try to straighten his back when he saw us watching his progress. But sympathy wasn't likely to do him as much good as getting outdoors in the sunshine. So when he drew down his bushy eyebrows at the idea of accompanying us on the picnic, I told him I wasn't having any nonsense from him. I bundled him into an old jacket and got him out the door without listening to his string of protests.

"We've all got things we should be doing," I scolded as we headed for the car. "Ben should be at work, the children should be getting a jump start on learning algebra, and I should be doing aerobics to build up my stamina to finish the spring cleaning on my own, now that Trina McKinnley has given me the boot. But there's more to life, Jonas, than being productive."

Hearing that Trina had flown the coop wiped the sour expression off his face. Like me, he didn't relish the idea of anyone replacing Mrs. Malloy. A sacrilege was what he called it. And he got into the car without any more grumbles to sit with Ben in the front while I got in the back with Abbey and Tam.

"Miss McKinnley find the job too much?" he asked as Ben started the engine.

"I'll tell you about it later," I said, making sure the twins' safety belts were secure. "Let's just have fun. Where are you taking us, Ben?"

"I thought we'd go to that little cove you're so fond of." He was driving through the gates as he spoke, turning left away from the village in the direction of Bellkiek, our closest market town. I had always loved the area from my visits to Merlin's Court as a child, and the hint that we were getting close had always been that first tantalizing whiff of the sea. Living here, I'd grown used to it except on occasions such as this when my childlike enthusiasm for magical sunny days and picnics reasserted itself. Rolling the window down, I breathed deeply, savouring the salty tang blown in by the breeze, and the sun on my nose.

The cliffs sheared down to our right, a climber's delight, but a problem for normal people wishing to get down to the ribbon of beach below. Ben told the children we would have to put them in the picnic basket and lower them by rope, which made them giggle. Jonas didn't think much of that idea because they'd squash his egg sandwiches, so I looked for the spot where we always parked the car when going to our special cove. When we came within sight of the house Tom Tingle had recently bought, I knew we were close.

There were only three or four houses on that stretch of road. Tom's was built of red brick and dated from the turn of the century. It was a lovely place, with ivied walls, mullioned windows, and lots of gables. It stood well back from the road, surrounded by rock gardens that I envied.

I wondered if Tom would host a Hearthside Guild meeting in the coming months, or if he had been too put off by what had happened at the last one to even attend in future. Ben stopped the car at a grassy circle shaded by a couple of trees that looked as though they knew their job, having done it for years. Here the cliffs became considerably less steep. There was a path that Ben and I sometimes walked down, but since it was overgrown in parts and there was a waterfall to negotiate, we always took the children down by way of a flight of steps leading down to the sea.

Ben now led the way, with me taking up the rear. The

beach was deserted but for ourselves. It was shaped like an armchair, with seaweed-covered rocks scattered about like large cushions. Today the sea spilled towards us in gentle ripples of white-edged foam. Gulls wheeled overhead, uttering their hoarse-throated cries. The sun smiled down as if pleased to see us. And Abbey and Tam were already tugging at their sandals, eager to wiggle their toes in the biscuit-coloured sand.

I handed them their buckets and spades, promising to help them build a castle after we had eaten, and told them they couldn't go paddling until Daddy or I had tested the water. Then I watched them scamper off to position themselves beside their favourite rock. It was always rimmed with a couple of inches of water, making it easy for them to damp down the sides of the sand they emptied out of their buckets and decorate these little edifices with seaweed. Their happy voices floated our way as I unfolded the chair for Jonas to sit in before spreading out the old plaid rug and anchoring its corners with stones gathered from the cliff bottom. Ben got busy setting out our picnic.

And a delicious-looking feast it was. In addition to the egg sandwiches made especially for Jonas, there were ham and cheese ones on wonderful crusty brown bread, a spinach and walnut salad, mushroom pasties, savoury eggs, a tray of sliced fruit, and the chocolate cake with Abbey's and Tam's names on it. There was lemonade for the children and coffee, along with the bottle of wine, for the grown-ups. Even Jonas admitted that he wasn't sorry he had come.

"We should do this more often," I said. "Irresponsibility is good for the soul. I feel a bit like Mole in *The Wind in the Willows* when he said, 'Hang spring cleaning' or something of the sort and went scurrying out of his dark little house into the sunlight."

Ben adjusted a final sprig of parsley on the egg plate. "Before we call the children over to eat, I want to hear all about Trina McKinnley—and don't leave out the part about how Bunty fits into the picture, because it was clear to me, Ellie, your friend was up to her pretty neck in whatever was going on." He set out plastic plates and cups and I told him and Jonas, who actually leaned forward in his chair to catch every word about Bunty and Joe.

"The two-timing scumbag!" Ben said of Leather Jacket.

"Actually he's three-timing." I settled down on the rug. "There's a wife in addition to Bunty and Trina McKinnley. But the real scoop is that Trina inherited over fifty thousand pounds from Mrs. Large. Can you believe that? The daughters got nothing—well, a hundred pounds each, just enough for them to choke on." I went on to explain about Mrs. Large's husband and the insurance policy.

Ben pursed his lips in a soundless whistle. "But I'm not clear where this Mrs. Smalley fits into things."

"I'm sorry, I was a bit garbled about that part. Mrs. Large arranged for Mrs. Smalley to be the trustee. She gets to dish out the money at her discretion, in order, I suppose, to prevent Joe from helping Trina go through it all in one fell swoop."

"I ain't clear why Mrs. Large left her the money." Jonas tugged on his moustache while the breeze lifted what little grey hair he had on his head.

"She wasn't close to her daughters," I said. "Mrs. Smalley told me when I met her the other day that they hardly gave Mrs. Large the time of day. It's possible all the members of the C.F.C.W.A. viewed Trina as a daughter or niece of sorts. Mrs. Smalley certainly made it clear she was very fond of her."

"Don't make no sense to me." Jonas huddled down in his chair and drew up his jacket collar when the sun drifted behind a cloud. "Wasn't Roxie Malloy a friend of Mrs. Large? Why not leave her something, her and all the other women in this—what did you call it?

"The C.F.C.W.A.—" I had begun to explain when the twins came flying across the sand towards us, Tam eager to tell me about the jellyfish he thought he had seen and Abbey holding out a pink shell she had found. They were quickly distracted from these enthusiasms by the sight of the chocolate cake taking pride of place among the other treats set out on the rug. Tam wanted to know if they could eat it first because picnics weren't the same as real meals and Abbey asked if some of the writing said "Happy Birthday." She knew it wasn't hers and Tam's, but she looked hopefully at Jonas. She had asked me recently if people got to be old by having more birthdays than other people.

"I think this should be a birthday party for Jonas," I said, smiling at him. "Everyone deserves an extra one now and then, and what makes this one special is that you aren't a year older." The children whooped with delight and had to be ordered off the rug before they trampled the food, which gave Jonas a moment to pull himself together and try not to look pleased.

"Daddy, do we got any candles?" Abbey liked things to be done right.

"No, but I'll light a match and Jonas can blow it out."

"And he still gets to make a wish," I promised. "Now we'd better eat if we want to get to the birthday cake before the sun goes behind the clouds for good and we have to go home."

"About time. I'm starving." Jonas took the egg sandwich Ben handed him and actually bit into it with relish. For the first time in weeks I felt optimistic about Jonas; I wished Freddy hadn't been at work and could have seen the sparkle in the old man's eyes as he proceeded to eat several mouthfuls of spinach salad and a few slivers of apple and orange.

"Eat up, Ellie." Ben passed me the plate of mushroom pasties, of which he knew I was passionately fond. "And you've hardly touched your wine."

"For once in my life I'm mostly enjoying watching other people devour everything in sight." I brushed a strand of hair out of my eyes and smiled at him. The sun was back out and all was right with my world. But I did sip my wine and take a pastie. Actually I took two, since they were even more delicious than usual, being seasoned with salt air.

"What birthday is it when you stop getting bigger?" my son wanted to know.

"Will me and Tam need all-new clothes when we wake up on our birthday and we're four?" Abbey asked.

It was clear they were getting impatient for the cake, so Ben unearthed a box of matches from the picnic basket and lit one, holding it up for Jonas to blow out.

"Don't forget to make a wish," I told him.

Jonas leaned forward in his chair and the movement was enough to make the flame go out before he could blow, before he could . . . but no, I had to believe that he had made a wish. This wasn't a day for bad omens. The fact that it had suddenly clouded up meant nothing, I was certain. We gathered up the remains of the picnic and stowed them in the basket, and Ben suggested we look for shells before heading for home. The four of us set off, leaving Jonas to take a catnap.

"We'll just walk around to the next cove." Ben took my hand as we made our way onto the damp, coffee-coloured sand, where it was easy to spot the shells. After helping the children select several to put in their buckets, we skirted a narrow strip of beach around the cliff shoulder, where shadows darkened our faces for a few moments before we entered another armchair-shaped beach. It was smaller than the one we had left, and there were more rocks, but what was most striking was the man seated at a table.

It was laid with a white linen cloth. The man had his back to us, but over his shoulder we could see the wine-glass being raised to his lips, the silver bud vase, and the soup tureen.

"Good heavens!" Ben whispered in my ear, "and I thought I'd gone all out!"

The scene was so completely unreal that I wouldn't have been surprised if the gull wheeling overhead had dropped to earth, shaken its feathers, and assumed human guise before producing a table for four and begging the Haskell party to be seated. So it was disappointingly anti-climatic when the man turned his head and stared at us without surprise, and certainly without enthusiasm.

"Why, it's Tom Tingle!" I felt silly just saying the name, so imagine how he felt living with it. "His house is almost directly above here." My eyes shifted to the cliffs as Ben, the children, and I trailed across the sand to beard the man at his table. On closer view we saw the remains of the smoked salmon, salad, eggs mayonnaise, and bread and butter that made up his meal, along with what I supposed was soup in the tureen. What a production it must have been getting everything down here! And impossible, I would have thought, to keep the soup even lukewarm.

"Out taking the air?" inquired Tom T., looking like a middle-aged gnome, cursed to sit there forever. His large head was sunk in the collar of his earth-coloured jacket.

"We've been having a picnic on the other side." Ben pointed back the way we had come.

"You two haven't met, have you?" I was feeling flustered for no sensible reason. "Darling, this is Tom Tingle, a new member of the Hearthside Guild. And Tom, I'd like you to meet Ben and our children—Abbey and Tam."

He remained seated, his stubby fingers splayed out along the edge of the white tablecloth. And he mumbled something barely audible in response to Ben's "A pleasure, Mr. Tingle."

"Mummy, is he real?" Tam's whisper carried much further. "Or is he just pretend?"

"Him's a sea fairy," Abbey's face glowed. She tiptoed forward, eager for a closer look, but careful not to rush in case she made him disappear.

"They think it's magic." Ben ran his fingers through his dark hair, probably to massage his brain back into working order. "How did you get the table and all the dishes as well as the food down here? I suppose you came by the path rather than the steps, but even so, some undertaking."

"I used a handcart," Tom said quite pleasantly. "It's over there behind those rocks." He gestured towards a couple of giant boulders. And I found myself wondering what they had been in their former lives before some wicked witch turned them to stone.

I scrambled forward to collect Abbey, who was now standing behind Tom and inspecting his ears. "Well, we'll go and leave you to your meal before it gets cold."

"Yes, wouldn't want the salad to cool off, or the smoked salmon, for that matter." He laughed at his small joke. "Even the soup is meant to be served cold. I call it potato leek, but it's got one of those fancy French names."

"Vichyssoise," supplied Ben, and Tam's eyes grew big—understandably so, because until now he had thought "Abracadabra!" the only magic word his father knew.

"I made it from one of those packet mixes." Tom was clearly making an attempt at conversation. "It was my only shortcut because I wanted the meal to be perfect."

"Is it your birfday?" Tam and Abbey asked together.

"As a matter of fact it is." Tom looked embarrassed and his eyes shifted away from ours to look out over the sea, which had lost some of its smooth sparkle and made louder whooshing sounds as it came frothing up on the sands. The sky had turned grey in patches and the sun looked ready to hole up behind the clouds. Something had definitely gone out of the day. It was suddenly clear that Tom was a sad and lonely man. Abbey and Tam asked if he would like to come and have some of Jonas's birthday cake, and his face brightened before he shook his head.

"Thanks but I think it's going to rain."

"I'm afraid you're right," I said. And feeling rather as though I were abandoning a baby on a church doorstep, turned to go.

Ben, the children, and I trod in single file along the strip of sand leading from one beach to the next, getting our feet wet as the waves made little foam-lipped rushes at us.

"I think he's a sad fairy." Abbey was looking back over her shoulder, although it was no longer possible to see Tom. We were back on our own little beach. Jonas was dozing in his chair, with a handkerchief spread over his head to protect it from the sun, which now posed little threat. He started awake at our approach. At the same moment the handkerchief blew away—flapping itself into wings. The children went happily scampering after it.

They didn't look nearly as merry when we all started trudging up the stone staircase back to the car. Abbey thought she had lost one of her shells and Tam kept saying, at every second step, that he didn't see why he couldn't go paddling. Keeping my temper wasn't easy. My son's constant stopping meant I was always in danger of bumping into him as I made up the rear of the procession with the buckets and spades. The traveling rug kept sliding off my arm as if determined to get itself stepped on. Just as I pitched forward for the third time and let out an unnerved scream we reached the top. Ben set the chair and picnic basket down on the gravel-strewn grass while he opened up the boot of the car.

The breeze tugged at my hair, spilling some strands over my eyes, but it felt good standing there, even with my skirts slapping against my legs as if chivying me into getting into the car. Three or four gulls glided overhead. I stood listening to their hoarse cries, wondering if they ever had anything cheerful to say when humans weren't around. And then I heard someone—or something—else cry out. The sound blew in from the sea below; there was suddenly a deep silence as even these gulls shut up to listen and the wind held its breath. I had just decided I was imagining things when Ben hurried up beside me.

"What was that?" He gripped my arm.

"I don't know." I stood stock-still.

It came again, a thin thread of a wail, followed a few seconds later by a more robust shout that Ben and I both instantly recognized as a cry for help. Dodging back to the car, I told Jonas to stay with the twins. "Someone's in trouble down on the beach or in the water." Someone! I had little doubt that it was Tom Tingle. "Here, take the traveling rug." Jonas thrust it into my hands as I raced after my husband. Already it seemed ages since we had first heard that cry. It was raining hard when I reached the cliff steps.

But I couldn't worry about losing my balance as I made my blurry descent; my mind was filled with the image of Tom Tingle floundering in the sea, spewing out water like a fountainhead while trying to catch his breath.

All my energy went to chasing Ben's shadow around the armchair curve of cliff separating the two beaches. The narrow strip leading from one to the other was now ankle deep in water and to prevent myself from stumbling I had to keep grabbing at the boulder wall. At last I could see Ben again. He was standing where the sky and the sea merged, kicking off his shoes and wrenching off his jacket.

"Be careful!" I yelled. And then he was splashing into the water, his arms extended as he prepared to leap into the waves. He wasn't a great swimmer, and there was said to be a vicious undertow beyond the breakwaters. My life flashed before me—my life as a heartbroken widow with two small children to bring up alone. Would Abbey and Tam even remember their father? Would I ever come out of mourning and stop cursing fate?

I could no longer see him through the rain, but I heard him shouting out to the other person in the water, and over the loud knocking of my heart I heard an answering cry. It didn't sound too far off. Hope reared its head as I hovered at the water's edge, my hands cupped fruitlessly over my eyes. There was nothing to see but grey. The sea moved and the sky didn't, that was the only difference. I had dropped the plaid rug a few yards away. Now I forced myself to go pick it up and shake off the sand. Then I got Ben's jacket. My nerves were ticking like a clock and my hands shook. I had never been more frightened in my life. For what seemed like ages I didn't hear anything. Then there came a shout. But I couldn't recognize the voice.

I had just reached the calm of icy desperation, when suddenly the nightmare was over. First I heard a splashing, and then something dark and hulking emerged before my eyes. It was Ben, my one true love, staggering under the burden of carrying someone in his arms. Someone who looked to be a deadweight . . .

"Darling! Are you all right? Is it Tom? Did you get to him in time?" I gabbled, weaving my way like a drunkard towards them with the traveling rug and his jacket.

"Yes, it's him." Ben spoke slowly, panting as he rose after laying the other man on the ground. "He was alive a couple of minutes ago. Thank God he didn't struggle and try to drag me under as I towed him in. I told him I'm not much of a swimmer and he kicked quite productively when I got him under the armpits."

I helped Ben put on his jacket, but he was still shivering when we both bent over Tom Tingle. Fully clothed except for his shoes, he looked waterlogged and had his eyes closed. But he was definitely breathing. If his heaving chest meant anything. Spreading the traveling rug over him and tucking in the edges, I whispered to Ben.

"I wonder?"

"About what?"

"If he meant to drown himself." The rain was thinning out and it was now possible to see the table and chair where he'd sat making his solitary birthday meal. Ben started to speak, but before he got out half a word, Tom Tingle's eyes opened and he spoke either to us or some vision inside his head.

"It was an accident. But how can a halfway decent man live with that?"

# CHAPTER NINE

*Wash bone-china dinner services
and tea sets during spring cleaning.
It is necessary that this be done
once a year to prevent cracking.*

ON THE FOLLOWING THURSDAY FREDDY SHOWED UP
early in the afternoon and stayed to watch me mix up a
batch of furniture polish from the instructions in Abigail's
little book. Eager for validation, I bragged about having
made some silver polish the day before, at the prospect of
which my cousin looked suitably awed. Had I, he inquired,
thought of mass-producing an entire line of housecleaning
products? And if so could he please be the one to start selling door to door? Such enthusiasm warmed my heart. I
actually liked his idea until I thought about turning the
kitchen into a one-woman factory. No hope of Freddy,
however enthusiastic a salesman, agreeing to do part of
the menial work.

He did offer to eat a slice of the chocolate cake left over
from an ill-fated picnic. In fact he had two slices, saying it
would be negligent to let it go to waste. Scratching his
beard, he looked at me in what I'm sure he considered a
meaningful way.

"I haven't forgotten," I assured him, swallowing my last

mouthful of cake, "about going to see Dr. Solomon about Jonas."

"When's he due back from his holiday, coz?"

"Today. But I thought I'd go tomorrow morning when the twins are in play school."

"Bad idea. Doesn't do to procrastinate." Freddy ambled over to the refrigerator to stand with the door open, peering inside with all the intensity of an anthropologist studying culture as evinced by an igloo. Finally, before his nose got frost-bitten off his face, he took out a bottle of milk and the makings of a ham sandwich and unloaded these spoils on the table. "You see," he said cheerfully, "you can take yourself off, Ellie, without fear I will starve to death in your absence."

"You just had half a cake," I reminded him.

"Did I?" He was busily unwrapping the sliced ham and squeezing the bread to make sure it was fresh. "As I was just saying, Ellie, procrastination is a bad thing. Always get a head start, that's my motto." Should I take his advice and go along to Dr. Solomon's surgery now? But I hated leaving the kitchen such a shambles. Besides, I didn't like the idea of leaving my polish-making paraphernalia sitting out where the children could get hold of it.

"Go," urged Freddy through a mouthful of sandwich. "I'll clean up this mess before the twins get up from their naps. Take all the time you want. As Mrs. Malloy was fond of saying, I only charge by the hour."

"Well, if you're sure," I said, "about there being no rush, I'll take Jonas's mirror to be repaired and return Brigadier Lester-Smith's raincoat. I really do need to get Ben's coat back." I was getting into mine as I spoke and taking a scarf from a hook in the alcove to put in my pocket.

"Don't forget your handbag." Freddy tucked it under my arm after I had collected both mirror and raincoat, then ushered me out the door as if I had come trying to sell my furniture polish. "And remember don't stint yourself on time. I can survive on what you have in the house at least until tomorrow morning."

"Don't forget the children and Jonas." I kissed his fuzzy cheek. "They'll need something to eat when they get up from their naps."

"Never fear, Freddy's here!" He waved me off, eager to return to his mid-afternoon snack, and I headed for the old convertible. It was a little chilly, but the skies looked innocent enough. I set off, but instead of turning towards the village on exiting our gateway, the car turned as if of its own volition in the direction of Bellkiek, as we had done on the day of the picnic.

I had thought a lot about Tom Tingle in the last few days. What had he meant in saying "It was an accident"? Ben thought Tom must have been speaking about putting both their lives in danger. But I wasn't convinced.

Within seconds Tom had been on his feet, apologizing in a shamefaced voice for making a nuisance of himself, thanking Ben for the rescue, and insisting he could make it back to his house on his own. He did not explain why he had gone into the sea with his clothes on. When we insisted on seeing him to his house, he turned the handle of the unlocked front door, bobbed us a nod, and went inside without even asking Ben if he would like to dry off.

It wasn't until the children and Jonas were in bed that Ben and I talked about the incident. And I posed the question, was it possible Tom had been talking about Mrs. Large? Did he believe himself responsible for her death? Had he perhaps opened the study door at Tall Chimneys and knocked the poor woman off her ladder? Was he consumed with guilt that he hadn't seen that a doctor was fetched? Or confessed his involvement to the police? Ben had told me I was letting my imagination run riot. At which point he had sneezed. Whereupon I decided one should always think first of the living. Which in this case meant feeling my husband's forehead to make sure he didn't have a temperature. Then making him another cup of cocoa before insisting he get between warm bedclothes and have a good night's sleep.

But I had continued to worry about Tom Tingle. Suppose his entering the water had been an attempt at suicide? And he tried again? The thought turned my legs wobbly as I now drove towards his house. There was no blaming Ben. Men don't think like women. They're much more inclined to take a man at his word when he says that nothing's wrong. Real men don't read each other's minds. They consider it an invasion of privacy. But there was no excuse where I was concerned. Driving along The Cliff Road I wondered how I'd been able to go about my own life without returning sooner to make sure Tom Tingle was still among the living.

My less-than-courageous answer came back pretty quickly. If he had, however accidentally, killed Mrs. Large, he might be completely irrational when wondering just how much he had blabbed down on the beach. And I had no desire to encourage him in the belief that the fewer people who knew his secret the better.

I could now see his house. Its warm red brick was certainly hospitable-looking. Would its owner slam the door in my face when I came knocking? My knees did a bit of that as I parked where the drive divided into two arms encircling a small lawn in front of the house steps. Next to the bell was a sign that read "Out of Order." So it had to be the knocker.

I rapped once—tentatively, as if flapping a leaf against a tree trunk. Realizing I could stand there all day at that rate, I got up the nerve to try again. I still didn't make much of a bang, but presumably Tom had ears like a cat. He immediately opened the door. He looked dubious, but I announced firmly that I had come to see how he was doing while putting my foot in the door like someone selling floor polish. And after a moment's hesitation he invited me to come in.

"Did I catch you in the middle of making dinner?" I asked, noticing as we stood in the wide hall that he was wearing an apron wrapped around his middle and that his hands were floury.

"I was just finishing up a steak and kidney pudding," he said. "If you mean to stay more than a minute or two, we'd best head for the kitchen. I'm not the best cook in the world. But I know how to read a recipe, and this one calls for steaming over gently boiling water at least three hours. So I've got to look sharpish if I want to eat before seven."

He led the way down the wide hall. Its carpet was shabby, the wallpaper needed replacing, but the windows on the staircase wall let in floods of light, and I imagined how handsome it might look if redecorated. We passed a couple of open doors on our way to the kitchen. One gave a glimpse of the dining room and the other of a book-lined study. The furniture looked old and there was a faintly musty smell. Even so, my heart warmed to the place. The quirky contours of the rooms and the sunlight twinkling on wainscotted walls already mellowed with age gave a sense of a house where people had once been happy and might be again. What was needed was cooperation from Tom.

When we entered the kitchen, my hopes rose on his be-half. Surely no one could have made such a floury mess preparing one steak and kidney pudding without getting some enjoyment out of the process. The old pine table was covered with a jumble of what seemed to be the entire contents of the pantry, fridge, and utensils drawer. There were milk bottles—one full, the other almost empty—onion scraps, Oxo cubes, an empty suet packet, chunks of raw meat—all having been caught off guard in a dry blizzard. Little wonder the pudding basin and rolling pin looked as though they didn't have a clue where to start. But luckily, their lord and master did not appear to be at a loss.

As I hovered across from him, Tom gave another twist to his rolled-up sleeves and got busy kneading the sticky mass in the mixing bowl he had unearthed from under a floury tea towel. If he didn't look as expert at the job as Ben, he lost no points in letting his ingredients know who was boss.

"You look well," I told him.

"I'm jogging along." He picked up the overturned bag of flour, scattered more of its contents, slapped down the suet pastry, divided this in two, and rolled the larger piece into a circle. "But I suppose you're referring to my dip in the sea the other day." His face reddened. "It was awfully good of your husband to come in after me. I'm very appreciative, but there was no need for you to come all the way over here. I didn't catch a deathly chill. And I hope your husband suffered no unpleasant repercussions." Tom had lined the pudding basin with pastry and now dumped in the meat and chopped onion. "I know I should have got in touch, but I'm afraid I allowed my embarrassment to get in the way of good manners."

"What"—I had to ask the question—"made you go into the sea with your clothes on?"

He finally looked at me. "Good gracious! You've been thinking I was trying to kill myself. Yes, I can see how you could have got that idea. It wasn't much fun having a birthday party by myself; but I promise you, Mrs. Haskell, that you have got the wrong end of the stick. I plowed out into that icy water to save the life of another, not to end mine."

"I don't understand."

"I heard someone scream and—"

"Oh, goodness!" I had to sit down. "I'll bet that was me when I almost tripped going back up the cliff. But you thought someone was drowning."

"I'm not very good at locating sound." Tom stood like a flour-covered gnome waiting to be dusted off and put back in the perennial border. Besides which, I"—picking up his pudding and taking it over to the steamer—"I may have been overly eager to charge to the rescue and perform deeds of daring-do. The fact that I can't swim more than a few strokes didn't seem important until I was out of my depth and going down for the third time."

"I think you behaved very nobly," I said, "but there's still something puzzling me."

"What?"

"It's not important." Suddenly I was feeling like an impertinent fool.

"Obviously it is." Tom turned from the cooker to fix me with surprisingly shrewd eyes.

"Well, it's just that you said something immediately after Ben got you out of the water . . . that . . . it was an accident, but that didn't make it easy for a man of conscience to live with."

"And you thought I was trying to make excuses for my silly behaviour that put your husband in danger?" Tom sat down across from me and put his floury hands on his knees and I couldn't bring myself to mention Mrs. Large. "All I can think"—he studied the mess on the table—"is that my life must still have been flashing before me, and I was remembering an incident from my schoolboy days."

"Yes?" I prompted.

"It was when I was in the fourth form. We were playing cricket and I was at bat. Bill Struthers—I think that was his name—bowled a fast ball that I actually managed to hit and it went for six. Or it would have done if it hadn't caught the headmaster on the head just as he peeked over the fence to see how we were doing. He got a nasty concussion and my parents, both keen sporting types, were mortified."

The story rang true, especially when I remembered Tom telling Sir Robert Pomeroy at the Hearthside Guild meeting that he disliked sports. It simplified things for my conscience where Mrs. Large was concerned. Also there was something about Tom that touched me. I found myself thinking about that old picture book, the one I had found in the attic about the wicked gnomes who had holed up in the old lady's rockery. Maybe if I had read it to the end, I would have discovered the little men were unhappy at being dug up all the time and the old lady was a fiend with a hoe.

"You have a beautiful garden," I told Tom, as I drank the cup of tea he poured for me. "Have you done much to it since you moved in?"

"Things are the way I found them." He got up to refill the pot. "I always lived in a flat with not so much as a window box to fill with geraniums. But the garden was the main reason I bought this house, and now spring's here, I'd like to get my hands in the earth. Trouble is, I don't know where to start. I could be pulling up plants thinking they're weeds."

"You should come and talk to Jonas—he's the original green thumb," I said. "Really, you'd be doing him a favour, because he can't work much in the garden anymore and he misses it."

"And you must miss having a gardener," Tom replied.

"Oh, Jonas is much more than that to our family." I

drank the last drops of my tea and stood up. "What we mind is that he seems to be failing. That's why I'd better get moving. I'm going to see his doctor. To find out what can be done to help him."

"I see." Tom removed his apron and took me back through the hall to the front door. "Perhaps I'll stop by at Merlin's Court sometime. I could bring some books of wallpaper with me, seeing I've heard you're in the decorating business and I could use some advice so as not to make things look worse rather than better."

"I'd be glad to help." I refrained from adding that I would love to oversee the renovation of the entire house one day. And so I left, thinking that life was indeed odd. I no longer believed Tom Tingle was a menace to himself, let alone anyone else. I even hoped we would get to know each other better.

It was after three when I got into the car. Even so, I doubled back past my own house, just to make sure there wasn't smoke billowing from the windows or any other sign of trouble. I was just picking up speed again when I saw Clarice Whitcombe approaching The Cliff Road from Hawthorn Lane. Stopping, I rolled down the window to say hello. I hadn't seen her since Mrs. Large's funeral.

"Hello, Ellie." Clarice looked embarrassed; her eyes didn't quite meet mine and she was fidgety. She was neatly turned out as always, in a raincoat and sensible shoes, but the woolly hat she wore was slightly askew and she had on only one pearl earring. "I've been meaning to have you round," she said, "only I don't know where the time goes. It's not as though I'm busy like you. No husband or children to keep me occupied . . ." Her voice trailed off. Clarice was now peering up and down the road, on the lookout, I supposed, for the bus that stops close to the vicarage gates at half-hour intervals.

"Have you been able to get back to your piano playing?" I asked, and she jerked around to face me as if I had slapped her.

"No, I haven't. Not once." She wrapped a hand around her wrist and wiggled her free fingers. "I'm still having trouble with this silly old arm. Actually I'm going down to see the doctor about it—that's where I'm headed now." Her face was turning pinker by the minute. "But I really do want to have you over, Ellie. I've been thinking about you quite a lot and hoping perhaps you would be kind enough to advise me, because one of my problems is I've absolutely no eye for colour."

"It's really not difficult," I reassured her. "You just need confidence in picking what you like. Then everything falls into place. And it's relatively easy to coordinate fabrics with the wallpaper and so on."

"But I wasn't exactly thinking about home furnishings." Clarice was looking more awkward by the minute. "What I'd like to know is how to choose the right shade of lipstick and eye shadow." She dabbed at her lids. "To help smarten me up, make me more attract— Well, just to look better, really. I know I'm past the age of being a glamour girl, but I thought that with you being younger and always seeming so pulled together . . ."

"Me?"

"Oh, but you are," she said. "You're lucky having such pretty hair and that fresh complexion, but you also know about the other stuff. Walt . . ." She exhaled shakily. "Brigadier Lester-Smith said once that a lot of women could take tips from you on how to wear makeup without making clowns of themselves."

"That was very nice of him."

" 'Just what a woman should be,' is how the brigadier described you. But not in any wrong way, Ellie. He made it clear he didn't . . . wouldn't . . . hadn't even for a minute harboured an improper thought in his head where you, a married woman, were concerned." Clarice was now so red her face could have stopped traffic. Could it be she protested too much? Was she perhaps concerned that Brigadier Lester-Smith harboured forbidden feelings for me? It was hard to imagine he had said anything to foster such an idea. Unless—my mind ran rampant—he had been trying to make her jealous? Schoolboy behaviour from a man closing in on sixty. But as my mother once told me, men in love often behaved like oversize children.

"Clarice," I said, "you don't need makeup tips from me, or from anyone else for that matter. You look wonderful the way you are, as your own self. Don't risk losing that. Other people"—the brigadier's name hung in the air between us—"might be very sorry if you did."

"Or he . . . they might think I was trying too hard to please." She shuddered visibly. "Yes, perhaps you're right, Ellie. But I would appreciate your advice on the house, how to make it more inviting—well, livable, I suppose, is the word I'm looking for." Clarice again looked down the road. "And now I'd better be getting to the bus stop or I'll be late for my . . . my appointment with the doctor."

"I can take you," I told her. "I'm going to Dr. Solomon's surgery."

"Oh, but he isn't my doctor," she said quickly.

"That doesn't matter. I'm not in any great rush; I'll be glad to take you where you need to go."

"But it isn't in Chitterton Fells." Clarice sounded panicky. "If it's all the same, Ellie, I'd rather take the bus; that way I wouldn't feel I was putting you out and could enjoy the journey. I've got a good book with me." Patting her handbag, she inched away from the car.

"Well, if you're quite sure."

"Oh, absolutely." She almost nodded her head off. I drove away, feeling uncomfortable at having put her on the spot. My guess was that she had an appointment with a psychiatrist. Something readily understood, given her parents' joint suicide. That must have been the most awful shock, especially after spending her life at the beck and call of two people who had been totally absorbed in each other. Poor Clarice Whitcombe! Surely if there were any fairness in life, happiness would be forthcoming, for both her and Brigadier Lester-Smith. He'd had his own share of sorrows. The two of them were still on my mind when I left Jonas's mirror at the repair shop.

Dr. Solomon's waiting room was packed, mainly with elderly people coughing and younger women with toddlers staggering around their chairs. The receptionist looked harried and the magazines were so dated only an antiquarian could have found them of interest. For the first twenty minutes I had to stand, wedged in between the children's book rack and the window. When I did get a seat, it was by the door, so I kept getting banged into by patients coming and going. The wall clock ticked out the minutes with excruciating slowness. I spent the next hour checking my watch—hoping the two timekeepers would get into a race, because surely the place would thin out by four-thirty. Then four-thirty came and went, and I began to fret; with several people still ahead of me, what if Dr. Solomon closed the surgery without seeing me?

It was well after five when a weary-looking woman with a child squirming under each arm staggered out of his office, and the receptionist called my name. She actually had to say it twice because by now I had forgotten it, along with why I was there. But the doctor, no doubt refreshed from his holiday, was in great form. He waved me into a chair, repositioned himself behind his desk, and greeted me as if I were the first patient of the day. I explained that I had come about Jonas, spent five minutes voicing my concerns, and waited for him to say something brilliant.

In fact he didn't say much. But he said it at considerable length, going back and forth over the same ground like a farmer trying out a new tractor. The gist of his conversation was that he didn't think there was anything wrong with Jonas other than old age slowing him down. What Jonas needed was good food, adequate rest, and something to stimulate his emotional and physical energy.

"Try and get the old boy out more," Dr. Solomon suggested. "Take him on car trips to places he's always liked."

"Jonas hates riding in a car for any distance." I knew I sounded uncooperative, but it was the truth. "And the only place he likes is home."

"Then encourage him to potter outside, find someone he can talk gardening with; old people love to pass on what they know to the next generation. Keep his spirits up, that's the best medicine, but I will stop in and look him over." The doctor flipped through his calendar and said it would have to be early the next week. I thanked him and rose to leave. Dr. Solomon walked me to the door, where he placed a kindly hand on my elbow. "Ellie, Jonas has had a long and healthy life, you have to face up to losing the old boy one of these days."

"But not now? Not soon?"

"I'd say he's got at least a couple of good years left to him." The doctor patted my shoulder. I said good-bye, feeling hopeful, if not entirely reassured.

I asked the receptionist if I could use the phone to ring home and got Ben at the third ring. He said he'd been back for half an hour, that Freddy was still there, and the twins wanted to help cook dinner. Everything being well under control, I felt no need to rush home. I told Ben about wanting to return Brigadier Lester-Smith's raincoat, but promised not to dawdle over endless cups of tea.

It was a short drive to the brigadier's house on Herring Street, only two doors down from where Mrs. Malloy had resided. Roxie. Not only had she failed to show up for Mrs. Large's funeral, she hadn't returned my subsequent phone calls, either. Both times I had talked with Vanessa, who had promised without enthusiasm to relay the message. My lovely cousin hadn't been forthcoming about the baby or her husband, let alone how she enjoyed having her less-than-aristocratic mother-in-law on the premises. Of course, Vanessa had a master's degree in self-absorption. The only topic she broached was the possibility of landing a tip-top modeling assignment.

Looking anything but a fashion plate in my nondesigner raincoat, I parked the car in front of the brigadier's terraced house with its neat square of garden. There were flowers in the borders and a dwarf cherry tree that shivered in the breeze. I was just about to push open the green-painted gate when I heard footsteps, and I turned to see a woman of about thirty-five or forty scurrying towards me. She was wearing a flamingo-pink sweater over tight slacks. Her arms flapped as she came, making her look like a long-legged bird attempting flight.

"Come to see the brigadier, have you, love?" she panted.

"I'm returning his raincoat." I rearranged it over my arm.

"Is that so?" Her false eyelashes flickered. "Nice to meet you. I'm Marilyn Tollings from across the street." The name didn't ring a bell, although Mrs. Malloy might have mentioned her. "And you are?" The woman took hold of the gate to prevent it swinging against her legs.

"Ellie Haskell."

It was clear my name also drew a blank and equally obvious that Marilyn Tollings was a nosey parker. "You wasn't
here earlier, was you? Just a half hour or so gone it must
have been. No?" She sized up my shake of the head. "Well,
if that doesn't take the biscuit! Two women coming to
see our prim and proper brigadier, almost back to back!
But don't worry." Marilyn Tollings gave me a poke with a
fingernail, which was sharpened to a point. "She's not
there now. I was at the bedroom window, you see, on the
lookout for my hubby—he works funny hours. That's how
I happened to see her—the woman you say wasn't you—
going up the Brigadier Hoity-Toity's path. She was wearing
a raincoat just like yours." Marilyn gave me another jab.
"Only now I think about it, she had on one of them woolly
hats, although I couldn't say as to colour. My eyesight's
not that great."

If this was true, she had probably weakened it spying on
her neighbours through a pair of binoculars. Saying I had
no idea who the woman might be, I reached for the gate,
but Marilyn Tollings didn't take the hint. "Funny thing is
she went halfway down the path, then stopped like she'd
found herself in the wrong place and went back out to the
street."

"She must have realized she had the wrong address."

"I suppose." Marilyn didn't sound eager to be convinced.
"Trouble is, I'm the sort that's inclined to worry about people. Even ones I don't know from Adam. And it seemed to
me that woman was scared half to death. And when I
thought you was her come back, I had to nip over to see if
everything was all right. You hear such dreadful things
these days about women being raped and murdered while
people that could have helped turned a blind eye. Doesn't
bear thinking about, does it?"

"No." This talk of crime did make me I realize I had
left the car keys in the ignition. But I would be in the

brigadier's house for just a couple of minutes. Besides, it would take someone really desperate to steal the old crock.

"I always feel sorry for women that live alone." She shook her head. "As I said, my hubby's gone a lot. But that's not the same as being a single woman, is it? They're a target for crazies, I always say. There was a Mrs. Malloy that was on her own living next door but one to the brigadier. She's gone to live with her son and daughter-in-law in London. Much the best thing for her and, I'll say it as shouldn't, likewise best for Brigadier Lester-Smith. Roxie Malloy liked to think she was in thick with him, and that sort of thing can be annoying to any man, let alone an elderly bachelor." Marilyn Tollings edged closer and the waves of musky perfume would have brought round bodies in the morgue. "He does have that hyphen in his name, but that's nothing to me; not when I was brought up going to Spain every year for my holidays and had an auntie that had a downstairs toilet."

"Really?" I fought an insane urge to whap Marilyn Tollings with the brigadier's raincoat.

"What went to Roxie Malloy's head was having friends in high places. She was in with the woman who dropped dead the other week. A Mrs. Large, that worked up at Pomeroy Hall for Sir Robert and her ladyship. You've heard about Lady P., haven't you? The new one he married just a few months back. Maureen Dovedale, she was. And what a change for her! Gone from working in that poky little corner shop with a post-office counter to being a lady of the manor! I'd be scared stiff of putting a foot wrong and mucking things up for myself. But then, there's them that can hold their own in this world better than others. The woman that's staying in Roxie Malloy's house doesn't mix with anyone on the street. Not so much as a hello or good-bye if she sees you. That's a big mistake in my book, because it makes sense for neighbours to look out for each other. Like I said, awful things can happen to a woman living alone."

I nodded while trying to remember which of her Magna Char chums Mrs. Malloy had said would be looking after her house until it went on the market. Then, as if having heard enough of Marilyn Tollings's chatter, the skies lowered themselves with a bang of thunder and a few portentous drops of rain landed on our heads.

"Look's like Brigadier Lester-Smith will be getting his raincoat back in the nick of time." I gave Marilyn Tollings a farewell smile and pushed on the garden gate. "Nice to have met you."

"Same here, love." She sounded suddenly forlorn, and I felt a twinge of pity. Was she always sticking her nose into other people's business because her husband was never home—on account of the funny hours he worked? Another clap of thunder sent her scurrying back home and me down the brigadier's path.

I was struck all at once by the blank stare of the house. Blank because all the curtains were drawn and because the house didn't have much facial expression, anyway. A very ordinary narrow-faced house, identical to almost every other one on the street. Was Brigadier Lester-Smith away? Or had Clarice Whitcombe returned when Marilyn Tollings was somehow absent from her post and, overcoming her shyness, made it all the way down the extremely short path to the door? Had Clarice rung the bell and been welcomed in with open arms by the brigadier? Were they even now sitting in the half dark, afraid that a chink of light would reveal to the entire world that there was a tryst in the making? I was certain that Clarice was the woman Marilyn had seen in the raincoat and woolly hat. And equally convinced that they were two middle-aged people caught up in the near-paralyzing terror of teenagers falling in love. I hated the idea of interrupting what might be a breakthrough in their relationship. Still, I didn't feel I could leave the brigadier's raincoat on the doorstep, and I needed to get Ben's back.

I rang the bell and waited. It was raining harder now and I wasn't getting much cover from the narrow overhang that substituted for a porch. A full minute went by and I was debating whether to try again when the door inched open and I found myself almost nose to nose with the brigadier. He was wearing a dressing gown and had a towel wrapped around his head. The smile he produced in greeting missed his eyes completely. It also missed his lips by inches.

"Brigadier, I'm sorry." My voice rattled along with the brass chain he was slipping from its slot. "Obviously I've caught you at a bad time. But I did want to return your coat."

"My what?" He now had the door properly open.

"The raincoat Ben took by mistake."

"Ah, that one." He sounded not one whit enlightened. "Sorry about this." He looked down at his dressing gown, saw a gap that shouldn't have been there, and in the process of tugging himself into order almost dropped the towel off his head. "I was washing my hair. I always do it on a Tuesday." He sounded flustered, and I didn't like to point out that this was Thursday.

"I won't keep you. You take this." I handed him the coat. "If you'll let me have Ben's, I'll get out of your hair."

Far from smiling at my feeble joke, he looked panicky as he invited me to step inside. Was it possible Clarice was in the house? I just couldn't see her and the brigadier getting to the dressing-gown stage in such unseemly haste. Then there was that towel on his head. Could it really be no more than a prop?

"I'm not quite sure where I put Ben's coat." Brigadier Lester-Smith poked at his collar with unsteady fingers before retying the dressing-gown cord yet again. "Why don't you go into the sitting room, Ellie, while I have a look round for it?" This was utterly unlike him; the brigadier was not a man to misplace things. I began to hope that lovesickness was his only problem as I perched on the arm of a chair, waiting for him to return. I found myself growing increasingly jumpy. Perhaps it was because I'd already spent too much time sitting today in Dr. Solomon's surgery. Anyway, I felt like a schoolgirl, desperately needing to go to the loo and being unable to ask to be excused because the teacher had left the classroom. After several minutes of this, I got up and went back into the hall.

"Brigadier?" I called.

There was no answer. After trying again, I decided I really couldn't wait any longer. Luckily I was familiar with his house, so I nipped up the narrow staircase and across the tiny landing to the bathroom. He'd had the wall knocked out between it and the once-separate toilet, making things less cramped. He had also put in new fixtures. At first I didn't look towards the frosted-glass shower doors. But a few moments later, while I stood washing my hands at the sink, I glanced sideways and noticed that the doors were pushed to the side, and I could see reddish-brown stains spattering the wall and even deeper dribbles of . . . the red . . . stuff going down the white tile to puddle by the drain.

"Ellie?"

On hearing the brigadier calling my name, I levitated a couple of feet off the ground, then staggered out onto the landing to collide with him at the top of the stairs.

"Sorry! I had to use the loo," I babbled. The expression on his face gave him away. He knew I had seen. And he knew he had to offer some sort of explanation. But even as the bloom faded from his peachy cheeks, he was saved by a piercing scream from outside. Looking like a man in a turban forced into battle against his religious beliefs, Brigadier Lester-Smith hurried down the stairs ahead of me towards whatever horror had paid an evening visit.

# CHAPTER TEN

*Clean brass trays, fenders,
and other flat pieces with
half a lemon dipped in salt.
Rub well before rinsing in
cool water and polishing
with a soft cloth.*

A COLLAGE OF DARK SHAPES EMERGED THROUGH THE
drizzle to group in the middle of the road, where they
fleshed out into real people, all jabbering away about having heard the scream. Marilyn Tollings's voice rose above
the rest with her announcement that she'd had one of her
funny feelings on and off all day that something terrible
was about to strike Herring Street. A male voice drowned
her out, saying it was probably nothing, just some fool of a
woman thinking there was a man hiding under her bed.
The group now shuffled uncertainly, murmuring amongst
themselves.

It was then I noticed the lights were on in Mrs. Malloy's
house. When I'd first arrived, I had thought how sad
and deserted it looked, even though one of Mrs. Malloy's
C.F.C.W.A. cronies was supposed to be staying in the
house. But whether the caretaker was Trina McKinnley,
Winifred Smalley, or Betty Nettle continued to escape my
mind. It was hard for me to picture Trina being a woman
to run screaming into the road whatever the provocation,

or even sticking her nose out the door if she heard some-one else do so. But either one of the others? Yes, it was definitely odd that Mrs. Smalley or Mrs. Nettle wasn't out in the street with the other neighbours.

I turned without saying anything to Brigadier Smith—I had blocked him right out of my mind along with what I had seen in his shower. But he followed close behind me as I hurried over to Mrs. Malloy's house. My heart was pounding while my brain did nothing at all as I raced up the path to ring the bell. Nothing. Then I pounded on the front door.

My hand reached for the knob. It turned, and there I was in Mrs. Malloy's hall with Brigadier Lester-Smith at my elbow, in his dressing gown and towel turban. Straight ahead was the kitchen, its door half open, and from within came the sound of a woman's voice. It wasn't talking to us. And it didn't sound panic-stricken, but I couldn't shake the feeling that I was walking in on someone or something horrific. There was no point in dillydallying, hoping for a poker to appear in my hand. I took the few remaining steps towards the kitchen. Cautiously!

The hall had been reduced to shoulder width by the amount of furniture Mrs. Malloy had miraculously squeezed into it. A clothes tree protruded, along with several what-not tables and an ancient aspidistra in a very large, very ugly pot. China poodles and Indian brass pieces had been scattered about with a generous hand, all geared up to come toppling down at the least nudge. I should have had enough sense to walk sideways, as I discovered with a leap of alarm when a decorative plate came clattering off the wall, propelling me and Brigadier Lester-Smith into the kitchen.

There were two people in that kitchen. One of them was Trina McKinnley, but she wasn't talking. She was lying facedown with a knife stuck in her back, her neck twisted around so that she appeared to be looking up at us in glassy-eyed inquiry. There was blood . . . The kitchen faded out and for a moment I thought that I was back in the brigadier's bathroom . . . until his hand came down on my shoulder. I sat down with a jolt in a chair already pulled out from the table. It was hard to concentrate, but I made myself look at the woman in the fake leopard coat and the black velvet toque standing with hands on her hips like a mannequin in a shop window.

"If I'd known you was stopping by, I'd have had the kettle on and some crumpets toasted," said Mrs. Malloy, coming abruptly alive. Something poor Trina McKinnley would never do. "But as you can see"—waving a hand at the corpse on the floor—"things is rather at sixes and sevens here, Mrs. H. Some homecoming this has turned out to be. But it doesn't do to complain, does it? We've all got troubles."

I could only stare at her.

"And what's he doing here, dressed up like something out of the Taj Mahal?" Mrs. Malloy demanded, suddenly appearing to notice Brigadier Lester-Smith standing behind my chair.

"We'll get to that later," I said, hoping desperately that I sounded casual, because when one is in the room with a possible murderer, it makes sense not to unduly put the wind up that person. "Mrs. Malloy, you have to tell us what happened here. You have rung the police, haven't you?"

"Well, it was like this." Mrs. Malloy began slowly unbuttoning her coat, perhaps to give her hands something to do. "I came up from London on the coach, it's not quite as quick as the train, but it puts me down within walking distance of home. And I'd only the one suitcase with me, so it was no bother." Still standing in her coat, she pointed at the suitcase leaning against the wall by the back door.

"The coach was about fifteen minutes late, so I suppose I got off at around six, and by the time I got here it must have been close to twenty past because I'd stopped to buy a bottle of milk at the shop down the road. It's there on the table, and lucky I didn't drop it." Mrs. Malloy wobbled for the first time.

"And you walked in to find Trina dead."

"Don't be daft, Mrs. H.! I came storming in bent on finding fault with how she'd been taking care of the house during my absence, and when I saw the state of the kitchen, I picked up the carving knife and let her have it good and proper." Mrs. Malloy snorted a laugh that broke into pieces, so that the next moment she was shaking and sobbing. And I found myself helping her into the chair I had vacated, while the brigadier mumbled something about brandy.

"Who could have done this to her, Mrs. H.? That's what I was asking myself before you walked in." Mrs. Malloy shook her head, dislodging the toque so that her hair was revealed. The maroon shade she had switched to after becoming a grandmother was no more. She was back to her tamer jet black, with the requisite two inches of white roots—much better suited to a woman in mourning. "A nice girl like Trina! Well, maybe she wasn't all that nice, but that's not the point, is it? We in the C.F.C.W.A. was fond of her. She could be a laugh, could Trina. Bossy, I'll give you that, and a bit on the grab when it came to money, but that's no reason to chop her, is it?"

"Absolutely not," agreed Brigadier Lester-Smith, who was gingerly stepping around the body to open the pantry door. Mrs. Malloy, understanding what he was about, said he'd find a bottle of medicinal gin on the second shelf.

"We have to figure out who done it." She was fanning her face with her hand, a face that was beginning to show signs of emotional wear and tear in the mascara smudges under her eyes and the droop of her butterfly lips. "And we'd better do it on the double, Mrs. H., or as sure as my middle name's Nelly, the police will think it was me."

"We don't know how long she's been dead," I pointed out. "It may turn out to have been several hours, putting you in the clear."

"Or, with my bleeding luck, it could have happened minutes before I waltzed in the door."

"Do you think the knife is one of yours?"

She nodded. "Looks like the one I used for the Sunday joint. I always left it out by the cooker."

"You didn't touch it?" I said.

"Now why would I do that?" she shot back.

"People do. You hear about it all the time. The person who finds the body goes to pull out the knife or makes contact with it while they're feeling for a pulse, or . . . whatever." My voice petered out.

"You're a fat lot of help, Mrs. H.! What I need is for you to get me off the hook by pointing the finger at someone else right this minute." A crash turned the last couple of words into an exclamation point. We both jumped. Brigadier Lester-Smith had dropped the bottle of gin. Amazingly, it didn't break. Or Mrs. Malloy might have turned into a murderer then and there. And from the expression on the brigadier's face, he wouldn't have been surprised if either one of us had turned on him.

"I rather fear Ellie thinks I did it, Mrs. Malloy," he stammered through lips that twitched as if pulled by puppet strings. "Regrettably, she saw some suspicious-looking stains in my shower just before we came over here. And it is not to be wondered you took them for blood." He turned jerkily towards me. "I remember thinking that's what it looked like after I stepped out of the shower and realized it hadn't rinsed away, probably because the showerhead wasn't at the right angle. And I was just about to clean it up when the doorbell rang."

"And if it wasn't blood, buster," Mrs. Malloy, too, had read her share of American crime novels, "what was it?"

"Hair dye."

"Hair dye?" Mrs. Malloy repeated scornfully. "You really think Mrs. H. here and yours truly are chumps enough to believe that cock and bull. Better pull the other leg, Brigadier, it's got bells on!"

"See for yourselves!" He unwrapped the towel and, understandably, hung his head.

"Well, blow me down!" Mrs. Malloy let out a whistle that should have brought the police running if they weren't on their way already. The brigadier's hair was a damp, sticky crimson.

"How long are you meant to leave it on for?" I asked, almost forgetting about poor Trina.

"Five minutes."

"And how long has it bloody been?" put in Mrs. Malloy, sounding downright vexed. "Oh, don't bother answering that! Too long. Green hair is what you'll get. And serves you right!"

"What I don't understand," I told him, "is why you came down when I rang the doorbell."

"I thought it might be some . . . thing important." He was rewrapping the towel around his head to prevent more drips going down his neck. And my heart, even at that inappropriate moment, went out to him. He had thought—hoped—it was Clarice Whitcombe at the door. She for whom he had coloured his hair in hope she would find him more attractive if he looked younger. I remembered now that his crinkly locks *had* looked redder at the Hearthside Guild meeting. I had put that down to a trick of the sunlight coming through the windows. But it hadn't been an illusion. Perhaps he had experimented with colour shampoos before moving up to a real dye job. I also remembered his urgency to get off the phone when I rang to say Ben had his raincoat. Hadn't he gasped and said something about "ten minutes"? Poor Brigadier Lester-Smith, who would be heartsick if Clarice Whitcombe found out, but still had been unable to resist going downstairs in his towel-draped head to answer the door in case it was her outside.

"Perhaps, Brigadier," I said, "you shouldn't wash it out before the police get here. It gives you an alibi of sorts, doesn't it? Because we may be asked to describe our movements during the last hour. Although, if it turns out that Trina has been dead longer than that, it shouldn't matter." I turned back to Mrs. Malloy. "Why aren't they here already?"

"Who?"

"The police."

"Oh, them." She resettled in her chair. "Maybe I forgot to phone them. Could be I sort of blanked out. Everything is pretty much of a blur until you two walked in." Her butterfly lips worked and her rouged cheeks showed signs of cracking, so I didn't press the issue. Instead I looked around for the telephone, remembering that Mrs. Malloy had one in the kitchen, but having no luck spotting it until she helped out by saying it should be under the tea cosy. I spied the cosy lying flat on a little table with the phone beside it. While I dialed, the brigadier picked up the bottle of gin.

"Do you think you should have any of this just now, Mrs. Malloy?" he said. "It might give a wrong impression to the police."

"You think they'd rather walk in to find me sitting knitting, with a body on the floor with a knife in its back?" she flashed back.

"No, but you don't want them thinking you've been at the bottle, Mrs. Malloy."

"I'd appreciate it, Brigadier," replied Mrs. M. at her most uppity. "Indeed, I'd appreciate it most awfully if you'd stop standing there like a genie let out of that gin bottle and pour me a good slug. If the police can't understand I've never needed a drink more in me life than at this buggering minute, then they should be the ones sitting home knitting."

It was hard to hear myself talking into the phone, let alone make out what was being said on the other end. But apparently I explained myself sufficiently well, because within minutes of my putting down the receiver, the house began to fill with policemen. Or maybe it only seemed that way. Perhaps there were only two at first. But they did so much tramping about and fired so many questions that I quickly felt I was in the middle of a stampede.

I was worried about Mrs. Malloy. She had been accompanied into her tiny sitting room by a Detective Galloway. The door closed behind them and did not reopen. Meanwhile, the brigadier and I took refuge in the hall, which had lost several of its china poodles in the past hour. We were questioned briefly: What time had we arrived at the house? How did we find the body? What, if anything, had we touched? And last, but most important, what had brought us to 27 Herring Street?

The brigadier explained that he lived two doors down, I had stopped at his house to return a raincoat, and we had both heard someone scream. I explained I was curious why the person looking after Mrs. Malloy's house in her absence wasn't out in the street with the other neighbours. Our personal policeman wrote things down, looking as though he believed us. Part of basic training, no doubt.

"You thought the scream came from out in the street?"

"Yes." The brigadier and I both nodded, he nearly losing his turban in the process.

"Sir, why do you still have that towel on your head?" The policeman cocked an eyebrow.

"You're going to have to explain, Brigadier," I said.

"Quite so." He gulped before manfully meeting the policeman's eyes. "I appreciate that, under the circumstances, this"—tapping his turban—"could look suspicious. But I assure you, sir, that I am not trying to hide a head wound caused during an attack upon Miss McKinnley. I don't think I have spoken to the woman above a couple of times."

The policeman was looking impatient, and Brigadier Lester-Smith, apparently being of the same persuasion as myself—that you only had to tick off a member of law enforcement to find yourself handcuffed, tried, and sentenced to life imprisonment all in the space of minutes—glumly removed the towel.

"Good God!" said the cop.

After that little episode I asked permission to telephone my husband. When I got through, it was Freddy who answered, saying Ben was putting Abbey and Tam to bed.

"What is this?" My cousin sounded genuinely alarmed. "Cleaning women dropping like flies all over the place!"

"Trina's murder may have absolutely nothing to do with what happened to Mrs. Large."

"And you've been reading Gullible's Travels!"

"Freddy, tell Ben I'm fine, but I'm not sure how long I'll be. Mrs. Malloy may need me for a bit. Sorry, I have to go now."

I found Brigadier Lester-Smith washing the dye out of his hair at Mrs. Malloy's sink. No doubt in fear and trembling as to whether he would even have a scalp left. The results, surprisingly, weren't as ghastly as might have been supposed. He was more crimson than carroty, but that was surely better than having hair that was frog-green.

Mrs. Malloy came out of the sitting room—looking, I must say, as cool as a cucumber sandwich. Putting detectives in their place was all in a day's work for her. She had removed her coat, and the taffeta frock she wore would have been suitable for a cocktail party, or at a pinch—being black—for Trina McKinnley's funeral. Not a word did she speak to me or the brigadier. About half an hour later, Trina's body was removed, and the house was suddenly bereft of policemen.

"Bloody hell!" Mrs. Malloy splashed gin into a glass and downed it in a gulp. "I'm too old for being suspected of murder."

"They can't think you did it," I said. "If they did they would have asked you to accompany them to the police station."

"I'm sure that's so," agreed the brigadier.

"I suppose they searched the place while I was in with that Detective Galloway—checking to make sure I hadn't switched clothes and hidden the bloodstained ones away if I hadn't had time to get rid of them." Mrs. Malloy gave one of her snorts before pouring another gin. "Flaming cheek, but it's not like there was anything for the buggers to find, leastways that I know about."

She went instantly from bravado to looking worried. The purple and bronze shadow she was wearing on her lids reflected in dark smudges under her eyes, which widened as she glanced over at the little telephone table. Dropped down beside it was a black plastic handbag. Mrs. Malloy's own bag was on the kitchen table—fake alligator with a flashy gold clasp. The other just wasn't her sort of thing at all. It was cheap and utilitarian. Trina McKinnley's? Where had I seen it before?"

"Whose bag is that?" I asked.

"Mine!" Mrs. Malloy knew which one I meant. "Can't a

woman have two bleeding handbags without you making something out of it?" Her hands shook as she poured herself another glass of gin.

"Silly of me," I replied quickly, "I'm not thinking straight." Obviously, she wouldn't say anything in front of Brigadier Lester-Smith. The trick would be hustling him out the door without arousing his suspicion. Luckily the brigadier looked preoccupied, as well he might after such an evening. He did, however, very kindly invite us back to his house for a restorative cup of tea and a bite to eat.

"Thanks ever so, Briggy old stick." Mrs. Malloy mustered a wan smile. "But just for now I'd like to sit here with Mrs. H. and have a good sniffle. Can't do that in front of a man, can I? Make me lose all me sex appeal, it would. And say what you like, you'd never feel the same about me."

She had said just what was needed. Giving his dressing gown another tug, Brigadier Lester-Smith headed for the door, murmuring that he wouldn't intrude one moment longer.

"Like as not I'll come by for that cuppa later," Mrs. Malloy offered by way of consolation. He departed with his stained towel draped over his shoulder. I was reminded of a boxer leaving the ring—bloodied and not exactly prancing on the balls of his feet. The moment the back door closed behind him I turned to Mrs. Malloy.

"Now let's hear about that handbag that isn't yours."

"And who made you Scotland Yard?" She reached again for the gin bottle, but I got to it first and planted it at the far end of the kitchen table.

"Not another drop until you start talking."

"Oh, all right, I'll tell you!" She caved in more readily than I had hoped. "You and me go back a long way, Mrs. H., you could even say we was family with my George being married to your cousin Vanessa." The name stuck in her throat, but she finally spat it out. At some point I would have to ask Mrs. Malloy what had kept her incommunicado for so long, but I wasn't about to distract her now. "I suppose what it really comes down to, Mrs. H., is I trust you. Leastways," she had to add, "more than I do most people."

"Butter me up all you like," I replied bracingly, "but you don't get another drop of gin until you spill the beans."

"Oh, bugger!" She heaved a soul-wrenching sigh. "I can't carry this thing on me own! But you've got to swear, Mrs. H., you won't go running to the police."

"I can't promise that. Not until I know what's involved."

"Oh, to hell with it! I've already given the game away, so I guess I might as well tell you the lot and hope you see things the way I do. You're right—that bag's not mine, and it didn't belong to Trina, neither. It's Winifred Smalley's and it weren't over there by the phone when I got here. It was right there next to the body."

"And that's when you went screaming out into the road?"

"I did nothing of the bloody sort." Mrs. Malloy ruffled up like an outraged chicken. "I'm not one of them hysteria types, and well you know it, Mrs. H.!"

"Then it must have been Trina when she saw that knife coming at her. I don't know why I was so sure that scream came from outside."

"Or it could have been Winifred. Not the bravest woman in the world, she isn't. But that's all to the good in this case. Because if she'd done it, she wouldn't have gone screaming outside to alert the neighbours, now would she?"

"People don't necessarily behave rationally when they've just killed someone. Think it through, Mrs. Malloy. If Mrs. Smalley walked in on Trina's body, why didn't she stay and phone the police?"

"Always got to put a spoke in the wheel, that's you,

Mrs. H.! I'm telling you, I know Winifred Smalley. The woman wouldn't hurt a fly, let alone Trina. They was like mother and daughter. Besides, where's the motive? Answer me that, Mrs. Clever Dick?"

"Maybe they got into an argument about Mrs. Large's money." I saw Mrs. Malloy's face go blank. "You don't know about the will, do you? Why don't I make us a pot of tea and we'll take it into the sitting room. If that's all right?"

It was a mark of how truly worried she was that Mrs. M. allowed me to bugger about her kitchen without so much as pointing me in the direction of the tea caddy or telling me to wipe off the kettle before putting it on to boil. She did wince when I rattled the cups and saucers while putting them on the tin tray with the thatched-cottage design. But she followed me meekly into her sitting room, where her coat lay on a chair—a leopard-patterned easy chair with a garish yellow footstool dangling scarlet tassels. We could have been in a sultan's pied-à-terre. There were cushions on the floor, incense burners, a statue of a Greek god sporting a fig leaf, brass urns, and sparkly sequined elephants with gold fringe. The latter reminded me of the set of fake ivory ones I had unearthed during my assault on spring cleaning. I decided to give them to Mrs. Malloy for her next birthday.

It helped to fasten on the mundane pleasures of life. It made murder seem far-fetched. But there is no living in a dream world for long. I poured our tea, stirred in milk and sugar, and handed Mrs. Malloy her cup.

"What were you saying about Gertrude Large's will?" She put her feet on the yellow footstool and eased off her shoes. "And I don't want no talk about how there'd be no need to ask if I'd come back for the funeral."

"I didn't get the details that day." I sat down on the

faux-lizard-skin sofa. "Mrs. Large's daughters did mention when I saw them at the service that they were heading down to see their solicitor. But it wasn't until they met with him that they got what must have been the surprise of their lives."

"Spit it out, Mrs. H.!"

"That Mrs. Large had left almost everything she had, something like fifty thousand pounds, to Trina McKinnley—insurance money from her husband's accident."

"Well, I'll be blowed!" Mrs. Malloy put down her teacup before she dropped it. "I knew about the insurance; we all did in the C.F.C.W.A., but I'd no idea it was such a bloody windfall!"

"Does it seem odd to you that she left it all to Trina, except for a hundred pounds each for her daughters?"

Mrs. Malloy pursed her lips and thought for a moment. "No, I can't say it does. You see when Frank—that's Gertrude's husband—was laid up, she gave up working for a while to take care of him. But you know how hard it is to nurse a man with the hiccups, let alone one that's bedridden. And from the sound of it, Frank wasn't what you'd call jolly when he was well. So after a bit Gertrude went back to work to get out of the house. There was a visiting nurse that came in regular, but Trina pitched in, too. She'd shifted her work schedule around so that she could stay with Frank a couple of hours two or three times a week. And she used to go in and help turn him and whatever on weekends."

"That explains it," I said.

" 'Course," Mrs. Malloy picked up her teacup, "it would've been nice if Gertrude had left me and Betty Nettle and Winifred Smalley a little something to remember her by—say a few thousand for old time's sake."

"She made Mrs. Smalley the trustee."

"Meaning?" Shooting up in her chair.

"That she got to ration out the money to Trina. And there, in my opinion, is what makes it particularly bad for Mrs. Smalley that you found her handbag by the body. When that comes out, the police may think she killed Trina over a row about the money."

Mrs. Malloy shook her head at my numskull thinking. "The trouble with that bright idea is that it should have been Trina doing the stabbing. Hoping that with Winifred out of the way she'd get control of her inheritance."

"I realize that," I said, "but what if it turns out that in the event of Trina McKinnley's death, Mrs. Smalley herself would be the one to inherit?"

"Just who was it gave you the scoop on Gertrude's will?" Fear flickered in Mrs. Malloy's eyes before flaming into annoyance.

"I'd rather not say."

"You don't have to." She laughed scornfully. "It was that Bunty Wiseman, weren't it? I remember now! Her ex was Gertrude's solicitor. And I never did think that man could keep quiet, short of padlocking his mouth. He ought to be struck off or unfrocked or whatever they call it."

I remained determined to name no names. "Nothing was said to me about what would happen to the money if Trina died. But it would certainly complicate matters for Mrs. Smalley if she becomes the beneficiary by default."

"Making it even more bloody important the police don't find out about her handbag!" Mrs. Malloy leaned wearily back in her chair. "They'll never buy the notion of Winifred walking in on the body and dropping her bag before she ran off in fright."

"What if it was Trina who picked up that knife in the first place." I sipped at my tea without tasting it. "Just to scare Mrs. Smalley into seeing the sense of shelling out the money in large amounts. And in the course of struggling to get it away from her, Mrs. Smalley struck the fatal blow?"

"Oh, I'll give you Trina had a filthy temper if anyone pressed the wrong buttons. But"—Mrs. Malloy shook her head—"she loved Winifred like she was her own mum. The only thing they ever argued about was Trina's boyfriend."

"Joe." I got up to refill our cups.

"That's right." She twisted her lips disparagingly. "Joe Tollings, Mr. God's gift to himself."

"Did you say 'Tollings'?" I spilled tea all over the tray. "I just spoke to a woman named Marilyn Tollings when I was going into Brigadier Lester-Smith's. I thought I'd never get rid of her. Don't tell me she's Joe's wife!"

"Been married to him these past ten years at least."

"I met him with Trina at Mrs. Large's funeral." Forgetting the tea, I sat back down. "It was Mrs. Smalley who got Trina to take over from Mrs. Large at Merlin's Court. And there was an awkward scene on Monday. Bunty Wiseman was there when Joe arrived to pick Trina up. And, no surprise, he's also been carrying on with Bunty. When Trina came into the kitchen and saw them together she picked up on the vibes. But she didn't cut Joe down to size in front of me. It was Ben who heard the two of them arguing as he drove through the gates on his way home for lunch."

"And you couldn't have told me this sooner?" Mrs. Malloy looked as though she would have liked to hurl the yellow footstool at me and follow it up with a couple of sequined elephants. "Because if this don't shed a new light on the miserable business, I'm a monkey's Great-Aunt Mabel. Joe Tollings always did have a violent streak. I think that's a good part of why Trina fancied him. She saw herself as a lion tamer, cracking her little whip."

"Dangerous."

"A suit and tie never was no challenge to Trina. I can't say as I worried about her like Winifred did, but I weren't all that easy in me mind when Trina offered to come and stay here while I was gone. 'What if his wife finds out the two of you are carrying on?' I says to her. I don't want me front door being kicked down or rocks thrown at me windows by the woman scorned. But cocky as anything, was Trina. She saw it as some bloody game—dangling herself in front of Marilyn Tollings's nose, so to speak. And look where it got her! Joe goes and chops her when he finds out he can't shake the money tree. It was just bleeding back luck that Winifred walked in and found her."

"Let's say that's the case." I stirred in my chair, having grown cramped and chilly. "Why didn't Mrs. Smalley go to a neighbour's and phone for help?"

"Because she was buggering scared she'd be blamed!" Mrs. Malloy spoke as if to a dimwit.

"But what if it's worse than that?" I suggested. "Suppose when Mrs. Smalley arrived, the killer was still on the premises, either in the house or lurking outside. Waiting to make sure no one was about when he took off down the road. And when Mrs. Smalley screamed upon finding the body he—we'll say it was Joe—grabbed her and dragged her away with him." My voice ground to a standstill. Awful images swam around in my mind. I should not have put ideas for which there was no foundation in Mrs. Malloy's head.

"I guess I'd better give Winifred a ring." She heaved herself up, looking as though she had been hit with the yellow footstool, and I trailed after her into the kitchen to stand hovering as she dialed her friend's number. "No answer," she said bleakly, hanging up.

"That doesn't mean something's happened to her," I tried to sound nonchalant.

"No, she's just bleeding done a bunk."

"I really think you have to phone the police." I put an arm around Mrs. M.'s black taffeta shoulders. "You should tell them about the handbag and let them take over. If there's the smallest possibility that Joe, or whoever else it might be, has made off with Mrs. Smalley, we can't waste time!"

"Oh, go on with you!" She shrugged away from me. "We're letting our heads cloud our judgment, Mrs. H., or however the saying goes. What I ought to do is call an emergency meeting of the C.F.C.W.A. That shouldn't take long, seeing there's only Betty Nettle left to call. Although I guess we could make you an honorary member, just for this evening."

"Mrs. Malloy, you mustn't shilly-shally."

"I'd better have a drink," she said, and on reaching for the gin bottle discovered it was empty. "Bloody hell!" She padded across to the pantry on her shoeless feet and emerged seconds later, her face at half-mast. "That was the only bottle. Now what am I to do?"

"Phone the police."

"Nothing doing! You nip down to the brigadier's and ask to borrow a cup of gin. Can you remember that, Mrs. H., or do I need to write it down for you?"

"All right." I was about to let myself out the back door when a thought occurred to me. "How would Mrs. Smalley have got into the house if Trina was already dead?"

"She had a key. All members of the C.F.C.W.A. had keys to each other's houses." Mrs. Malloy sighed deeply. Two of her friends dead and one of the others up to her neck in trouble. It had stopped raining, but the night was thick with cloud and the wind nippy as I hurried out onto Herring Street. There were no neighbours hanging about. They'd probably all trotted back inside after the grand finale—Trina's covered body being removed from the house.

One car did slide past me as I was about to step inside Brigadier Lester-Smith's gate. I was thinking how Marilyn Tollings had rushed across the street to ask if I were the woman in the woolly hat and raincoat she had seen earlier. Sheer nosiness had been my assumption. But might she not have had another motive? There was no doubt Joe's wife had reason to hate Trina McKinnley if she knew about the affair. Had she been craftily covering her tracks in saying she didn't know the woman living in Mrs. Malloy's house? My God! What if she'd gone there to have it out with Trina and ended up sticking a knife into her back? Then just suppose that when she was leaving the scene of the crime she saw my car pull up. And thinking it unlikely she could get all the way into her house without my seeing her, she had with wickedness aforethought made a big production of talking to me! A gutsy sleight of hand.

I stood for a moment at the gate where I had talked to Marilyn Tollings, seeing myself getting out of the old convertible, trying to picture exactly when I had first seen her. And suddenly my heart gave a thump that actually jolted me sideways.

My car was no longer parked outside Brigadier Lester-Smith's house. It was nowhere in sight. It was gone. That fact took longer than necessary sinking in. And then I found myself running back to Mrs. Malloy's house. Suddenly the front door opened and she was standing there. To hell with her cup of gin, I thought, and was about to spill out this latest development, when she broke in ahead of me.

"Good of you to come back, seeing as your hubby just rang up, Mrs. H. And you'll need to phone him back, because he's all of a twitter. Seems the police paid him a visit to say they found your ruddy car on a deserted lane not far from here. And a few feet away, half in a ditch, was the body of a woman. No identification in her coat pockets, but one of them policeman knew her by sight."

"Mrs. Smalley?" I whispered, rushing forward. And Mrs. Malloy could only nod brokenly before sagging into my arms.

# CHAPTER ELEVEN

*When cleaning out cupboards,
set aside unneeded items to be
donated to the church bazaar
or other charity. Then reline
with oilcloth or waxed paper.*

"WHO IS THIS MRS. SMALLEY, AND WHY ARE WE TALK-
ing about her at this time of the morning?" Jonas sat up in
bed and scowled first at me, then at the bedside clock,
looking even crosser when he saw it was almost ten A.M.

"She was a friend of Mrs. Malloy's."

"So what's that got to do with the price o' tea in China?"
My grouchy friend folded his striped pajama arms and begrudgingly shifted his feet so I could perch on the edge of
the bed.

"I met her in Bellingham's cafeteria just after Mrs.
Large died and again at the funeral. She seemed a very
nice woman." I was having trouble getting to the point.
The words kept skipping about inside my head, instead of
lining themselves up into neat little sentences. Not surprisingly, Jonas grew more impatient by the second.

"Nice! I'm woke up to talk about some nice woman! If
you've a mind, Ellie girl, to marry me off to this Mrs.
Smelly, you'd best think again. I've long ago forgot all I
ever knew about the birds and the bees and I ain't working

myself into a froth trying to remember. Stares me in the face, it do, that you want to be rid of me." His face settled into even deeper lines. "And can't say as I blame you. A useless old man, that's all I be these days."

"I don't want to get rid of you." I got up and kissed the top of his bald head. "And how can you talk about being useless when I need you more than ever?"

"What's happened?" Jonas shot up higher in the bed. "Something wrong with Ben or the little ones?"

"No, it's about Mrs. Smalley. She is—was—a friend of Mrs. Malloy's, a member of their little housecleaning organization. Last night she was knocked down and killed by a car. My car. I'd left it parked outside Brigadier Lester-Smith's house with the keys in the ignition, of all stupid things, and whoever took it ran the poor woman down. If that isn't dreadful enough, Trina McKinnley was murdered—stabbed to death in Mrs. Malloy's kitchen. I was with Mrs. Malloy when the police arrived in Herring Street and I didn't leave until after they finished. By which time Mrs. Smalley had been found in a ditch off Bramble Wood Lane, just a few yards from the abandoned car. I'm not a suspect"—I choked on the words—"because I have an alibi for the time of death. So I suppose there is one small bright spot in all this."

"Mrs. Malloy's back home?" Jonas fastened on this piece of information as he covered my hand with his and studied my face with anxious eyes.

"I still don't know what brought her back, or why she didn't get in touch after Mrs. Large died; we never got round to talking about that. All I know is she took the coach from London yesterday evening and walked in to find Trina's body with a knife in the back."

"That do be three." Jonas kept hold of my hand.

"Yes." I nodded. "All members of the C.F.C.W.A., and

only one of their deaths appearing to have been accidental. And now Mrs. Malloy is riddled with guilt because she
didn't mention the handbag."

"Whose handbag?"

"Mrs. Smalley's. And Mrs. Malloy kept quiet because
she didn't want the police thinking her friend had murdered Trina. I think she may even have wiped off the knife
handle, in case Mrs. Smalley had touched it. When Ben
phoned about Mrs. Smalley, Mrs. Malloy rang the station,
pretending she'd just found the handbag. By then it was
clear what had happened. Mrs. Smalley must have walked
in on the murderer and either ran from the house to be
chased down the road by the killer in my car or she was
dragged outside and into the car to be taken to Bramble
Wood Lane and dumped in the road. Oh it's too awful!" I
covered my face with my hands. "To think of her being run
over as she tried to get away."

"Try not to think on it, Ellie girl."

"She was such a frail little person."

After an almost-sleepless night I didn't have much energy to spare. Ben had got the children up and dressed,
given them their breakfast, and taken them to school on
his way to work. I had hoped he would at least take
the morning off, but I hadn't said anything. Even talking
to Ben had been too much for me at that point. Instead
I'd drunk most of the pot of tea he left for me, nibbled
around the crust of a piece of toast, and after forcing
myself to take a bath and wash my hair, came up to see
Jonas.

"Do you think the police have any ideas?" He resettled
himself in the bed and sat stroking Tobias, who had leaped
out of nowhere to land on his middle.

"They didn't take me into their confidence, but I think
it very likely they'll want a word or two with Trina's mar-

ried boyfriend, Joe, and his wife. She may have known what was going on and decided not to stand for it." I got up and moved around the room, straightening things that Jonas wouldn't want straightened and looking at the faded rectangle of wallpaper where his mirror had hung.

"I hates to see you upset, girl." Jonas lay back against the pillows. A shadow cast by the wardrobe door that Tobias had nudged open darkened the smudges under his eyes and deepened the hollows in his cheeks.

"I shouldn't have bothered you with any of this." I bent over to kiss his papery forehead. "You were sleeping so peacefully before I woke you up. There was the loveliest smile on your face. I think you must have been having good dreams."

"I was." He turned his face towards me but his eyes held a faraway look. "It was a beautiful spring morning, like yesterday before it turned to rain. The sky was bluer than hyacinths. There was flowers everywhere you looked, and buds on the trees and grass so green you'd think God got up before the crack o' dawn to plant it fresh. My mother was in that garden, Ellie girl." His voice dwindled to a whisper and I knelt down by the bed.

"What was she doing?"

"She was on the lawn, looking up at the sky. She had hold of a kite on a long, long string, and all of a sudden she let it go and watched it fly away."

"Were you with her in the dream, Jonas?"

"I was the kite." He struggled to open his eyes, but sleep had returned for him like a firm but gentle presence tugging him away from me. I felt a moment's terror, but he stirred and squeezed my hand. "I be glad you talked to me, Ellie girl. What of Mrs. Malloy. Did you bring her back here last night?"

"I offered, but she insisted on staying in her own

house." He was nearly asleep again, and after smoothing out his sheet, I tiptoed from the room. Then, after taking only a couple of steps towards the stairs, I turned around and went back to make sure he was still breathing.

Nerves! I told myself. It was only to be expected that I would be jumpy. But I was bound to feel better if I ate something. After that I would go and see how Mrs. Malloy was doing and if she'd heard any more from the police. Crossing the hall, I heard footsteps downstairs. My heart skipped a couple of beats. And then I realized the intruder would of course be Freddy staking out the refrigerator. Only it wasn't. When I pushed the kitchen door I found myself face-to-face with my husband.

"Ben!" I ran into his arms as if we had been parted for decades and separated by oceans and continents and all the hostile forces of the world. "I've wanted you so all morning, but I didn't like to ring you at work, making a pest of myself when you had to be busy. In this day and age, a woman should be able to cope with the aftermath of murder without sniveling on her man's shoulder." I proceeded to demonstrate how far I had to go before finding true liberation, and he stroked my hair and kissed me in the most soothing way.

"Are you sure you like the idea of having me home?" he asked presently.

"That's a silly question."

"But I'm not just talking about today." He stood, hands on my shoulders, his brilliant blue-green eyes looking intently into mine. "How do you feel about having a husband underfoot day in and day out?"

"What are you saying?" I was frozen in place, unable to think, let alone blink an eyelash.

"I've retired. Hung a 'Closed' sign on Abigail's door and tossed the key in the air."

"Ben!" was all I could manage.

"Oh, it's all right; it landed in here." He patted his jacket pocket. "So I can always go back if you throw me out."

"Never!" I came jerkily back to life. "Tell me, what made you decide? Was it the picketers?"

"No." Ben swung me around in a waltz only slightly restricted in its exuberance by the kitchen table and chairs getting in our way. "And I haven't become a born-again vegetarian, Ellie. You'll just have to blame my madcap behavior on spring fever."

"I can't." I sagged against him feeling giddy, while at the same time life came sharply back into focus. "You did this for me. You're worried about how I'm going to react to three deaths in such a short space of time. And it's true, walking in on two bodies and having another woman die as a result of being hit by my car is a lot to deal with. But that's no reason for you give up your career. When we talked about it before, you were adamant about not throwing in the towel, as you called it."

"That's true." He sat down on the rocking chair in front of the fireplace and drew me onto his lap, his dark head resting on mine. "But I've been thinking things over since then, sweetheart. It's been growing on me gradually that I was sticking it out at the restaurant just to prove a point— as much to myself as to Mrs. Barrow and her picketers. And those deaths did play a part in the decision I've made. They made me realize life is short and there's so much more I want to do. Write another cookery book, have Jonas teach me how to garden. The grounds have been getting too much for him for a long time. Rather than hire someone to help him, I could pick up the slack."

"Jonas will love to teach you," I said. "In fact it might be just what the doctor ordered to help put him on his feet again. "But, Ben, won't you miss Abigail's?"

"Of course." He leaned back and the rocking chair gave a nervous groan under our combined weight. "But I'm excited about experimenting with new dishes for a cookery book. That's something I haven't done much of lately because customers come back for their favourites and don't appreciate too much chopping and changing. And I'm not saying I won't reopen in time. Perhaps just doing lunches and tea. I don't know, Ellie, what I'm going to want down the road. And in the meantime we shouldn't have a problem getting by on the income from Uncle Merlin's legacy. Do you think you can live with that?"

"We'll do fine, so long as I remember to be reasonably frugal."

"Me too"—Ben smiled—"and I'll try not to get too much underfoot."

"Don't worry." I wound a dark tendril of his hair around my finger. "I'll make sure you take afternoon naps."

"By myself?"

"Not always." I snuggled in close and then thought of something. "Ben, what about Freddy?"

"Don't worry, sweetheart, I think he's been itching to leave Abigail's, but thought he owed it to me to stay on. He told me he's in pretty good shape financially—he's been able to save most of his wages living rent-free at the cottage and eating almost all his meals either here or at the restaurant. Give him twenty-four hours and Freddy will come up with a scheme for making us all rich and infamous."

It would have been one of these golden moments, but for Trina McKinnley, Mrs. Smalley, and of course dear Mrs. Malloy.

While Ben went upstairs to encourage Jonas to share a potter in the garden, I dialed Mrs. M.'s number. No answer. And no need for me to be worried. But I was. Why hadn't I overridden her insistence that she was perfectly all right staying in her own house and brought her here with me last night? What if she had tried to drown her sorrows in gin and taken a tumble down the stairs or overdone the sleeping pills? I looked her friend Betty Nettle's number up in the directory and tried ringing her. Again, no luck. She could well be at work, although I would have thought that with two members of the C.F.C.W.A. so suddenly dead, she might have taken the day off.

Returning to the kitchen, I found Freddy there along with the children. True to form, he was supervising them in a game of jumping on and off chairs.

"Mummy." Tam took a flying leap into my arms that sent us both hurtling against the hall door. "We're playing zoos; Abbey's a monkey and I'm a lion."

"And who's Freddy?"

"He's the keeper man." My daughter bounced around the room, her mouth spread wide to expose her teeth while she scratched at herself with one hand and held a half-peeled banana in the other.

"I was just about to lock them in the pantry, honestly I was, Ellie." My cousin tried but failed to look virtuous.

"But he was afraid I'd bite him." Tam, still clinging to me, giggled into my neck.

"And I kept 'scaping up trees." Abbey proved her point by climbing from a stool onto the edge of the sink.

"It's not my fault." My cousin collapsed in a chair. "Neither you nor Ben bothered to ask what I thought when you decided to have children. But I try to pitch in and help make something of them. Think of all the outings I've offered to take them on."

"You wanted to take Tam to get his nose pierced."

"There you go, coz, raking up the past."

"Me? You're the one who suggested taking Abbey to a hypnotist who would regress her into former incarnations."

"I thought it would fun for her." Freddy swiveled round

to face the sink. "You'd have liked that, wouldn't you, Abbey, finding out you were a princess in one of your former incarnations?"

"I am a princess," came her response.

"I thought carnations was flowers." Tam slid out of my arms and crawled across the floor to growl up at his sister.

"Only think, Ellie." Freddy stood up and stretched. "How lucky for all of us that Ben has liberated me along with himself from the shackles of the workforce. As a man of leisure, I shall be forever at your disposal. An hour will not pass without my popping up to offer to take some burden off your shoulders. If you'll teach me how to plug in the Hoover, I'm sure I could learn how to push the thing."

"There shouldn't be any need for that sort of sacrifice," I said, "not if Mrs. Malloy is back for good."

"How is the old girl?" Freddy's face sobered. He flopped an arm around my shoulder and planted a scratchy kiss on my cheek. "The village was abuzz with the news this morning. One of the waitresses was saying that Trina's boyfriend Joe . . ."

"Tollings," I supplied.

"That's right. It seems he and his wife . . ."

"Marilyn."

"Thank you." Freddy clamped a hand over my mouth to prevent further interruptions. "According to Deirdre—that's the waitress—the husband and wife were invited down to the police station early this morning, and I suppose we can assume it wasn't for tea and biscuits. Deirdre is engaged to a constable, and according to him it's just a matter of deciding which of the Tollings did it."

"I'm glad to hear the police aren't letting the grass grow under their feet," I said, going over to lift Abbey down from where she now sat with her feet in the sink.

"So why do you look so grim?" my cousin asked.

"I'm worried about Mrs. Malloy."

"Now look here, coz." Freddy clapped a pontifical hand on my shoulder as I straightened up from setting Abbey down on the floor. "She's a tough old bird is our Mrs. M. She'll get through this."

"I suppose so." I was getting the children's lunch when Ben came into the kitchen and offered to take over. And Freddy said he might as well hang around for a while, which meant he got in the way making numerous grandiose suggestions as to what we should eat.

"But I don't like snails," objected Tam just as Jonas came shuffling into the room. What little hair he had was standing on end, but he looked reasonably assembled in a plaid flannel shirt and a pair of baggy trousers of no particular colour.

"Snails is good for the garden," he informed my son before depositing himself at the table. "And that be just one of the pearls of wisdom I suppose I'm meant to pass along to—"

"I'm the new undergardener." Ben gave him a sideways smile while continuing to stir a saucepan of Welsh rarebit. "I hope you plan to be patient with me, Jonas, because I've always been quite daft when it comes to the outdoors."

"Me too," chipped in Freddy. "It's a pity we live in modern times because I'm sure I would have cut quite a figure striding up and down the lawn with a scythe."

"You'd be far more likely to cut off both feet." I settled Abbey at the table, fetched over the salad and dish of sliced beetroot Ben had prepared, and within a few minutes we were all eating our lunch. It pleased me to see Jonas sounding animated for the first time in weeks as he lectured Ben and Freddy on the right time to plant runner beans. Much as I loved my cousin, I hoped Freddy would allow Ben and Jonas to have their first gardening session on their own.

He must have read my mind, since he remained rooted to his chair as the garden door closed on Ben and Jonas's comradely chatter. "Is it going to take you a while, Ellie, to get used to having Ben home?"

"I haven't had a chance to really think about it," I said, washing off Abbey's and Tam's faces, "but of course it will be an adjustment for both of us. It's exciting, a little scary." I stood with the facecloth in my hands, remembering how eager I had been to redecorate my bedroom. But that morning when I had woken to its familiar furniture and wallpaper, I had wondered what could have possessed me to want to change anything. There was so much comfort in the known, particularly when life demonstrated that it could turn topsy-turvy all in a moment. Now I found myself wondering where Mrs. Smalley had lived, and Trina McKinnley—when she wasn't staying at Mrs. Malloy's house.

"Freddy, would you mind staying with the twins while I go and phone Mrs. Malloy? There was no reply earlier."

But there was still no answer. I couldn't just wait, worrying that she, too, was lying dead in a bucket of suds. I was just about to go and check on her in person when the garden door opened and Ben reentered the kitchen with Tom Tingle at his heels.

"Look who's here," announced my husband cheerfully. "Mr. Tingle came by hoping to have a chat with Jonas about gardening and I've invited him to join me in my first lesson."

"That's lovely," I said.

"You seemed to think it might be a good idea when we talked yesterday." Tom sounded nervous, as if preparing himself to be ordered back outside with perhaps a couple of Wellington boots sent hurtling after him. "And I brought those books of wallpaper we talked about, so if it's not too much trouble . . ."

Or had he really come to find out what I knew about the murders? It was nasty of me, but you can't sing in the bath in Chitterton Fells without half the residents knowing the title of the song and how many verses you got through. I told them that I was going out, but should be back shortly.

"To Roxie's?" Ben asked, raising his eyebrows.

"Umm," I said, trying to be cryptic. For all yesterday's conversation Tom Tingle was still a virtual stranger. And who knew what he wanted to glean from this little visit?

"Freddy said he'll watch the children," I told Ben, "so there's no need for you to interrupt your afternoon in the garden."

"But we want to go outside and play with him." Abbey was inching ever closer to Tom. She wasn't a child who readily took to strangers. So I found myself feeling ashamed of my suspicions. And I found myself picturing him as a sad little garden gnome who got continually showered with pebbles instead of rain and rarely got a glimpse of the sun.

"Darling, you can play with Mr. Tingle another time." I picked up my daughter, who was suddenly all flounces and fury.

"Not another time. Now!"

"Me, too," piped up Tam.

"Perhaps your mummy will bring you to my house one day." The smile Tom Tingle gave my children was surprisingly disarming. "I'd like that. It gets lonely all by myself."

"We'll come," I promised as the door closed behind him and Ben.

"Was he at the meeting where Mrs. Large . . . left abruptly?" asked Freddy.

"Yes," I replied, my mind full of questions again and no answers. I was trying to remember if I'd left my handbag in the drawing room or upstairs in my bedroom when someone knocked on the garden door. Before I could take a step towards it, Bunty Wiseman whipped into the kitchen.

"Thank God!" She flew at me in a whirl of black miniskirt and jaunty matching jacket, her short curls a silvery blur and her voice wavering on the brink of hysteria. She was ever a woman who knew how to stage an entrance, but I sensed her alarm was at least two-thirds real. "I was so afraid you'd be out having a romantic lunch with Ben."

"Ben's in the garden."

"I saw three men standing under a tree, but if he was one of them, I didn't notice, which is hardly a surprise, seeing I'm off men entirely at this moment. Even Lionel. You wouldn't believe how chilly he acted when I went to see him just now and told him about how my getting mixed up with Joe Tollings has properly landed me in the soup."

"Calm down, Bunty. Take a deep breath."

"That's easy for you to say." She flung herself into a chair. "Here am I, suspected of a double murder and about to get the sack if I'm back late from lunch again. And don't tell me it's my fault for carrying on with married men, Ellie. I might murder you. And that won't put me in well with a judge and jury."

"The police think you killed Trina McKinnley and then stole my car and rode over Mrs. Smalley?" I plopped down in the chair across from her.

"You bet I'm a suspect! Why wouldn't I be, after Joe blabbed to them about us? He told the police I'd found out about him and Trina, and I was jealous enough to kill her. The lying creep! He knew I didn't give two hoots who he slept with. For me it was just the occasional night out and a bit of a giggle. I told you, Ellie, I wanted to make Lionel sit up and take notice."

"Don't the police think the murders were done by either Joe or his wife? That's what Freddy heard from the girl-friend of a local constable."

"They're up there on the list—him and his Marilyn." Bunty ran manicured nails through her impish curls. "But that didn't stop a frigging detective inspector from banging on my door as I was getting ready for work and asking questions about my whereabouts last night. And wouldn't you know, for once in my life, I was home with no way to prove it. I even left work early—at a little after four, because I had a rotten headache. Me, who never gets headaches! After making myself a cup of tea I went straight to bed. Nobody phoned. So where does that leave me? Looking guilty as sin, is where."

"I'm sure you're worrying unnecessarily," I said lamely, knowing that in her position I would be planning farewells to my nearest and dearest. "You can't be placed at the scene of the crime if you weren't there."

"Darling, Ellie, you're so naive." Bunty's impossibly blue eyes welled up with tears. "How do I know that Joe didn't leave a couple of strands of my hair by the bodies? Or that Marilyn didn't strategically drop a hanky with B.W. em-broidered on it. If she knew about Trina she could have known about me. Murderers do that sort of thing all the time in books. Of course"—Bunty brightened just a little—"I'm not at all sure Joe can read." She sighed again and grabbed my arm. "Ellie, you have to help me."

"How?"

"Oh, I don't know." She got up and prowled around the room, found the dish of beetroot among the luncheon left-overs by the sink, and nibbled a couple of slices, dripping juice down her hand. "Crikey! Does that look like blood, or am I really going round the bend?" Turning on the tap, she slooshed herself off before leaning dispiritedly against the sink. "You're my friend. And I'm depending on you to get me out of this jam. I don't care how you do it. Confess to the murders yourself if that seems easiest. Bugger!" She looked up at the clock. "I've got to catch the bus and get back to work or I'll have to go to jail a pauper, and I've heard the inmates pick on poor people unmercifully."

"Bunty, I'm sure you're going to be all right." I trailed after her to the door.

"I suppose so." She did a fairly good job of propping her pretty mouth into a smile. "I really only came by for a little moral support after Lionel failed to offer any. Damn him! I never want to see him again."

I stood looking at the door that had closed behind her, wondering if I should telephone Lionel and urge him to at least provide her with legal advice, when a different idea flashed into my head. I raced out of the house to catch up with her in the courtyard.

"Bunty!"

"Yes?" She turned so fast, she fell into my arms.

"Do something for me."

"What?" Taking a couple of steps away from me.

"Use your real estate connections to find out what you can about why the Miller sisters, Clarice Whitcombe, and Tom Tingle all moved to Chitterton Fells."

"I don't know how that's likely to help me." Bunty pursed her lips and shrugged. "But if it's important to you, I'll slip old Mr. Ward a sleeping pill and poke through the files."

Bunty flitted off down the gravel drive, and I went back inside determined to find my handbag and set off for Mrs. Malloy's house before something else interrupted me. I had just unearthed it from under a sofa cushion in the drawing room and was debating whether to bother with a raincoat when the garden door banged open, and Mrs. Malloy herself marched into the kitchen with Betty Nettle trailing two paces behind.

"Where are you off to, Mrs. H., all done up to the nines for dinner?" So much for the woman I'd been picturing dead in her dining room. It was true my shoes were only slightly down at the heel and my dress was clean and pressed, but *she* was done up like a dog's dinner in a purple brocade suit with black satin trim and rhinestone buttons. The hat perched on her head sported a spiderweb veil befitting a woman in mourning. Mrs. Nettle was suitably drab in shapeless black, as became any friend of Mrs. M., but I didn't see her as a woman who would willingly sit on the sidelines of life. Not with those shrewd eyes and beaky nose.

"You've done something different to your hair," observed Mrs. Malloy, plonking her bag down on the table and stripping off her lace gloves. "Combed it, maybe that's it, Mrs. H. But Betty here and I didn't come to ask if you'd like to pose for the cover of *Vogue*—like your cousin, my daughter-in-law." She stood nibbling on the corner on her purple lip before beckoning to Mrs. Nettle. "You two met at Gertrude Large's funeral, so there's no point in me going into lengthy introductions. Enough to say, Betty's a woman of sense, Mrs. H., so I hope you'll listen to her like you would to me and make up your mind to help us see justice done."

"It's a pleasure to see you again, Mrs. Nettle," I said, "and a great relief to know that you're all right, Mrs. Malloy. I rang you a couple of times this morning and was just about to go to your house."

"Me and Betty was out having a meeting at a café near where she lives, and we come to an important decision, Mrs. H."

"Yes?"

"We want to make you an honorary member of the C.F.C.W.A. Or rather"—amending the pronouncement before I had time to get above myself—"we worked out such was our only course under the circumstances, because whatever your faults, you're a woman who's not afraid to stick her nose in where it's not wanted if the situation demands. And right now, three noses is definitely better than two."

"Thank you," I said, offering Mrs. Nettle a seat. Does this have to do with the murders? And if so, do you think Mrs. Large was the first?"

"What a question!" Mrs. Malloy snorted. "It makes me wonder if you haven't gone soft in the head since I've been away. 'Course Gertrude was murdered! Trina, who for all her funny little ways was sharp as a thumbtack, must have found out who done it and decided to put the squeeze on whoever it was. It don't seem right to use words like *blackmail* when talking of the dead." She heaved a sigh that threatened to pop the rhinestone buttons. "But there's no getting round Trina was a greedy guts when it come to money."

"But she'd just inherited a bundle from Mrs. Large."

"And Winifred Smalley wasn't going to dish it out big while Joe Tollings was in the picture," Mrs. Nettle put in. "Now, if he'd murdered Winifred first, I could be persuaded the police was on the right track. But men like that don't bump off girlfriends that's about to lay the golden egg. Not even if they have had a row."

"Then it could have been his wife," I felt bound to say as I paced the kitchen. "And the police have already questioned my friend Bunty Wiseman, who was also seeing Joe."

"Poor innocent lamb!" Mrs. Malloy somehow managed

to convey an accusing look in my direction even with her head bent.

"Well, of course I don't want Bunty accused." I banged the kettle down on the cooker and began foraging in the cupboard for cups and saucers. "Nor, for that matter, do I want Joe, unlikeable as he is, or his wife blamed for a crime they didn't commit. I can't help thinking that Mrs. Large may have been the first victim of foul play. And that the person who killed her was one of the people she worked for. Perhaps someone she had found out something about. Something damaging to their reputation or general happiness. And I wouldn't doubt for a minute that Trina, who counted every knickknack on every piece of furniture in this house the one morning she worked for me, found out why Mrs. Large died and who was behind it."

"Trina rung me up evening before last," supplied Mrs. Nettle, "and I wish I could remember exactly how she put things. Trouble is, she caught me in the middle of me favourite TV program, but I'm now sure she was talking about blackmail."

"Give Betty a cuppa, Mrs. H.," said Mrs. Malloy, "and see if that unclogs the pores in her brain."

"That's it!" Her friend sat up to attention. "Trina said something about pores—leastways I think that was it. I didn't catch the first part because I had the receiver away from me ear because it was getting to a really good part—lots of lovey-dovey—in the program. But then she laughed loud enough to get me attention and said—now let me think." Mrs. Nettle drew in her bushy eyebrows and her beaky nose probed the air, sniffing out the memory. "Yes, it's coming back to me. Trina said like it was the best joke in the world, 'It never rains but it pours pennies from heaven. And I'm sure old Gert would tell me to stick it to the rotten sod.'"

"So she never said nothing about pores, like on your nose." Mrs. Malloy had to nitpick.

"No, but it was you mentioning the word that jolted me memory, and I just wish I'd paid proper attention to what Trina said before the bit I've told you, because it seems to me she did mention finding something. But there you are—I wasn't listening when I should've been."

"You didn't ask Trina what she meant about the part you did hear?" I asked, handing Mrs. Nettle a cup of tea.

"No, 'cause she hung up, like she wanted to leave me wondering, I suppose. But one thing's for sure, Mrs. Haskell, if Trina said that much to me, she'd have spilled even more of her guts to Winifred. Them two was like mother and daughter."

"Maybe she invited Mrs. Smalley round last night," I suggested, "so she could tell her the whole story face-to-face."

"That would be Trina." Mrs. Malloy gave a grudging nod as she took her teacup. "Always a one that liked to build up the suspense. Not to speak ill of the dead, but I can see her enjoying telling Winifred she wasn't going to be entirely dependent on Gertrude's money. They'd get into spats, just like a regular mum and daughter, Trina and Winifred, but they always come round in a day or so."

"Lots of people saw the wrong side of Trina." Mrs. Nettle pulled a hanky from her black breast pocket and blew her nose. "It's easy to see people only one way, make some into saints when they're not and the other way round. But most of us is a pretty mixed bag."

Mrs. Malloy sipped at her tea, for once without complaining that it had too much or too little milk. "The point is, no one gets to murder my and Betty's friends even if they do slip up of a now and then and decide on a bit of blackmail. Not and get away with it, they don't. So there you have it, Mrs. H.; you sit yourself down and I'll read you the bylaws of the C.F.C.W.A.—skipping over the big words so as not to confuse you. Then if you're ready to commit body and soul to the C.F.C.W.A., which basically means wearing an apron with pride and never admitting to using spray polish, you get to be a member until this matter is sorted out."

"But what about the gavel?" queried Mrs. Nettle. "We can't open a meeting without one of us banging on the table for order."

"I thought you'd have it." Mrs. Malloy rounded on her.

" 'Course not, it went in the coffin with Gertrude, as was only proper seeing she was president."

"Then we'll have to make do with a rolling pin for the time being. I'm sure Mrs. H. has one as she can spare until we can get us another proper gavel. And there's no sense in arguing about who gets to use it, Betty. I elected meself president last night. Now don't go hanging your head, because you get to be everyone else—vice president, treasurer, recording secretary, and ways and means charwoman. Think of it this way: I get the glory but you get to do all the work."

I handed over the rolling pin to our invaluable president. "What I want to know is just how the three of us are going to solve the murders. What can we do that the police can't?"

"Go and clean them houses where Gertrude worked." Mrs. Malloy gave the table a rap that sent our teacups into orbit. "See if we can't find whatever it was she came across in digging out drawers or cupboards that had her all upset. The only problem as I see it is not arousing suspicion by you taking up a life as a char, Mrs. H."

I resettled my cup in its saucer. "It so happens that I may have the answer to that. You see, Ben retired from the restaurant business this morning, and it's not as though I have been setting Chitterton Fells on fire as an interior decorator. Also there is something I could contribute to working with you ladies. Abigail Grantham's homemade cleaning products."

# CHAPTER TWELVE

*Sort through contents of linen
cupboard, checking for any
needed repairs. After making
these, return to thoroughly
cleaned shelves. And put
fresh lavender in bags.*

THE FOLLOWING WEEKEND SAW THE KITCHEN AT MER-
lin's Court turned into a miniature factory. Ben claimed
he was beginning to prefer cooking up batches of furniture cream to whipping up soufflés. Jonas and Freddy
pitched in when they weren't helping out by keeping an
eye on the twins. And Mrs. Malloy and Mrs. Nettle also
came for a three-hour stint on Saturday afternoon. It wasn't
that we really needed four dozen bottles of silver polish
or gallons of mildew remover, but our production efforts
made me feel halfway official, instead of like a woman
about to participate in the biggest housecleaning scam of
all time.

Ben had certainly voiced objections when I first broached
Mrs. Malloy's plan to him, and I had to admit that I'd had
second thoughts myself after the exuberance engendered
by being made a member of the C.F.C.W.A. had ebbed a
little. But I pointed out to my husband, as Mrs. Malloy
had done to me, that I could sit on my conscience and let
a possibly innocent person take a murder rap. Or I could
put on my pinny and set about helping put the world to

rights. The thought of Bunty Wiseman being hurled into the clink was probably the part of my argument that swayed Ben. He found her exasperating at times, but in an adorable sort of way. What man wouldn't? And he agreed that our Bunty wasn't likely to take enthusiastically to prison food or to the horrid outfits produced by obscure designers that they make women wear.

"But I still don't like the idea of your snooping through people's personal possessions," he said when we had the kitchen to ourselves during a momentary lull. "Especially people we know, like the Pomeroys and Brigadier Lester-Smith and even Tom Tingle. He really seemed to enjoy his afternoon in the garden with me and Jonas. And I quite like him. He's an interesting chap."

I was having trouble getting the label to stick on a bottle of silver polish, the duster wrapped around my head kept sliding down over my eyes, and I was feeling just a little testy. "Naturally you've become fond of him, Ben. You saved Tom Tingle's life. That's bound to create a bond, but at times like this we can't afford to be sentimental."

"And you won't mind in the least if your pal the brigadier turns out to be a triple murderer?" Ben had now upgraded himself from bottle filler to foreman and was inspecting the products lined up on the kitchen table, making sure that the lids were properly tightened.

"Dear, Brigadier Lester-Smith has nothing to hide, other than the fact he has taken to dyeing his hair. I know him well enough to be certain of that." I finally got that label to stick. "And anyway, if he's a murderer he can't marry Clarice Whitcombe, and I've set my heart on them living happily ever after."

"You know hardly anything about her, Ellie."

"True, but I like what I've seen." I was sticking on another label. "She likes animals, is eager to embrace life, in a tentative sort of way, and asked my advice on lipsticks, which naturally I found engaging. And she's very modest—shying away from talking about her piano playing. She's never mixed much. Her parents kept her at home."

"Until she was what? Forty-five or fifty?"

"It does sound rather gothic," I agreed. "From what she said, her parents weren't exactly unkind to her, just completely wrapped up in themselves. It was convenient for them to have Clarice around to run the household."

"Her only outlet being to sit in the attic in a white nightgown at dead of night playing mournful tunes on the piano while praying that Mummy and Daddy wouldn't live forever?" Ben knocked over one of the bottles, sending half a dozen others plonking backwards. Righting them, he continued: "It really wouldn't come as much of a surprise to me, Ellie, if it turns out Clarice doctored her parents' heart medicine or whatever they took, and that's the dirty little secret Mrs. Large uncovered."

"Clarice told me they committed suicide together."

"Considerate of the old dears."

"Perhaps you're right to be skeptical," I conceded slowly. "Much as I don't like to think it, she *does* present possibilities. But let's not overlook Tom Tingle. I've got to say I found myself taking to him when I went over to his house the day Trina McKinnley and Winifred Smalley were murdered. But I'm not sure I buy his explanation as to what he said on the beach about it being an accident, and I sense he's always seen himself as a misfit."

"Because he's short, I suppose."

"He could have any number of insecurities. Those ears of his, for instance. They really are very pointed."

"And Mrs. Large found evidence that bodies tended to pile up everywhere he went?" Ben said even more skeptically.

"I'm not saying that." I leaned wearily against the sink. "But he is a virtual stranger, as are Clarice and the Millers. And believe me, those sisters are also high on my list of possibles. Madrid is a slave to her deceased Norfolk terrier's memory. As for Vienna, sturdy though she appears to be, it would hardly be surprising if she cracked under the pressure of being her sister's mainstay. Maybe she falsified the dogs' pedigrees so they will sell for more money, or . . . well, it could be anything. Perhaps it's not fair, Ben, but I find it preferable to suspect virtual strangers rather than people I've known for years. Which is why I asked Bunty Wiseman to use her real estate job to find out what she could about the newcomers who were at the Hearthside Guild meeting the day Mrs. Large died."

"I understand why you're focusing on them." Ben rubbed a hand through his hair, further disheveling his dark curls. "They were on the spot. But it could have been someone else."

"Jonas was out in the garden and he didn't see anyone going into the study through the French windows or leaving the same way."

"He wasn't there the whole time. Didn't he go into the kitchen for a cup of tea after he had finished the pruning?"

"Yes, and of course, the murderer could have entered through the front door. After all, Clarice did. She said it was unlocked and no one had come when she rang the bell. But there's another thing, Ben."

"What?"

"Mrs. Large worked for everyone present at that meeting—the Millers, Sir Robert and Lady Pomeroy, Tom Tingle, Clarice Whitcombe, and Brigadier Lester-Smith. And her only other clients, according to Mrs. Malloy, were a bedridden woman of ninety-odd and a couple who have been in New Zealand for the past three months visiting their married daughter. And Mrs. Large stopped working for Mrs. Barrow at the beginning of the year."

"What happened there?"

"The queen of picketers decided it was morally irresponsible to have someone in to do the housework. So, you see, darling," I said, "that does narrow the field. And given the fact Mrs. Large thought about presenting her concerns at a C.F.C.W.A. meeting, that being at least part of what she wanted to talk to Mrs. Malloy about on the phone, we know whatever was troubling her had to involve one of her clients. Then there's Trina McKinnley. The reason she gave for being able to give me only a couple of hours a week was that she was taking on all of Mrs. Large's people. Which means she went to work for the murderer."

"And look what happened to her, Ellie!"

"Exactly! But you and I will be careful not to blackmail anyone."

"Five houses to check out." Ben shifted me away from the sink to wash his hands. "I'll go along with that, on condition I make up part of the work team. It'll help speed things up, and I'll be able to supply brute male force should we get caught snooping by whoever it is who's bound and determined to keep his or her secret. Although I've got to say, I really don't think there's much likelihood of our finding anything. Surely any competent murderer would have gotten rid of whatever it was Mrs. Large discovered by now."

"Not necessarily." I handed him a dish towel to dry his hands. "It could be something the killer can't bear to part with or now feels safe to keep."

Our conversation came to an abrupt halt when Mrs. Malloy and Mrs. Nettle bustled in, the former looking ready to unionize us on the spot and the latter expressing mild disappointment that we didn't have a conveyor belt on which to transport the product from the bottling station to the labeling plant. Freddy appeared and offered to make one out of a board placed on a pair of roller skates he thought he might have at the cottage, but no one greeted this idea with enthusiasm. So he busied himself making cups of tea that nobody found time to drink and talking hopefully about the millions we could make if we would stop thinking small and buy a proper factory run by robots while we all sat in the executive dining room discussing advertising strategy. Mainly to get him off that topic I told him about Ben's intention of helping out the C.F.C.W.A., and was immediately interrupted by Mrs. Malloy.

"My making you a honorary member of the organization went to your head quicker than I'd have thought possible, even of you, Mrs. H.! Asking your hubby to join us without even having the decency to put the invite in the form of a motion! That beats anything I've heard in all me . . . few years on this earth! In future I'll thank you to remember who's president here," she fumed. "Betty, I want you to write Mrs. Haskell a letter of censor on our official notepaper. And don't go putting no kisses at the bottom."

"I'm sure she didn't mean any harm, Roxie." Mrs. Nettle went right on mixing up a solution to put the colour back in those whitish moisture rings that are the ruin of many a sideboard or table. "And I can see the sense in Mr. Haskell helping out. The more hands and eyes the better, I say, considering we're looking for a needle in a haystack, so to speak."

"Then count me in." Freddy gave his ponytail an enthusiastic toss. "I've always been frightfully keen on this cloak-and-dagger stuff, haven't I, Ellie?"

"He's staked out any number of refrigerators in his time," I told Mrs. Nettle, "and held up quite a few pantries without being caught."

"Lads will be lads," she responded, looking as indulgent

as was possible for a woman who closely resembled a bird of prey.

"Oh, all right." Mrs. Malloy endeavoured to make the best of finding herself stuck with a suggestion she probably wished had been her own. "But you, Freddy, and Mr. H. have to face up to the fact that you're just temporary reinforcements; you're not entitled to no voting privileges and there's no good hoping you'll be invited to the annual Christmas do, because the goings-on at said function isn't suited to mixed company."

"Speaking of voting"—Mrs. Nettle wiped up a spill— "the C.F.C.W.A. decided in your absence, Roxie, not to wear armbands for Gertrude; we went with black bows instead, to wear in our hair. What do you think, should we do the same for Trina and Winifred? To me it don't seem quite enough, but I'll go along with whatever you say."

"Bows?" Mrs. Malloy puckered her purple lips. "I don't remember as Trina was wearing one when I found her. And she had on one of them white uniforms of hers. That started when she took up helping nurse Frank Large. Liked to look important, did Trina. Power mad, as I've said before. But a bow in her hair . . . I'm sure I'd have noticed. But maybe you'd all stopped wearing them by that time, Betty."

"No, it was agreed we'd keep it up for six weeks. And then maybe wear purple ones for another month. I just haven't put mine on since the . . . last two went, because it didn't seem right to acknowledge Gertrude's passing and leave them out. And three bows in the hair seems a bit much for women our age, Roxie."

Mrs. Malloy did not look thrilled by this observation. She said briskly that the present situation obviously called for armbands, which she would be happy to donate seeing she had a lifetime supply left over from the funerals of husbands number two and three. She went on to say that she'd just telephoned Lady Pomeroy, who said she would be delighted to try out our new service, which meant that Mrs. Malloy had now called all Mrs. Large's former clients—the ones that counted, that is. And they'd all agreed (without asking any rude questions about my being part of the work crew) to the times and days she had suggested for our first domestic onslaught.

"I said the first time, four hours each, would be free, so they could see how they liked the products, but really to hook them good and proper. Besides"—Mrs. Malloy assumed a virtuous expression that went well with her purple ensemble—"I thought that was only fair, seeing as we're up to tricks."

"I just hope the murderer doesn't twig to why we're being such good sports," I said, looking from Ben to Freddy and reading the same thought on their faces.

"And make sure there's nothing for us to find," inserted Mrs. Nettle, who was now rinsing out her funnel.

"It don't do to overestimate people like that." Mrs. Malloy waved an airy hand. "Cocky as all get out. Stands to reason, or they wouldn't think they could get away with their high jinks. Many's the day we've all thought about knocking someone off, but most of us stays humble."

No one came up with a quick answer to that, and then Jonas came into the kitchen with Abbey and Tam. It was good to see how Jonas had improved during the last couple of days; all the activity had acted on him like a tonic. Freddy even took me aside to say how well the old man was looking, and Jonas himself mentioned with begrudging pleasure that Tom Tingle wanted to come back for more gardening lessons.

Evening arrived. Mrs. Nettle went home a little ahead of Mrs. Malloy, and when Roxie got up to leave, I walked her outside, grasping at the opportunity to talk to her about what had happened in London. What had made her decide to come home? How was dear little Rose, and of course, George and Vanessa? But there was no getting anything out of her. After a few noncommittal mumbles her face—not just her mouth—clamped shut. Watching her walk the rest of the way down the drive and through the iron gates, I pondered what could be wrong. Surely if she'd had a blazing row with Vanessa she would have told me. Mrs. Malloy knew my cousin and I weren't exactly soul mates. What was she keeping from me?

For a while the murders receded to a back cupboard of my mind. But by Sunday afternoon I was back to thinking about very little else. Even trying to stay busy in the kitchen factory or playing with the children didn't help, because the morrow hung over everything like a black drape on a coffin.

Mrs. Malloy, Ben, and I were to go to the Miller sisters at nine and on to Clarice Whitcombe's at one. Unfortunately, Dr. Solomon had promised he would come and take a look at Jonas on Monday. But the doctor rang early on Sunday evening from his car phone to say he was in the area.

"Would it be convenient for me to stop by?" he asked, "because tomorrow looks like a tight squeeze."

"That would be great," I said.

When he arrived, he told Jonas, who was not best pleased, that he had been wondering if his favorite patient had had any more trouble with bronchitis, and brooking no argument, he bustled my friend off into the study. Afterwards, Ben walked Dr. Solomon to his car. Fabulous news.

"Jonas is in better shape than many men half his age," was his pronouncement. "Make sure the old boy gets regular doses of the prescribed medicine—moderate exercise, plenty of mental stimulation, and fresh air. And you can tell your wife to stop worrying."

At any other time my heart would have sung, but I was feeling more jittery by the minute, which made Freddy's boundless enthusiasm for our prospective adventure—as he insisted on calling it—hard to take. Even though I was grateful that he and Mrs. Nettle were the ones who would be doing Brigadier Lester-Smith's house, along with Tom Tingle's. I wasn't cut out to be a spy, which surely was a job more suited to skinny people, who are better able to fade into the woodwork or wallpaper if things went wrong.

It had been agreed that the two work parties would meet at Merlin's Court at eight-thirty on Monday morning, for a quick cup of tea and a final boost of moral support. Freddy showed up early, looking disgustingly chirpy and eager to know whether he would look more like a proper char if he stuffed his ponytail under a hair net and wore matronly earrings. Ben was suggesting a floral pinny when Mrs. Nettle arrived. But where was Mrs. Malloy?

We drank our tea and I went upstairs to see how Jonas was coping with the twins. He was reading to them from one of their favourite storybooks, and I told him there was cereal and a compote of plums, peaches, and figs for breakfast. And a quiche and salad in the fridge for lunch. But it was clear Abbey and Tam wanted to hear more about the little dragon who lived in the time between long ago and right this minute. So after hugging them and reminding Jonas yet again that he must telephone if there were any problems, I returned to the kitchen. Still no Mrs. Malloy. And it was now a quarter to nine.

"It's just not like her." Mrs. Nettle stood looking hollow-cheeked and beaky-nosed, hands clasping her giant bag of Abigail's Homemade Cleaning Products. "Punctual to a fault, that's Roxie."

"Perhaps she missed the bus," offered Freddy.

"Could be." Mrs. Nettle started tapping her foot, picking up the beat from Ben, who'd been at it for several minutes.

"We'll give her another five minutes," he said, looking, I noticed even in my distraction, like any woman's dream char. His teeth were as white as the open-necked white shirt he wore under a thin navy sweater, and Beau Brummell's tailor might have fitted his crisply ironed khaki slacks. My dress was also navy, dug out from the back of my wardrobe, because I'd decided it would make me look serviceable. I'd also twisted my hair into a housekeeper's bun at my neck. It would have been disheartening to reflect how easily I had succeeded in making myself into the archetypal domestic. But as the clock ticked closer to nine, all I could think about was that nothing short of calamity would have kept Mrs. Malloy from being here.

"We'll have to go on without her," said Ben. "Perhaps she got mixed up and thought she was to meet us at the Millers."

"Oh, but she wouldn't have," I protested. "We went over the arrangements more than once."

"I don't know." Mrs. Nettle brightened a little. "She hasn't been herself, Roxie hasn't. I've got the feeling it started before the murders. Look how she didn't show up for Gertrude's funeral, after saying she'd be there."

"That's right." Ben visibly relaxed and I struggled to look positive, even as my insides continued to tie themselves into knots which would never come undone.

"Did anyone think to phone her?"

"I did," replied Freddy, "twice, while you were upstairs, coz. Both times the line was engaged."

"Or off the hook," I managed.

"But then I rung back," proffered Mrs. Nettle, "and that time there was no answer."

"So she got a late start and probably has gone straight to Tall Chimneys, assuming we'd have the sense not to wait for her." I was breathing just a little easier as I followed Ben out to the old convertible. Freddy and Mrs. Nettle took the other car and, when we reached the gates, took off in the opposite direction.

It was a fresh, breezy morning under clear blue skies, but Tall Chimneys looked as it always did—a house stuck permanently in the winter of the soul. Its narrow-eyed windows squinted on a world they would have preferred always shrouded in dense fog and chilling rain. And those chimneys were sufficiently off-kilter to suggest they were deliberately cocked, the better to listen for the malevolent cawing of crows and the howling of wolf-like dogs.

The Millers' Norfolk terriers were certainly woofing their heads off from the back of the house as Ben and I approached the front door. Vienna promptly admitted us with a deep-voiced greeting.

"How professional you look, and so punctual!" Understandably, she looked a little uncomfortable at the switch from meeting us as social acquaintances to our showing up as the household help.

Were rumours already flying around Chitterton Fells that Ben and I were on the brink of financial ruin? If so, it would keep suspicious minds from wondering why we had taken up this line of work. With every step I took down the hall to the kitchen I kept hoping to hear Mrs. Malloy's chattering voice—to no avail. She had not arrived. And Vienna said she had not heard from her.

Madrid almost immediately materialized in the kitchen in a flutter of gauzy garment that sadly emphasized her middle-age spread and mocked her flowing Lady of the Lake hair. Ben and I might have been a couple of spectral figures she saw only as floating transparencies until Vienna said, in a voice that was at once firm yet cosseting, "You look chilly, dear. Why don't you wrap this around you?" She plucked the shawl Madrid had been wearing on my last visit from the back of a chair. "You remember Ellie and her husband . . ."

"Ben," he supplied, his gallantry making him appear increasingly miscast for the role of someone who was about to don a pinny.

"So nice to meet you properly." Vienna smiled warmly at him while not taking her eyes off her sister. "Madrid, there's a little bit of a mystery. Mrs. Malloy was meant to have been here."

"She won't be coming."

"Really, dear?"

"Clarice Whitcombe rang to say Mrs. Mallone"—Madrid paused but none of us corrected her—"had tried to get in touch with us, but our line was engaged. You know I was on the phone for ages working out the final details."

Her sister nodded and explained that they had to be in London tomorrow and the following day for a dog show.

"Clarice said Mrs. Malone had also tried to ring the Haskells but couldn't get through to them either."

"We were trying to call her," I said.

Madrid was now floating about the kitchen, half draped in the shawl. "So I was to pass on the message that something has come up and she can't be here. Does that put you in an awful bind?" Her gaze actually zeroed in first on me, then on Ben. "After all, I suppose being a proper char, she was supposed to do the work while you two showed her how to properly apply these cleaning products you've invented."

"Oh, we can manage." I hoped my voice did not sound as hollow as I felt.

"Are you sure?" Vienna was now steering her sister away from the cooker, as if afraid it might be too taxing for Madrid, were she to attempt to put on the kettle. "If you'd rather come back another day with Mrs. Malloy, that would be perfectly all right."

"We wouldn't think of it." Ben began unpacking our bag of products produced in the Merlin's Court kitchen factory. "You'll want the house shipshape when you come back from your trip."

"That's true." Vienna sounded relieved, even as the awkwardness in treating us as employees as well as social acquaintances again became visible. "I'm always so busy with the dogs, and Madrid isn't sufficiently fit for housework, so that things have really got behind here. Dust everywhere you look. When Trina—such a terrible tragedy—returned from her holiday and took over again from poor Mrs. Large, she wasn't able to give us as much time as before. Just half a day a week, because she took on her friend's clients. Trina said she felt she owed it to her, and of course Madrid and I had to respect that. A very decent young woman in her own way."

"Absolutely," I agreed.

"Ellie and I will do everything we can to pick up the slack." Ben managed to sound enthusiastic without overdoing it.

So, saying she knew we must want to get started, Vienna conducted us on a quick tour of the house with Madrid alternately trailing behind or disappearing in the middle of a sentence. It seemed hours, although it was probably only ten minutes, before Ben and I found ourselves alone. It had been a relief to hear that Vienna would be occupied most of the morning grooming the dogs. And Madrid had announced that after breakfast she was going out for a long walk, something she did most days because she had always felt at one with the outdoors.

"It certainly doesn't sound as though they suspect us of being here to snoop." Ben smiled encouragingly at me as he surveyed the sitting room, where we were watched only by the portrait of Jessica above the fireplace.

"There's no reason for the sisters to think we're up to something if their consciences are clear," I whispered.

"A dog with a ring painted on its paw." His eyes were riveted.

"It's a ruby, her birthstone."

"Wacky, but then there's something creepy about the entire house." Ben pulled a face and opened a bottle of furniture polish.

"It feels worse today." I shifted up close to him. "But maybe that's because I'm so on edge about Mrs. Malloy. I'd feel better if one of us had talked to her."

It was difficult to get my mind back on track and my body into action, but somehow I managed to put myself on automatic. In the next hour, while Ben briskly polished, wiped, and Hoovered, I poked through desk and dresser drawers, searched cupboard and wardrobe shelves, growing increasingly convinced that we were knocking ourselves out for nothing. I was wishing I could go home and sit quietly, trying to figure out where Mrs. Malloy could be, when in a tabletop box on Vienna's bedside table I found a small stack of love letters. They were dated twenty years earlier. Written by a man who claimed to love her deeply, even as he grew increasingly impatient because she wouldn't leave her sister—until the time was right. Obviously that time had never come. It sounded like a Victorian sort of love affair and I replaced the letters feeling impatient with all three people concerned. But there was no hint of anything sinister.

Ten minutes later I found a letter in a bureau in Madrid's room. It was dated a couple of years back—from a woman who was a member of a recovery group for people who had faced the loss of a beloved pet. I felt a faint stirring of sympathy for Madrid. Was it her fault that she didn't have the emotional strength to overcome what for her might have seemed equivalent to losing a child? It was still hard for me to identify with her, much as I doted on Tobias, but the fact that I was not proud of prying into other people's lives made me a little less judgmental.

One o'clock arrived and somehow Ben had managed to make the house look as though we had both been working. Vienna was warm in her praise and thanks. She paid us without looking too embarrassed, and my husband and I left Tall Chimneys without seeing Madrid again.

"That got us nowhere," was Ben's response as we drove the short distance to Crabapple Tree Cottage. From the sound of it, he, too, was losing his enthusiasm.

"There wasn't time for a thorough search." I leaned back in my seat, feeling spent. "But I'm not sure it will help however many times we go back. I'm beginning to think we've been barking up a tree where no cat is holed up."

I was to feel even more guilty when Clarice Whitcombe greeted us enthusiastically upon our arrival at Crabapple Tree Cottage. The furniture she had brought from her old home still looked too big for the place, but there were signs that she was settling in: a vase of daffodils on the hall table, fresh curtains at the windows, and a collection of comfortingly old teddy bears grouped on top of the kitchen cupboards. The grand piano still dwarfed the small sitting room, but it looked as though it had been recently polished.

Clarice did not display any of the embarrassment Vienna had shown. She offered Ben and me lunch, which we refused in accordance with the rules of the Magna Char—fibbing by saying we had already eaten. And afterwards, while Ben remained in the kitchen, she accompanied me into the sitting room, where I tried to look highly motivated.

"I'm so impressed," she said, taking the easy chair across from me in front of the diminutive fireplace.

"Why's that?" I spread the duster over my knees and straightened its corners, my mind on Mrs. Malloy.

"I've always been awed by people who take life by the horns, Ellie, because I'm not that sort of person. I just let the years roll over me. The neighbours where I used to live thought I was a saint, staying on to look after my parents, but the reality was I was born spineless. While you and your husband"—her face, as pleasantly old-fashioned as her skirt and blouse, lit up like a child's—"you are both so brave! Him giving up a successful business and joining you in this wonderful new venture. Not caring what other people think. Just living your own lives. I really don't know whether to clap or to cry."

It was my turn to feel embarrassed.

"I only hope you'll still be able to spare the time to help me redecorate," Clarice went on.

"Absolutely. The hope is that we will be able to incorporate the production of Abigail's Homemade Cleaning Products into my interior design activities. Perhaps even open a little shop, with space for Ben to serve morning coffee and lunches." All true, but—because I had come to spy on her, I was convinced I sounded the world's most inept liar.

"It all strikes me as wonderful." Clarice fidgeted with her hands. "Since coming here, Ellie, I have tried to break out of the old mold, become a shade more adventurous. I even went over to Walter's . . . I mean Brigadier Lester-Smith's house the other evening . . . after going to see the doctor about my wrist." Now clasping it with her free hand. "It seemed to me that in this day and age a woman should be able to make a friendly overture without being considered brazen. But after taking a couple of steps to his front door, I panicked and scampered away like a naughty little girl. Then I lay awake half the night wondering if he had seen me—or if one of the neighbours would say something and he would have to write me off as loony."

"We women do agonize about that sort of thing," I agreed. But had Clarice told me about that visit, not because she lacked real friends to confide in, but because she wanted to establish that her being in Herring Street had nothing to do with Trina McKinnley's death? Her account tallied with Marilyn Tollings. But a sneaky suspicion arose in my mind. What if Clarice had gone up the brigadier's drive by mistake? After realizing she was at the wrong house, had she scuttled off to her meeting with Trina, next door but one?

With a glance at the mantel clock, I suggested as nonchalantly as I could that I really did need to be getting to work, especially as Ben and I were lacking Mrs. Malloy.

"You did get the message from her that I passed on to Madrid Miller?" Clarice stood up, looking sorry that our chat was winding down.

"That there had been some emergency." I nodded. "Did Mrs. Malloy sound particularly agitated?"

"I thought so, but you can't really go by that, Ellie, because I don't know her, remember." Clarice's gaze wasn't on me as she spoke. It was fixed on a small bowl that I hadn't previously noticed on the carpet to the side of the door. Set down next to it was a box of starch, and without having time to analyze why, my heart started to thump.

"I forgot to take that away," she said.

"What's in the bowl?" My legs walked me over to it and I stared down at the milky liquid it contained.

"Just starch and water. My mother used to have me mix it into a thin paste for getting out . . ."

"Bloodstains?" I murmured too quickly—because now I wouldn't get to know if that was what Clarice had intended to say.

"Of course you would know about that old-fashioned remedy for one of life's little problems." She sounded genuinely admiring. "My mother was a fount of such information, even though I never knew her to do housework. We always had help until I took over. What happened here"—pointing at the carpet where the bowl and box of starch sat—"is that Mrs. Grey, the little cat from down the road, paid me a visit this morning. And it was only after she got into this room and I saw the streaks of blood on the floor that I realized she had cut one of her paws."

The telephone rang at that propitious moment and Clarice went off to answer it, leaving me feeling weak at the knees. Suddenly I saw it all. Mrs. Malloy had arrived at Crabapple Tree Cottage that morning, having got the schedule mixed up. Shortly thereafter, Clarice had let slip that she had murdered Gertrude Large, Trina McKinnley, and Winifred Smalley. Naturally Mrs. Malloy had taken umbrage, and not being a woman to mince words, had spoken her mind in no uncertain terms. Whereupon Clarice had added another woman to her list of victims. And, tut-tutting at the inconvenience of it all, had phoned Tall Chimneys to deliver a fake message from my beloved Mrs. M. I buried my face in the duster. It was too cruel! She had been restored to me only to be shoved headlong into eternity.

I tried to tell myself that the story about the cat could well be true, that I was allowing my imagination to overcome common sense. If Clarice had murdered Mrs. Malloy, she would surely have got rid of the bowl and the box of starch, particularly when she might guess I would know their purpose. But then again—the ugly thought would not be held at bay—she might have decided to leave that small task until she had completed the even more pressing one of disposing of the body. And that could have so distracted her that she had let a crucial piece of evidence slip her mind.

It was difficult to get back to sleuthing, since now every part of me, not just my teeth, seemed to be chattering. Ben came into the sitting room from the kitchen and I almost accused him of sneaking up on me. He realized something was up, but I muttered that I couldn't talk about it now. And while he again took over the real work I opened drawers and dragged out the contents. Nothing of interest turned up until I raised the top of the piano stool and lifted out its contents. To say I was shocked is to put it mildly. Clarice Whitcombe was not what she claimed to be. And I was all fingers and thumbs as I replaced the evidence. Not a moment to soon! She came silently into the sitting room and knew my face had to be on fire. I stood fanning myself, hopefully looking as though I had overexerted myself polishing the furniture, until my heart stopped pounding. Did she suspect, from the way I avoided looking at the piano, that I was on to her?

I was desperate to tell Ben what I had found but I retained enough sense to wait until we were away from Crabapple Tree Cottage. But when we got into the car in the late afternoon to drive home I couldn't bring myself to talk about it. Not until I'd had a cup of tea.

Abbey and Tam swarmed all over us when we came in the door. And we immediately had to see to getting tea for them and Jonas, who looked remarkably fit given his day with the children. Then we had to wait for Freddy and Mrs. Nettle to show up, which they did half an hour later. They appeared to be on excellent, even chummy, terms. Jonas took the twins into the study to watch a favourite television show. And we four sleuths sat down in the kitchen to talk.

"Clarice Whitcombe has misrepresented her piano-playing skills in a big way," I said. "I found sheet music for 'Mary Had a Little Lamb' and other beginner pieces. Along with a notebook containing instructions of the most basic kind from her piano teacher. Such as 'Paint a dot on middle C if that is the only way you can find it.' "

Freddy irritated me by laughing. "That's all you and Ben came up with after four hours of snooping at Crabapple Tree Cottage?" He gave Mrs. Nettle a conspiratorial wink. "So the poor dear is just a beginner instead of being able to pound out Beethoven, Mozart, and Bach without having to look at the music! Lots of people exaggerate their talents, coz!"

It was clear from Ben's and Mrs. Nettle's expressions that they were in agreement with Freddy.

"But given what I know of Clarice, she would die with embarrassment if she was found out. She probably got started in the pretense when Brigadier Lester-Smith saw that very grand grand piano taking up three-quarters of her sitting room and assumed she could play." I leaned forward, elbows on the table. "She wouldn't want to disillusion him, but then Clarice was in the soup because he wanted to hear her play. She had to come up with an excuse. Which was that she had injured her arm. Buying her time to start taking lessons and hope she would discover she had a God-given ability to make 'Mary Had a Little Lamb' sound like Mozart. I'll bet she was off to a lesson when I met her on the afternoon of the day Trina McKinnley was killed."

"But I don't think these deceptions amount to a woman leading a double life." Ben pushed a plate of biscuits my way.

"The trouble is"—my heart ached more than all the other muscles I had exercised that day because I had so wanted this love story to have a happy ending—"I can identify with Clarice's insecurities. She could have worked herself up into an irrational state where she felt trapped, with no way out of the lie, when cornered by Mrs. Large, who had found the evidence in the piano stool. She'd picture herself branded as a liar not only to the man she loved but to the entire village. Perhaps Clarice went into the study at Tall Chimneys to beg Mrs. Large not to spill the beans. And then lost her head."

Mrs. Nettle sat with her beaky-nosed face tucked into hunched shoulders. "I don't see that even if Gertrude Large had found out about Miss Whitcombe's deception, she'd have been all that bothered. Certainly not enough, if you'll forgive my speaking so plain, Mrs. Haskell, for her to wonder if she didn't ought to report the matter to the C.F.C.W.A."

"You don't think that, working for Brigadier Lester-Smith as she did, Mrs. Large might have been worried he would be lured into a serious involvement, even marriage, with a woman of deceptive practices?"

Mrs. Nettle grew pensive. "Put like that, I can see it could've made for a problem with Gert—her as was always honest in her dealings, besides being fiercely loyal to all those she worked for. Making it difficult, I suppose, for her to know where her duty lay."

"Brigadier Lester-Smith doesn't win any prizes in truthfulness himself." Freddy's words sat me back in my seat.

"What, just because he's taken to tinting his hair?"

My cousin grinned through the ragged edges of his beard. Then he sobered. "Sorry, Ellie, I know you're fond of the brigadier . . . as you call him."

"What's that supposed to mean?" Ben and I spoke one on top of the other.

"Mrs. Nettle and I also made a couple of discoveries today during working hours. One being a gold watch I found in Lester-Smith's bedside table."

"So?" It was now quite dark outside, but with the lights on, there was no reason the kitchen should suddenly have seemed to dim, or that Tobias jumping down from the rocking chair should have presented such an elongated shadow.

"That watch was engraved." Freddy made matters worse

by drawing the words out slowly. "It was a retirement gift presented to your friend, Ellie, after thirty years of employment as a law clerk. He's not a brigadier. He doesn't even have the hyphen. Lester is his middle name. So isn't it just as likely that Mrs. Large was worried that Mr. Smith was romancing Clarice Whitcombe under false pretenses and that she was agonizing over whether she had a duty to warn the poor woman before it was too late?"

# Chapter Thirteen

*Wipe mirrors with a flannel rag, wrung out of warm water and dipped in a little whiting. The gilding must be merely dusted, as the least dampness may injure it.*

LYING IN BED THAT NIGHT I TRIED TO FOCUS ON CHEER-ful thoughts. None springing readily to mind, I struggled to believe Freddy was wrong about Brigadier Lester-Smith—that the engraving on the gold watch meant nothing. Perhaps it was true that he had been a law clerk for thirty years, but had maintained a second career, working his way up to brigadier on the weekends or at night. And that in reward for his service to God and country he had received official permission to hyphenate his name. Unable to convince myself this was likely, I began making excuses for him. Probably the other boys at school had called him Carrots. A boy like that would yearn to show the world one day what a brilliant success he'd made of himself. And when that didn't happen, he'd made it up. To me, he would always be Brigadier Lester-Smith and I wouldn't—not for a second—listen to the voice whispering inside my head that there might be a grain of truth to the belief expressed by such as Mrs. Malloy, that a man who dyed his hair was not to be completely trusted.

Where are you, Mrs. Malloy? My mounting anxiety coupled with fatigue made it impossible to think clearly, yet sleep refused to come. So I replayed the other piece of information Freddy had brought back from his workday with Mrs. Nettle regarding Tom Tingle. They'd found his current checkbook in his rolltop desk and in looking through the entries saw that in recent months he had written several checks, each for ten thousand pounds, to the same individual—one Lucia Frondcragg. Also in the desk was a letter, one line of which had leaped to Freddy's eye: "I appreciate the help, Tom, but I feel as though I am taking blood money." Signed by Lucia—suspicious to say the least!

Finally, I latched onto a relatively cheerful thought. If either Brigadier Lester-Smith or Tom Tingle were the villain, there could be no reason for Clarice Whitcombe to have made up that phone call from Mrs. Malloy, let alone have murdered her. Ben and Freddy certainly hadn't taken my concerns seriously. Every fifteen minutes or so I began to doze, and each time I was jolted back to awareness as if some badly behaved nocturnal child had sent a ball slamming against the bedroom window. Unable to stand it any longer, I climbed out of bed and tiptoed over to the chair where I had left my dressing gown. A glass of milk might help me sleep.

As a rule I rather liked prowling around the house during the dead of night, but as I went along the gallery to the stairs I heard a rustle from above. Perhaps a bird had got into the attic. I wasn't about to go up and check because it seemed to me entirely possible that the shadows up there amused themselves by moving objects from place to place just for the fun of it. I found myself picturing that attic as a nursing home for aged, decrepit, or otherwise unwanted household goods. Their pasts now half forgotten, their futures as uncertain as the boards creaking under my feet.

Upon switching on the kitchen lights I recovered my sanity—what there was of it. I heated my milk and settled into the rocking chair with Abigail's green notebook. It was comforting to read about such prosaic topics as how to prevent fruit stains from becoming permanent: wet the stained spot with whisky before putting in the wash.

To clean hairbrushes and combs, use two teaspoons of supercarbonate dissolved in half a pint of boiling water.

Holding a piece of velvet in front of a steaming kettle will restore the pile.

One should stuff up mouse holes with rags saturated in a mixture of cayenne pepper and water.

We didn't have mice, as far as I knew, and if we had, Tobias would have expected me to mind my own business, but I savoured this and the other pieces of housewifely wisdom, anew, despite having pored over them many times in recent days. They brought back the kind and gentle ghost of Abigail Grantham, banished the spooks from the attic, and restored the past as an ally.

How hard people had worked before God gave us Hoovers! My eyes drifted shut. To imagine a pre-modern woman slogging through her housework would have been exhausting even in the middle of the day. It was now, however, two A.M. I knew I should finish my milk and return to bed before I had to crawl up the stairs. But the hard kitchen chair was so comfy I found myself nodding off again. My head slumped forward and must have hit the table because I heard a thump, actually two of them, before I was reclaimed by muzzy sleep and dreamed that someone was opening the garden door and creeping into the kitchen.

It wasn't a dream; it was brutal reality. I shot awake, my heart hammering away as I gripped the arms of the chair and forced myself to turn and face the intruder. What I should have done was pick up my cup and slosh the remains in his or her face. Unfortunately there was only about an inch left in the bottom. But at least it would have been something to do.

"Good morning, Mrs. H.," said the new president and fellow member of the C.F.C.W.A., as if arriving at a perfectly acceptable time of day. "The front of the house was dark, so I was forced to come round back."

"Mrs. Malloy!" I stumbled out of my chair.

"No need to look at me like I'm a ghost!"

"I'm just surprised." A huge understatement. For a good part of the day I had been picturing her dead and buried. But her fake leopard coat was undeniably real and the only thing even slightly unusual was that instead of her usual supplies bag she was carrying an enormous holdall that was unzipped halfway. It looked commodious enough to have accompanied her on board ship as she moved to Australia.

"A good thing I didn't give you back the key when I left Chitterton Fells," she continued while I was still trying to unlock my jaw. "When I saw the lights on through the glass in the door I knocked good and loud a couple of times, but you didn't rush to welcome me with open arms."

"I thought"—rubbing my brow—"that I'd bumped my head."

"That doesn't surprise me." Mrs. Malloy gave me a pained look from under her neon-coated lids. "Would you mind turning off the overhead light, Mrs. H., and just leaving the one on by the back door? I'm getting a headache that threatens to turn something cruel."

"Oh, what a shame!" Hustling over to the light switch, I agonized over what had brought her here in the middle of the night. Mrs. Malloy teetered over to the table to deposit the holdall and stand fussing with it before removing her coat, revealing a purple velvet dress underneath.

She rested a hand on the table as if to try and stop the room from spinning. "As I was saying, it wouldn't surprise me if you'd got a migraine of your own, because in your right mind, Mrs. H., you'd be pouring me a cup of tea and asking if I wanted any brandy in it."

"I've been worried about you." I scampered to put the kettle on and shuffle Tobias off the rocking chair so she could sit down. "I was sure there had to be something wrong for you to go off like that."

"Sorry, I should have sent a postcard saying I was having a lovely time. And I did try to phone, but the bloody line was engaged. And I had a train to catch to London." Her butterfly lips, coloured cherry red to clash with her frock, drooped. I fetched a bottle of brandy from the pantry and liberally laced her tea before handing it to her. "Here's to you, Mrs. H.," she toasted me by raising the cup to her lips and taking a deep swallow. "You're a port in a storm." A tear slid down her cheek, creating a channel between eye and chin.

"Have a little more brandy," I urged, torn between sympathy and the urge to know what latest catastrophe had befallen her.

"Just a couple of drops." Holding out the cup she roused herself to supervise. "That's not even a drip, Mrs. H.! Forty of them wouldn't make one drop."

"How's that?" Upending the bottle. "Now please, Mrs. Malloy, you have to tell me what's going on and let me help you if I can."

"I got back on the last train out of Victoria. Arrived in at a little before ten. And although I can't say I was feeling like a dog with two tails, I was doing all right—considering. Until I walked up me garden path. That's when it really hit me for the first time they was all gone. Gertrude and Winifred was good through and through, and I'm going to miss them like you wouldn't believe. Then there's Trina . . ." Mrs. Malloy reached into her purple velvet pocket for a hanky to wipe her eyes. "I was fond of her—well, as fond that is as you can be of someone you don't ever so much like. I'm not about to say now she's gone that she deserves a halo the size of a dinner plate. But Trina did do wonders for the C.F.C.W.A.; there's no getting round that. She got us thinking like professional women. It was her that organized the Christmas bonus club. No one can take that away from her, Mrs. H.!"

"Of course not."

"Going back into the house tonight was the first time I was really spooked. It come back in flashes to me, like finding Trina's body with a knife that I'd used time out of mind—stuck in her back."

"Awful!"

"I tried to get meself to sleep." Mrs. Malloy continued to dab away with the hanky. "But as if I didn't have enough to think of already, I kept wondering how you and the hubby, along with Betty Nettle and Freddy, got on today. So take a load off, Mrs. H.," she commanded magnanimously, "and tell me if you found out anything, without me there to give you all a poke in the ribs."

"Mrs. Malloy!" I protested. "I want to hear about your day first."

"Not till you've given me the scoop." She was adamant.

So I told her. And she nodded and pursed her lips as the particular revelations required.

"You turned up a sight too many secrets," was her comment. "Now we're stuck thinking any one of them— plain Mr. Walter Lester Smith as he turns out to be, Miss Whitcombe, *or* Mr. Tingle—could be the one we're after. True, you didn't find nothing much at the Misses Millers' house. But I say we put our money on them. Like I read in one of them crime novels, often it's what you *don't* find that counts big. But I'm with you on one point, Mrs. H., I'd just as soon it wasn't our brigadier. Bleeding shame!

Him thinking he had to play the part of the big-I-am to get by in life. The man should have talked to me. I'd have set him straight about how to deal with the stuck-ups!"

I couldn't tell from the look Mrs. Malloy gave me whether she included me among that obnoxious group; just in case, I got up and poured her more tea with another slosh of brandy.

She settled back in the rocking chair. "Well, it's not like we're done checking out the possibles. There's still Sir Robert and her ladyship to be put under the microscope."

"We're supposed to go to Pomeroy Hall today," I reminded her.

"That's been changed, Mrs. H.."

"Really?"

"Sir Robert rang up before I left the house this morning, or I suppose I should say yesterday, to say her ladyship was under the weather—a bad cold that's gone to her chest—and it would be better if we left the cleaning at least till the end of the week."

"Didn't you find that a trifle suspicious?" I stopped, cocked my head, and looked at Mrs. Malloy. "What was that?"

"What was what?"

"It sounded like a teeny-weeny sneeze."

"Power of suggestion."

"I suppose so." I got to my feet.

Mrs. Malloy was behind me, breathing heavily for a person who had done no more than stand up and take one and a half steps. "Mrs. H., there's something I've been getting round to telling you about, but I needed to get meself together before giving you another shock."

I didn't have to ask what she was talking about; I was staring at the holdall, which she must have unzipped when she set it on the table. The sides were spread open. Sleeping peacefully inside under a fleecy pink blanket was one of the most beautiful babies I had ever seen. No wonder my cousin Vanessa and Mrs. Malloy's son George had named her Rose.

"Little love!" Her grandmother bent forward to touch her damask cheek.

"She's adorable," I whispered. "But why is she here?"

"Because George isn't her proper father . . ."

*"What?"*

"No need to screech like that, Mrs. H., you'll wake her."

"Sorry!" I gulped. "But this is all such a surprise. I feel as though I'm taking part in a performance of *The Importance of Being Earnest.*"

"It all came out just after I went to live with them in London. George has always been the neat, orderly sort. Gets that from yours truly. And one Saturday afternoon when Vanessa was having a rest, painting her toenails and such, he thought he'd do a little spring cleaning. Don't it make you want to spit? But then I always did say no good could come of men thinking they was as good as women and had a God-given right to help around the house. Meddling is what I've always called it. And of course I make an exception for Mr. H., him working in the line of duty to help solve the murders. And I'm not saying as I blame George. Feed a man nonsense, and he'll eat every scrap." Mrs. Malloy heaved a voluminous sigh. "He came across a letter in a drawer to Vanessa from the other man. The bugger had spelled it all out—how he was sorry about the baby, but he wasn't the marrying sort and he was glad she'd found some chump to play the role of Daddy."

"Oh, poor George!" My heart ached for him as well as the beautiful baby in the holdall. "I really thought Vanessa cared for him."

"You'd have changed your tune might quick if you'd heard her when George confronted her. Believe you me, Mrs. H., I didn't need to stick my ear to the keyhole. You could've heard her a mile away. Turned everything around to suit herself, she did." Mrs. Malloy smoothed out the pink blanket with a trembling hand. "Talked about how George had all sorts of unfulfilled needs a wife could never meet, as well as throwing in how he'd insisted I move in with them. Well, that's when my boy flipped his lid good and proper. He told Vanessa straight, he'd been forced to ask me to help out because she'd shown not a jot of interest in little Rose from the word go."

"No wonder I hardly heard from you." I put my hand on her arm.

"George, being soft as they come under all that business sense, tried to patch things up. But Vanessa kept right on acting the injured party. The day of Gertrude Large's funeral there was another blazing row. No way I could walk out, not knowing what I'd come back to, because"—Mrs. Malloy's voice cracked—"even though it's turned out I'm not this here baby's gran, she's come to mean the world to me, has my Rose. I'd even got to the point of thinking, Bugger growing old gracefully, as they call it, and switched me hair colour back from that silly schoolgirl red and threw out me miniskirts. Then this morning, just as I was about to leave to come here, I got a phone call from George. All in a panic he was! Vanessa had bunked off to Italy in the night. The baby was howling her little head off. And he didn't know how to get the bottle in her mouth or the nappy on her bottom." Mrs. Malloy blinked away a tear. "Well, enough about me, Mrs. H., I need to give you this." Reaching into a side pocket of the holdall, she handed me a letter, which I unfolded. I recognized my cousin Vanessa's writing:

Dear Ellie,

It turns out I'm not cut out to be a mother. I know you like it, but then you never had a career such as mine to give up. So giving bottles and changing nappies all day and night probably seems like heaven to you. If you hadn't married, things might have been different. I could have hired you as a nanny for Rose. You'd have had your own room and television, and we'd all have been happy. As it is, I'm being offered some fabulous modeling jobs. Thank God flawless perfection is back in vogue again, instead of the shapeless nymphet look that was all anyone wanted for a while. I am off to Italy for three months, and even if I wanted to do so, it wouldn't be fair to drag the baby along. She'll be much better off with you, Ben, and your little people. And don't let me forget Freddy: for all his weird ways he's a whiz with children. I'm also sure Mrs. Malloy will be glad to help out. Even after what's happened she'd bound to have an interest in Rose. Now don't go thinking I'm sticking you with this responsibility for life, Ellie. Who knows? I could change my mind. Let's just think of the arrangement as temporary until I make up my mind. Don't hate me. I'm really not a complete cow. If I were, I would have sent Rose to my mother.

Love and kisses,
Vanessa


It took a while for the impact of that letter to sink in. I don't remember much of what I said to Mrs. Malloy, except that we agreed she would spend at least the next couple of days at Merlin's Court, helping the baby to adjust to a bunch of strangers. I have to admit I was relieved she wasn't willing to release her grandmotherly hold immediately. She dispatched me from the kitchen, saying I needed to talk to Ben while she gave Rose her next feed.

Entering our bedroom, I found him up and in his dressing

gown, even though it wasn't yet dawn. He'd just been about to come and look for me. Handing over the letter, I watched him read it through, his expression thoughtful.

"What do we do?" I asked.

"I don't see we have a choice." Folding up the pages, he laid them on the mantelpiece. "We wouldn't turn a stray puppy away, so how can we refuse to take this baby?"

"It would be different if we knew it was permanent." I started to pace at the foot of the bed. "We could raise her like one of our own, but being in this limbo makes me afraid. What if I really start to love Rose, the way a mother does, and Vanessa walks in one day and takes her away?"

"I don't know." Ben caught hold of my hand and drew me into his arms and stroked my hair as the tears welled in my eyes. "It's a risk. Look at what Mrs. Malloy has already lost. But one thing I can tell you, whatever you decide, we're in this together, Ellie. Let's take it one day at a time, shall we, darling?"

"What about Abbey and Tam?" Wiping at my cheeks.

"We'll tell them little Rose has come to us for her holidays and leave it at that for the time being."

"They'll like having Mrs. Malloy here. I asked her to stay for a while, Ben, which has the added bonus of our being able to keep an eye on her."

"You're really worried about her, aren't you, sweetheart?" Again he held me close.

"Put it down to lack of sleep." I kissed the edge of his mouth. "I know I'm probably being irrational, but I'll make sure she tells us everywhere she is going until these murders are solved. I promise to always keep someone apprised as to my whereabouts, too, darling."

"And just where do you think you're off to now, without so much as a backward glance?" he inquired as I retied the cord on my dressing gown and headed for the door.

"To have a bath, as it seems to be closing in on morning."

When I returned to the kitchen, Mrs. Malloy stood resplendent in a bottle-green brocade dressing gown, heating up Rose's bottle in a saucepan. But the holdall on the table was empty.

"You'll have to change the wallpaper in that bedroom you put us in, Mrs. H., if you want us to stay more than a couple of nights." She tested the heat of the formula on her wrist. "Blue's a chilly colour and that's not good for the baby."

"I'll move you."

"The wee mite's had enough of being bounced around." Mrs. Malloy's heavily powdered jowls tightened. "No use you standing around like a bus with seats to fill, Mrs. H. Why don't you make us a cup of tea while I go and give little Rose her bottle?"

"Could I do that?"

"I suppose." She sized me up. "But what about the twins? Won't they be down in a minute, wanting their breakfasts?"

"Ben's getting them dressed and he'll see to fixing them something." My hand wasn't completely steady as I took the bottle. "Where is Rose?"

"Jonas has her." Mrs. Malloy's face softened, a sure sign that she had been up most of the night. "He came in here a half hour since, and it was a treat the way his face lit up when he saw me holding her. I don't remember nothing so gentle as the way that old man sat down and held that little scrap. So after a bit I got them into the study and left them cooing away together like they spoke the same language. Go and see for yourself if they aren't a picture to hang on a wall."

Mrs. Malloy was right. My heart turned over when I tiptoed into the study. Jonas wasn't afraid to love this baby, even though it was next to impossible that he would live to see her grow up. And here I was, feeling my resistance mounting, as I looked down at her snuggled in the crook of his arm. It would be agony to give her up once the bond was formed.

"Vanessa's daughter, and promising to be a beauty herself." I set the bottle down on the table beside Jonas's chair and studied the baby's sweet face with its rose-petal cheeks. "Look at those eyelashes, and she's going to have her mother's tawny hair." I almost said "Lucky little girl," but caught myself in time. She was anything but, and a wave of anger flowed over me. How could Vanessa have handed her child over to me like a windup toy? Was she completely without feeling? Did she think *I* was?

"I reckon you be wanting to hold her." Jonas smiled, but his eyes were troubled. He knew me so well.

"In a minute." I tried to speak lightly. "I'm enjoying watching the two of you together."

"If I was a fairy godfather, do you know what I'd wish for her, Ellie girl?"

"Tell me."

"That she'll grow up to be loving and loved. That's enough for anyone in my book." The tenderness in his gruff old voice was for me as well as the baby, and I longed to drop down beside his chair and rest my head on his knees. I knew his gnarled hand would stroke my hair, but I didn't feel I deserved to be comforted. For what? Being asked to take care of a dear, innocent baby while her mother was off slogging down the modeling ramp in Italy?

There wasn't time for such nonsense. Rose stirred and began to mew.

"You give her this, Jonas." I handed him the bottle. "I think I hear the twins out in the hall." Opening the door, I beckoned to Ben, and he brought Abbey and Tam into the study. "Look, darlings"—I took hold of their hands— "here's your baby cousin. Her name is Rose, and her mummy has asked us to look after her for a little while."

"She looks like my doll," whispered Abbey, tiptoeing away from me to lean over Jonas's chair.

"What can she do?" Tam gravitated to his father's side.

"Not too much at the moment," said Ben.

"You mean she don't sit up or crawl or nothing?" My son screwed up his nose. "Then what good is she? Let's send her back, Daddy."

Dropping down beside him, I stroked his silky dark hair, "But, darling, Rose needs us to look after her. Only think what fun you and Abbey will have teaching her how to splash in the bath and play with toys."

"She don't get my red lorry." Tam had made his position clear. Knowing my little boy, I accepted that he had to be allowed to warm up to Rose at his own speed. Making things harder for him was the fact that his sister was enchanted with the miniature intruder.

"Careful, darling." I moved up close to her. "Don't jostle Jonas while he's giving Rose her bottle."

"She ain't bothering us none." Jonas came close to beaming. "Here, Abbey, do you want to help me hold the bottle?"

"Oh, yes!" Her eyes shone as she perched cautiously on the edge of the chair and reached out her hands. "Mummy, can't we keep her? Please! It won't be very 'spensive; she can sleep in my bed and wear all my dresses."

"Sweetheart, Mummy and I can't make that promise," Ben told her lovingly. "Let's just enjoy little Rose while she's here."

"I wish her was a boy," said Tam.

"A pity you ain't interested in her." Jonas looked around at him from under bushy eyebrows. "Babies make for lots of work, Tam Haskell. Could be you're too busy to help out, but that's a right shame, seeing as you already know so much from being on this earth three long years afore this little one come along."

"I s'pose I could teach her stuff, like how to play trains." Tam didn't exactly throw resentment to the winds, but he did inch forward. "Can I hold the bottle next?"

"It take know-how," said Jonas. "Not many people gets the knack right off." Abbey solemnly agreed. And Ben and I waited to see Tam join Rose's feeding team before slipping out into the hall.

Ben grimaced. "Ellie, I hate to do this, and it won't become a habit. But I have to go down to Abigail's. Freddy came up a few minutes ago to say that there are some details about payroll that need clearing up. I may be gone for a few hours."

"Say no more." I smiled into his eyes. "I promise to let you know if things aren't absolutely perfect here. Now, doesn't that set your gallant heart at ease?"

I don't think it did completely, but I strove to remain cheerful. After watching him drive away, I returned to the kitchen to find Mrs. Malloy, now dressed in one of her black cocktail frocks, laying the table for breakfast.

"You must be exhausted," I said.

"Speak for yourself, Mrs. H. You look like you've been round the world on a bicycle with two flat tires. Them bruises under your eyes do nothing for you, if you don't mind me saying so."

"I always go smudgy," I protested, "even if I just stay up late. It's you I'm worried about. It must have been awful finding out Rose isn't your granddaughter."

"Well, that's life." Mrs. M. turned her back to me and began splashing water around in the sink, rinsing out the saucepan she had used to heat the bottle. "I'll just bloody have to get on with it, won't I? Same as George. And talking about getting on with things, what's the next step in the criminal investigation?"

Before I had time to reply, Jonas appeared with the baby in his arms, followed half a second later by Tam and Abbey.

"Mummy, the baby needs her nappy changed." My son informed me in the voice of a social worker not entirely happy with the care being provided in case number 342.

"And then can me and Jonas and Tam put her in the wheelbarrow and take her for a walk?" Abbey clasped her hands imploringly as she pranced around me.

"First things first." I settled her at the table. "You and your brother have to eat your breakfast and—"

"I'll go and change little Rose," Mrs. Malloy took her from Jonas and hurried out into the hall.

"That be one precious baby." Jonas took his seat, eyeing the plate of toast on the table with enthusiasm. Then he noticed Abigail Grantham's green-covered notebook lying next to the milk jug. "A real trip down memory lane," he said wistfully as he opened it up and began turning the pages, although he had read through it several times before. As I filled the children's bowls and urged them to eat every spoonful of their porridge, he occasionally muttered a few lines aloud. And when I set his portion in front of him, he polished off the lot as he continued reading. He was even reaching absentmindedly for a second slice of toast when Freddy breezed into the kitchen apologizing profusely for being late for breakfast.

"I do better with bacon and eggs, Ellie; I can smell them frying before they even go in the pan. Porridge is more difficult." Freddy headed for the cooker and slopped some into a bowl with the wooden spoon. "I have to rely mostly on my psychic powers, which while formidable, are not infallible."

"Freddy"—Tam bounced towards him pogo-stick fashion—"Mummy and Daddy got us a new baby."

"Her's called Rose." Abbey slid off her chair, wiping her hands on her blue-and-white-check frock as she did so.

"My word, Ellie!" My cousin clutched the wooden spoon to his chest, getting porridge on his sweatshirt. "I knew you and Ben were fast workers, but this takes my breath away."

"She's Vanessa's baby." I busied myself clearing the table. "Mrs. Malloy brought her here last night. The idea is for Ben and me to keep Rose until Vanessa . . ."

"Finds time to be a mother?" Freddy tossed the spoon in the sink.

"She had to go to Italy on a modeling job." Brushing past him, I deposited the dishes on the working surface.

"And when is our adored cousin coming back to collect her bundle of joy?"

"That's up in the air."

"What does George have to say about this arrangement?"

I dried my hands on a damp cloth. "Freddy, we'll talk about all this later."

"Okay." He looked at the twins, then draped an arm around my shoulders. "Anything I can do to help, Ellie?"

"And I used to call you feckless Freddy!" Returning his hug, I blinked back silly tears and told him I would appreciate his fetching the cradle—the one I hadn't been able to use for the twins—down from the attic.

When he did so in five minutes, I took it into the drawing room to give it a wipe-down. The carved hood was as practical as it was beautiful in that it would protect little Rose from drafts. And the walnut had a lovely sheen even without my polishing it, but somehow it seemed important to do so—a sort of ceremonial purifying. So I went and fetched a bottle of Abigail's Homemade Furniture Cream and a couple of cloths. I also checked on Abbey and Tam, who were busy putting together a puzzle on the study floor while Jonas read in his chair. Mrs. Malloy was upstairs putting Rose down for her nap.

I was in the hall about to go back into the drawing room when the doorbell rang. Bunty Wiseman stood on the step. She blew inside like a breeze.

"Ellie, I love you, but do you always have to looks so disgustingly busy?" Her eyes went to the bottle of polish and the cloths in my hands, while I tried to decide if she looked like a woman about to be arrested for murder.

"Forget the compliments," I said. "Tell me how *you* are."

"In what respect?" Twitching her skirts, Bunty sashayed past me into the drawing room. "My love life? My ability to pay my bills on time? Or are you speaking about the little matter that had me so tweaked the other day?" Truly Bunty at her most exasperating. But I had to forgive her giddy behaviour. She was living on her nerves. And who could blame her? The police had questioned her again. And, understandably, she was unable to take much consolation from their impartiality in appearing equally interested in Joe Tollings and his wife.

"Are you scared, Bunty?" I put the polish and cloths down beside the cradle.

"Who, me?" She dropped into one of the Queen Anne chairs, adjusting a cushion behind her blonde head and crossing her shapely legs. "You should know me! I never do things halfway, Ellie! What I am is frigging terrified! But that hasn't stopped me from doing what you asked."

For a moment I wondered what she was talking about.

"Checking out the newcomers," she told me.

"That's right, I did ask you to do that."

"It was a labour of love." She continued to sparkle. "Anything to help put someone other than my precious self behind bars. And I found out some interesting tidbits from the gabby-mouthed employees of the real estate firms that handled the sale of the former residences of Clarice Whitcombe, Tom Tingle, and the Miller sisters."

"Let me get you a glass of sherry." I promptly did so and decided on having one myself.

"First, Clarice Whitcombe," Bunty spoke between sips. "The word on her is there was a lot of gossip when her parents died in a double suicide from overdosing on sleeping tablets. You know the idea, Ellie, repressed middle-aged daughter gets fed up with looking after Mummy and Daddy and decides to bump them off so she can finally be free to spend their money and kick up her heels. But if that's true, she seems to have got away with it. According to the verdict, the parents committed suicide while the balance of their minds was disturbed. The woman I spoke to said it was rubbish to think anything else. She liked Clarice and was convinced she was just the butt of gossip in a place where nothing had happened for decades on end."

"What else?" I asked Bunty.

"That's all on Clarice. Shall we progress to Tom Tingle?" My friend's eyes peeked impishly at me over the rim of her sherry glass. "He was definitely party to a death."

"He told me that he accidentally struck his headmaster with a cricket ball, but he didn't say the man died. And he was only a boy at the time."

"That's not what I'm talking about—but it does sound as though the man was cursed with an unfortunate knack for causing accidents." Bunty straightened her face. "A woman in the firm that sold his London flat told me that Tom was taking a walk one afternoon. He spotted an acquaintance on the other side of the street and shouted out a greeting. The other man stepped incautiously out into traffic, looking to see who was hailing him, and promptly got plowed under by a lorry."

"Was his name Frondcragg?"

"How did you know?"

"I'll tell you later," I said, not wanting to clutter up the conversation explaining about the letter Freddy had found at Tom's house. "Are you sure, Bunty, there was no doubt that the man's death was accidental?"

"I'm afraid so." She held out her glass for more sherry.

"There was no one standing anywhere near Mr. Frond-cragg when he stepped into the road. So if you're wondering if Tom's shout was the signal for an accomplice to give the fatal shove, you'll have to scrap that one. But alas, poor Tom! He thought of himself as a murderer. That was his reason for getting out of London"—she paused dramatically—"so I was told."

"No wonder he seemed so sad." I handed back her glass. "Anything on the Miller sisters?"

"There was some awful tragedy about a child dying. A little girl named Jessica."

"She was a dog."

Bunty's blue eyes widened in shock. "Ellie, that's not kind!"

"Jessica was a Norfolk terrier."

"Are you sure?"

"There's a portrait of her in the sitting room at Tall Chimneys."

"It's still very sad."

"But hardly sinister." I finished my sherry. "Unless . . ."

"What?"

"Unless Madrid Miller felt a need to vent her rage at Jessica's loss and found a convenient scapegoat in the vet, who may not have warned them sufficiently about postpartum complications. Or even more likely, she may have got even with the owner of Baron Von Woofer."

"Who? Bunty's blue eyes widened.

"The dog who got Jessica pregnant and failed to pine away after her death. And to be fair, Bunty, we can't leave Vienna off the suspect list. After all, she could have acted out of rage at seeing her sister turned into a walking me-morial to a Norfolk terrier." I was talking mainly to myself and not paying sufficient attention, so when I put my sherry glass on the mantelpiece I knocked over Fifi, the china poodle given to me by Mrs. Malloy when she went to live with George and Vanessa. I tried to catch it, but it hit the brass fender, shattering to bits.

"Was it priceless?" Bunty scooted out of her chair.

"Only of sentimental value."

"What's that, Mrs. H.?" The drawing door pounced open and in came Mrs. Malloy, looking as though she would have heard the crash had she still been living in London. "Only sentimental value, my foot, I paid all of two quid for that piece of bone china." She looked from me to Bunty and back again. Something in my face must have told her I had other things on my mind. "Well, I guess it's not the end of the world," she conceded. "After you sweep up the pieces we'll put them in a box and bury them in the back garden. The children—except for Rose, who's a bit young—might like to come to the funeral and we could ask the vicar to say a few words."

Mrs. Malloy vanished back into the hall, leaving Bunty to ask the obvious question.

"Who's Rose?"

# Chapter Fourteen

*To dye white doilies and chair
covers beige, steep in strong
cold coffee. Rinse well.*

"WHAT DID OUR BUNTY HAVE TO SAY?" FREDDY COL-
lared me as I closed the door behind her, but before I
could answer him the telephone rang. It was Sir Robert
Pomeroy asking if I would be so kind as to pay his wife a
visit at the earliest opportunity, for she was anxious to talk
to me. No mention of her cold.

"That's odd," I said upon hanging up. "Lady Pomeroy
wants to see me."

"Like me to come with you?" Freddy offered.

I stood on tiptoe to kiss his cheek through the scraggly
beard. "Thanks, but he'd hardly invite me to his house if
he didn't plan to let me leave. Besides, we haven't found
out a thing about either of the Pomeroys' making me a
threat to be removed."

"When do you plan to go?" Freddy looked at the grandfather clock. It was eleven.

"As soon as I've got lunch for the twins and spent some
time with Rose."

"Why not scoot off now?" he suggested. "I can see

252 • DOROTHY CANNELL

you're all on edge—hardly surprising after the last few days—and I can help Mrs. Malloy take care of things while you're gone."

"Perhaps I should," I said. "That way I'll be back when Ben gets home and it won't seem as if we're on different shifts. Make sure the twins take their naps even if they put up a fuss." I had already started up the stairs. "Tell them they need to set an example for Rose, who's having to get used to our ways."

"Aye, aye, captain!"

Hurrying up the remaining stairs, I concentrated on not thinking about anything except whether I had hung my sage-green cardigan in the wardrobe or put it in a drawer. There were so many pieces of all shapes and sizes rattling around my head. I needed to sit quietly in order to arrange them in a pattern that would make the picture on the jigsaw-puzzle box emerge. I put on a beige-and-cream dress, found the cardigan, shoved my feet into a pair of shoes suitable for a visit to Pomeroy Hall, grabbed up my handbag, and sped back down to the hall.

"You've got a strand of hair coming down at the back." Freddy appeared like a genie to offer this helpful observation.

"Thanks." I didn't mention that half his hair had come out of his ponytail, which was just as well because he had spent the intervening fifteen minutes on his hands and knees giving Tam and Abbey donkey rides, and with all his bucking and eyeore-ing, they'd naturally had to keep a very tight hold on his rein.

"I really don't know what I'd do without you." I stood with my hand on the front doorknob. "Explain where I've gone to Mrs. Malloy, and please make a special fuss over Tam, because I think he has a lot of mixed feelings about the baby, what with suddenly finding himself the only boy."

"He did ask me if everyone would miss him if he wasn't here, but I wouldn't worry about that, Ellie. Tam will be Rose's devoted slave in next to no time."

"I hope so. He's such a loving little boy." I was now standing on the steps leading down from the front door. The garden was veiled in mist, but I headed for the car without going back for my raincoat. It was Freddy who fetched it and came hurrying after me as I was settling behind the wheel.

"Sometimes I think you need a mother, coz." He reached in a hand to turn on the windscreen wipers and stood watching as I set off down the drive.

Fusspot! I thought. It wasn't as if I were driving the old convertible. Ben had taken it and left me the vehicle with a roof and turn signals that operated. But I found myself thinking of my mother as I headed through the village and along winding hedge-lined roads to Pomeroy Hall. She had died when I was seventeen, and although I had missed her terribly, my world hadn't fallen apart when she was gone. I always felt that said a lot about the sort of mother she had been. A little casual in her approach, often forgetting to make the beds or cook dinner when she was engrossed in a good book. By the same token she never got upset when I stripped the blankets off my bed and built a tent in the sitting room on the day she was having a party for her and my father's odd assortment of friends. She treated me like an adult from the time I was little—or rather like her concept of one, because she never quite grew up herself. So that in our home there was always a sense of the magic that makes for breathtaking possibilities at any given moment. Not a perfect mother, perhaps, but because she loved to spread her own wings, I knew how to fly instead of plummeting like a stone when I looked one day to see the nest was gone.

I was now driving alongside the high brick wall that enclosed Pomeroy Hall. On entering its noble gates, I proceeded down the broad sweep of drive flanked by oaks and cypress and parked in front of the centuries-old facade of buff-coloured brick and towering Grecian columns. Pigeons flocked the courtyard as if mistaking it for Trafalgar Square. One even escorted me up the steps.

No one answered my first ring of the bell, or the second. Just to be doing something with my hands I turned the huge iron handle and watched the door swing silently open to reveal the vast hall with its marble floor and granite fireplace straddling a corner under the hanging staircase.

"Hello?" I sounded like someone auditioning for a part in a play, hoping against hope it would be a nonspeaking one.

A door opened to my right and Sir Robert's head poked out. He looked at me without speaking, his red face perplexed. He beckoned me to join him in an enormous room where the furniture all looked as though it belonged in a museum cordoned off by red velvet ropes. The room was extremely chilly, making me glad I was wearing my raincoat. A tiny fire burned like a faltering candle in a grate sufficient to roast a whole herd of oxen. The Pomeroy forebears in their gilded frames all looked as though they were suffering from head colds. But even they didn't look as unhappy as Sir Robert. Tiptoeing behind me, he closed the door painstakingly. But at least he didn't lock it and pocket the key.

"Lady Pomeroy isn't well." He drew a finger to his lips. "And I don't want to wake her if she's resting. Frightfully sorry, Ellie, if you had to let yourself in. I disconnected the doorbell. The staff are all off this afternoon, to make things quieter for my wife. You know how irritating it is when servants, even the best trained of them, bustle around at such times. They mean well, I'm not suggesting they are inconsiderate, but they will insist on getting on with their work. And the next thing you know—*clang* goes a silver chafing dish."

"I'm sorry her ladyship is under the weather." I tried to speak calmly. After all, what was so frightening about being trapped with a batty baronet in a secluded mansion from which the entire staff was conveniently absent? Doubtless he was behaving in this peculiar way because he was worried about his wife's health. He and the former Mrs. Dovedale might even be said to be still on their honeymoon.

"Ah, poor Maureen! Not at all well!" Sir Robert's cheeks billowed out over his shirt collar before deflating in a sigh. "And usually the most robust of women. I'm in a quandary, Ellie, about what to do for her. She's shut herself away, refusing to eat or drink, and I can't get more than two words out of her."

"Oh, dear!"

"A mystery! What! What!" Sir Robert lowered himself onto one of the museum chairs, looking totally bewildered. "Never known the old girl like this. Always such a cracking good sport. Full of spunk. Never laughed so much in m'life as I did on our honeymoon. We made the hotel suite shake every night."

"You said her ladyship wanted to see me." My mind was now such a jumble of nerves and curiosity I could move only one thought ahead at a time.

"Did I?"

"On the phone."

"That's right! Knew you had to be here for some reason. I'll take you up to m'wife." Sir Robert heaved himself up and led the way back out into the hall, where he paused to make sure he hadn't lost me, before proceeding up the stairs like a man headed for the guillotine. Tapping on a door, he announced: "Maureen, my love, my own!

Ellie Haskell is here as you requested. I'll be downstairs should you need me." He ducked away, looking more like an underservant than the master of Pomeroy Hall. I entered Lady Pomeroy's bedroom wondering what role I was about to play.

It was a room fit for a Tudor queen. Dark with red plush, its walls were hung with tapestries glorifying the medieval hunt and pictures of dogs with dead birds in their mouths. The only light came from the bedside lamp and a chink in the curtains. I felt like a visitor to the Tower of London when it housed royalty for extended holidays before they had their heads cut off.

"Ellie," said a voice from the bed beneath the canopy embroidered with the Pomeroy crest. And I tiptoed forward to look down at her ladyship, who in that pale, shifting light looked ghastly enough to have been lying in state. "It was so nice of you to come at a moment's notice." She struggled to sit up. "Please pull up a chair and"—reaching out a hand—"I'll turn up the light so we can see each other better."

It wasn't better. The added illumination just increased the feeling that I was looking at a stranger. She had always been such a cheerful woman in her days behind the grocery counter, and a pretty one, too. Now her smile was stretched tight as a rubber band about to snap, the rosy freshness was gone from her cheeks, and even her eyes had lost much of their colour. So this was the secret Mrs. Large had uncovered, I thought—heart pumping like a washing machine until I could hear the blood slosh in my ears. Sir Robert had been slowly but surely poisoning his wife. He was tired of her already, he didn't like the way she ran the household, he had been appalled to discover she was opposed to foxhunting. Whatever the reason, he was a black-hearted villain who deserved to be sent to the

Tower. I was wondering if I would have to get her ladyship
out of the house by way of the bedroom window when she
squeezed my hand.

"Ellie, you have to help me."

"Of course, Lady Pomeroy."

"Oh, please don't call me that." Her smile seem to rip
into her face. "I'm still Maureen to you. We've got to know
each other well over the years, haven't we? I always felt we
could talk, and over the last few days I've realized I had to
tell someone."

"About Sir Robert?"

"He's so good."

"Yes." Well, that was some relief!

"That's why he could never, not in a million years,
understand how I—the woman he loves with all his dear,
loyal heart—could have done something so criminal." Maureen reached under the pillow. I couldn't budge from my
chair. Numb with shock, I waited for her to produce a gun
and confess to murder before shooting me between the
eyes. After fumbling for what seemed like an eternity, she
pulled out a handkerchief and blew her nose.

"Why don't you tell me about it?" I said, going limp.

"Do you remember, Ellie, how Robert talked at the
Hearthside Guild meeting about how much he detested
dishonesty?"

"Yes, it had something to do with flowers being sent on
behalf of the Hearthside Guild to someone who wasn't a
St. Anselm's parishioner."

"And do you remember how embarrassed I got?" Maureen tucked the handkerchief back under the pillow and
placed her trembling hands on the sheet as I shook my
head. "Well, maybe it didn't show, but I can tell you, I felt
awful, because just a week or so before, my past had gone
and caught up with me. And almost the worst part is I'd

forgotten about what I'd done until . . ."—her voice broke—"until that day when Gertrude was here cleaning and found them."

"Found what?" This was the big moment. The question that had haunted me and the members of the C.F.C.W.A. was about to be answered, and I didn't feel anything at all.

"A pair of fur gloves."

I undoubtedly looked as blank as I felt.

"They're in the top drawer of my dressing table."

"Maureen, I don't understand."

"Remember," she said, "a couple of years back when Mrs. Barrow got on one of her bandwagons and persuaded—you could say pressured—people to pack up their furs and send them off to an animal rights' organization where they would be put on a bonfire?" I nodded and she continued: "The post-office section of my shop was jammed for days with women coming in to post their parcels and tell me how good they felt about doing the right thing. And one day on her way home from work Gertrude Large brought in a package that Mrs. Barrow herself had asked her to send off. Gertrude was cleaning for her at the time, and being a good friend of mine, she told me what was inside."

"The fur gloves."

"Rabbit ones that had belonged to Mrs. Barrow's mother. And something came over me after Gertrude left the shop. It was a cold winter, one of the worst in years, and it seemed to me such a wicked waste to send those gloves off to be burned when there I was without a decent pair to my name. All the crying in the world wouldn't bring that rabbit back from the dead. That's what I told myself. Of course it's no excuse. And I couldn't enjoy the gloves because I was too afraid someone would see me wearing them. So after a couple of times I put them away and more or less forgot about them. You see, Ellie, I started seeing

Robert at about that time and everything else went by the board."

"Until Mrs. Large found the gloves."

"She recognized them and confronted me. It was awful." Maureen again reached for the hanky. "She was so terribly disappointed in me. And what I hadn't known was that when Mrs. Barrow didn't receive a letter of acknowledgment for the gloves from the fur-fighting organization, she accused Gertrude of keeping them for herself, instead of sending them off."

"Did Mrs. Large threaten to tell Mrs. Barrow what you had done?"

"Gertrude was too good a friend for that, Ellie. She urged me to confess. I refused, saying that I couldn't risk the scandal, because of what it would do to Robert. I was a postal employee and stealing from the mail is a government offense. I could have gone to prison."

"Oh, surely not!" I said. "Not for a pair of gloves."

"You know Mrs. Barrow, for all her talk about living in peace with all God's creatures, she would have had me hung, drawn, and quartered, and done a dance in the middle of Market Street to celebrate." Maureen twisted the handkerchief into a ball. "I thought about sending the gloves back to Mrs. Barrow anonymously. But the woman would have set up a full-scale enquiry and I'd have found myself having to own up to prevent someone else—most probably Gertrude—getting the blame."

"What was the result of your conversation with Mrs. Large?" My uneasiness was back full force.

"She felt a loyalty to Mrs. Barrow—that's how she was with all the people she worked for. She talked about a code of conduct set out in the Magna Char . . ."

"I know about that." I gripped the sides of my chair.

"And Gertrude felt that if I wouldn't say anything, she might be morally obliged to do so, but at the same time she hated to hurt me. She said she would talk to Mrs. Malloy, who had a kind heart as well as a sound head, and see if she thought the matter should be put before the C.F.C.W.A."

"And?"

"She died—Gertrude, who was my best friend. And I'll always believe I killed her"—Maureen turned her face away—"because she would never have taken that fall if she hadn't got into such a state about what I had done. She told me she wasn't sleeping and couldn't eat. And if I can't forgive myself, how can I ever hope that Robert will?"

"You're going to tell him."

"I have to. I can't live like this anymore."

"What can I do?"

"Tell all this to Mrs. Malloy." Maureen was now looking me squarely in the eye. "I owe it to Gertrude's memory to set the record straight amongst her fellow workers that her loyalty to the C.F.C.W.A. never faltered. And that I'm more sorry than I can ever say."

"I will." I got to my feet. "And I hope that in time, Maureen, you will be able to remember all the good times shared with your friend Gertrude."

"Even if she had lived, things would never have been the same between us. There's a saying: Broken friendship is like broken china, you can put it together again, but it will always show the crack."

"Maureen, your husband loves you very much. He'll forgive you." I then went downstairs to tell Sir Robert his wife wanted to see him. When I asked if I might use the phone, he pointed one out to me in an alcove off the hall. As I dialed my own number and spoke to Freddy, I heard the baronet's footsteps dwindle into a sad echo.

All I wanted at that moment was to get home, but I had explained to my cousin that I was going to make a stop first and that if I wasn't home within half an hour to come and rescue me—words lightly spoken because I didn't foresee any problems. I wasn't silly enough to walk into the lion's den when the lions were there. But it's true I wasn't thinking entirely clearly. A numbness had settled on me upon leaving Maureen Pomeroy's bedroom.

As I drove up The Cliff Road, the only thing I was sure of was that she hadn't killed Mrs. Large. I told myself that the reason for making a stop before going home was an attempt at putting the ghosts of my suspicions to rest. To face once and for all the fact that Mrs. Large's death had been an accident. It was raining hard as I got out of the car and walked towards the house. Tall Chimneys stared back at me with dark, unseeing eyes. The Miller sisters were away at their dog show. But I did not need them to let me in. I remembered Vienna had spoken about a spare key to the back door hidden under a flowerpot.

The house closed in on me as I entered the kitchen, and it wasn't until I blundered into the hall that I found a light switch. But even in the sudden brightness there remained something furtive about that hall and the way the stairs hugged tight against the wall. I didn't like the way the entire house pretended to echo my footsteps so that no one would guess what it was really saying. Although, to be fair, who could blame it? I was not much better than a burglar. As much a criminal as Maureen Pomeroy. I took off my raincoat because its cold dampness weighed me down, and hung it on the hall tree. Stepping out of my wet shoes, I jumped when a raincoat belonging to either Vienna or Madrid slid off the tree, to be followed by a felt hat.

Heart hammering, I replaced them. There was no denying that Mrs. Large made one ghost too many at Tall Chimneys. I braced myself to go into the study to relive the moment of finding her lying on the floor beside the toppled ladder, the dustpan and pile of ashes bearing silent witness to her recent activity. But I couldn't do it. Instead I moved towards the sitting-room door, which stood open. Its furniture looked as though it would tell on me if I shifted one foot off the hall floor. So I stood in the doorway, restaging those who had gathered there for the Hearthside Guild meeting. Our hostesses, Sir Robert and Maureen Pomeroy, Brigadier Lester-Smith, Tom Tingle, and Clarice Whitcombe. All assumed their places. Their faces and forms fleshed out; their voices grew in resonance as memory came flooding back. My spine prickled and my hand felt cold and sticky.

What was this room trying to tell me? Was a phantom Mrs. Large attempting to give me a mental nudge? Or was I unnerved by the portrait of Jessica—with the lilac bows between her ears and the ruby on her paw? She looked so alive, as if she might start barking if I moved a muscle. Suddenly I was in the drawing room at Merlin's Court, Bunty across from me sipping her sherry, and I was putting my glass on the mantelpiece, knocking over Mrs. Malloy's china poodle. In a flash of belated illumination, I knew why I had stood with my eyes glued to the floor. Looking at those broken piece had prodded a memory. And it was that half-formed realization that had brought me back to this house. Now the other pieces of the jigsaw puzzle fitted into place. It was rather like one of those times when you're talking and can't find the right word and all the poking around in your mind won't dig it up. So you tell yourself that if you leave it alone it will come to you later. And it does, popping into your head when you are thinking about something else entirely.

I leaped at the blast of noise, but it wasn't Madrid's beloved Norfolk terrier. It was the telephone. The shrill sound went on and on. Probably Freddy, I thought. The silly ass! There was no recovering my nerve when the phone finally stopped. Grabbing my raincoat off the hall tree and snatching up my shoes—to be put on when I got outside—I barely remembered to switch off the light before making a dive for the door.

I was still feeling sick as I backed the car into a skid and bounced out onto the lane. My shoes were on my feet, but I had tossed the raincoat on the passenger seat. Even with the windscreen wipers going full speed, I had trouble seeing through the fogged glass as I turned onto The Cliff Road. Cutting the corner too sharply, I stalled the engine, got it going again, and was breathing a little easier when the car slid into a ditch to settle with a soft bump—rather like a dog landing in its basket. Some five minutes later, having only dug myself in deeper, I faced up to walking home.

It was as I reached for my raincoat that I had my worst moment. The tip of a scarf protruded from the pocket. A scarf that wasn't mine. Meaning neither was the coat. As my loving husband had said, it was easily done. So many of them look the same. But this was not the time to regret that I hadn't gone for flaming red or royal purple. I was already half running, half slithering back around the corner and down the lane to Tall Chimneys.

I have to admit cowardice has its charms. Reentering that house was something I would not have wished upon anyone, not even the murderer of Trina McKinnley and Winifred Smalley. I was in such a daze of fright that it didn't strike me that the hall light was back on as I came through the kitchen. I had eyes only for that hall tree, which is why I didn't hear Vienna Miller come down the stairs.

"Well, Ellie, this is a nice surprise." She was standing two feet in front of me. If I still had a mouth, I couldn't find it. All I could do was stare at her. "I had to come back for Madrid's medicine," she continued. "My poor sister suffers terribly from springtime allergies."

It was only long afterwards that I was able to think of excuses that I might have made, such as I hadn't been able to find my handbag since coming here to clean and hadn't thought she and Madrid would mind if I came round to look for it while they were gone. Vienna might even have believed me, until in my stricken state I fiddled with the scarf dangling from my pocket, and as it slipped to the floor found myself holding something that must have been caught in its folds. A smallish black bow. And like a complete idiot I allowed realization to show in my eyes as they met hers. "What was in the dustpan, Vienna?" I heard myself saying. "Is that what Trina discovered?"

"So now you know, dear." It was the endearment that chilled me more than anything. Never had Vienna looked more sensibly tweedy. More kindly capable. More thoroughly resourceful. "I had to get rid of that unpleasant Trina McKinnley," she said calmly. She might have been talking about the increase in the price of coffee.

"Then it was you! Not your sister!" The bow was sticking to my hand.

"What, Madrid? She doesn't have it in her to murder anyone." Vienna smiled indulgently. "I've always had to take on the world for both of us. So when Madrid told me Trina was blackmailing her because she had knocked Mrs. Large off that ladder, it was big sister to the rescue as usual. Not that I intended to kill Trina when I went to see her in Madrid's stead that evening. I really thought I could reason with her—get her to see that what had happened to Mrs. Large was an accident. Madrid hadn't meant to kill her. Certainly she lost her temper and gave that stepladder a shove. It was an impulse and completely understandable under the circumstances, in the light of Mrs. Large's gross insensitivity to Madrid's grief and outrage. But there was no getting through to Trina. She was angry that her friend Mrs. Smalley was going to portion out her inheritance from Mrs. Large—which, when you think about it, she would not have received but for Madrid. Trina wanted money, lots of money. And of course she would have been back for more. So when she turned her back I did the only practical thing."

"That's one way of putting it."

"I was waiting to make sure the coast was clear before leaving the house on Herring Street, when who should walk in but Mrs. Smalley." Vienna's voice became if possible even more bland. "I got her outside, and she had the sense to behave until I spotted the old convertible a couple of doors down, with the keys in the ignition."

"It was mine."

"I know, dear. And I'm sure you've learned a valuable lesson. It was as I was getting us settled in the car that Mrs. Smalley screamed."

"So that's why I was sure the sound came from out in the road. You were directly beneath Brigadier Lester-Smith's bathroom." Talking helped. It made me feel a little less powerless. "The surprising thing is that you were able to drive away from Herring Street without being spotted. It was full of people standing about when the brigadier and I got outside."

"Several other cars were passing when I got the engine going, and I just tucked in between them."

Rage seized me—at that wretched car. All the times it had stalled for me, but oh, no! Not for a murderess making her getaway with an elderly waif in the passenger seat.

"Don't tell me how you killed Mrs. Smalley!" Tears stung my eyes. "I don't need the details. Let's get back to why Madrid pushed Mrs. Large off the stepladder."

"You still haven't figured that out, after all your snooping?" For the first time Vienna looked at me with dislike, and my spine stiffened. Looks couldn't kill and there wasn't room in the pockets of her tweed jacket for a weapon. In a hand-to-hand struggle, I would give as good as I got. There are advantages to not being a size 3.

"Mrs. Large broke something connected with Jessica that day, didn't she?" I took a deep breath and resisted clutching at the hall tree as Vienna's eyes narrowed. "My guess is a plaster or marble bust. Madrid told me that the man who painted Jessica's mainly did sculptures."

"Plaster." Vienna bent and picked up the silk scarf from the floor. "It was my sister's most treasured possession, even more important to her than the portrait, because she said it captured Jessica's soul. And when that oaf of a woman broke it, all she could say was that she was glad it wasn't valuable—couldn't be because the artist was still alive."

"Mrs. Large said something similar when she broke a mirror at my house," I said. "But even Jonas, to whom it belonged, wouldn't have pushed her off a ladder. He might have been tempted, but he would have restrained himself."

"Don't criticize my sister!" Vienna yanked the scarf tight between powerful hands. "You can't understand her. No one ever could but me. I didn't even contemplate the thought of letting her confess what she had done. She couldn't have dealt with the aftermath and I wasn't about to let her pay the price." Vienna took a couple of steps towards me. "It happened minutes—seconds—before the Hearthside Guild meeting was due to begin. Someone rang the bell as Madrid was explaining to me what had happened. I picked up the larger pieces of the bust and told Madrid to put them in the dustbin. I scattered the smaller pieces with fireplace ash and left the dustpan alongside, to look as though it had been disturbed in the fall. Then I answered the door."

"Unflappable you! I should have realized at once that Mrs. Large would not leave a full dustpan on the floor before starting to dust the bookshelves. I'm sure the rules of the C.F.C.W.A. instruct that one job must always be completed before starting another. But I suppose you couldn't risk going back into the study after people arrived in case someone saw you."

"That wasn't it!" Vienna studied me with mounting contempt. "I didn't have a moment to spare. Every minute was taken up trying to calm Madrid down so she didn't give the game away. My poor darling."

"I think she did remarkably well." I was trying not to look at the hall tree, because I was counting on giving it a shove when—if—I could catch Vienna off guard. "She had her wits sufficiently about her to tell me she was upset because it was the day Jessica had died. And being the fool you take me for"—attempting a smile—"I didn't realize her story couldn't have been true when you told me on my subsequent visit that Jessica had died on her third birthday. And the ruby she is wearing on her paw is the December birthstone."

"A little too late to think yourself clever, isn't it, Ellie?" Vienna's smile was much better than mine.

"Speak for yourself!" I placed my hand—unobtrusively, I hoped—on the hall tree. "Oh, I'll admit that you played your part very well, taking me into the study to make sure Mrs. Large's body was found while the Hearthside Guild members were still in the house. Luckily for you and your sister, every one of the members except me had left the sitting room at one time or another for various reasons. Although I'm not so sure it really mattered. The police had no reason to think Mrs. Large was murdered." I had forgotten I was still holding the black bow. The small token of mourning had become part of my hand.

"I tore that bow out of Trina's hair when we were struggling and must have picked it up along with my scarf, which had slid off." Vienna spoke in a conversational voice. "I didn't do a perfect job. Just the best I knew how to save my sister. When Trina came in to clean after the funeral—her first time back since her holiday—she noticed that the bust was gone from the bookshelf in the study. Nothing got past Trina McKinnley. So I told her I had put it away because I was beginning to think that looking at it was not helping Madrid's despondency. Unfortunately she realized I was lying when she found a piece of a paw that must have slid under the bookcase."

I stood looking at Vienna, suddenly wondering if things might have worked out differently if Mrs. Nettle had been paying attention when Trina phoned her and had asked what Trina meant in saying, "It never rains but it pours pennies from heaven." But there was no bringing Trina or her two C.F.C.W.A. colleagues back. I had to save myself, something I might not have needed to do if Freddy had followed instructions and come looking for me as we'd agreed. He was as feckless as he'd ever been. I was just working myself into a froth when Vienna caught me off guard by flinging the silk scarf over my head and, capitalizing on my few seconds of blindness, slammed me into the staircase wall.

I heard my head breaking into fragments just like Jessica's bust and Mrs. Malloy's china poodle before darkness dropped down over me like a blanket over a birdcage. "Stupid, stupid me!" I murmured before drifting away on a vast tide of nothingness. Although perhaps there was something: a vile and suffocating smell. What was it? Deciding that it mattered took a huge effort. My head throbbed and my eyes burned and I was curled up in a cramped heap on the floor. But it wasn't the floor in the hall. I was in the pantry at Tall Chimneys. Or was I dreaming about the time I got trapped in there? I told myself that if I blinked a few times, I would wake up fully to find myself in my own bed at Merlin's Court with Ben hovering over me, begging me to taste a mouthful of chicken soup.

Alas for happy endings, the noxious fumes told me this was all too real. Struggling to my feet, I cupped my hands around my mouth and after trying, and failing, to open the pantry door, endeavoured to take in my surroundings. I could see the marble shelf by the light filtering through the high window. But the ones stacked with tins and boxes were blurred. I was just able to make out a bucket on a shelf a good five feet above my head. It was from that bucket that the overpowering smell was coming. I knew exactly what was in that bucket. A mixture of bleach and ammonia. Abigail's book of household hints had contained a warning about working with such a combination—especially in a closed area. The fumes were toxic. Deadly.

My mind, if not my head, cleared as if by magic. It's amazing what self-preservation can do. I was even able to get a grip on my terror. Force myself to think. There had to be a way out. If Vienna had left the key in the lock on the other side, I might be able to nudge it out with a splinter of wood torn off one of the shelves and pull it inside on a piece of paper slid under the door. After winding the raincoat belt around my nose and mouth I knelt down and peered into the keyhole. It was empty. Vienna had outfoxed me. There had to be another way. I told myself that I had the advantage of having been locked in here before. Nothing is ever as bad the second time around.

I remembered suddenly that Vienna had said—after she had rescued me the first time—that she had been meaning to do something about the pantry door's sticking. Might I not reasonably assume that the problem had existed before she and Madrid moved into Tall Chimneys? In which case the woman who had lived here before might have had the same problem. The Lady in Black had been eccentric, but eccentricity is not the same as stupidity. If she'd ever found herself trapped in the pantry wasn't it likely she would have kept a spare key in here? Indeed, my grandmother had kept a spare key above every door in her house.

Hands shaking, feeling more foggy by the moment, I reached above the door. It was there! While I was giving silent thanks to the Lady in Black, my shaky hand fitted the old iron key into the keyhole. At last I heard the grate of turning metal. Would the door stick this time? I shoved with all my considerable weight against it and finally it gave way with a disheartened groan.

I sat on the kitchen floor until I could breathe again. I was about to stagger to my feet and flee through the back door when Vienna appeared, no doubt to unlock the pantry door, so that my passing could be regretfully described as another ghastly accident.

Mustering all my strength, I got to my feet. "You don't love your sister," I said. "You don't know the meaning of the word. You're one of those people who need so desperately to be needed that you suck the life out of those closest to you. Clarice Whitcombe's parents may have been selfish, they may have used her, but at least they allowed her to develop the capacity to function in the world. And my cousin Vanessa loved her baby enough to let her go when she wasn't sure she was cut out to be a mother. But you are a monster. I'm sure you encourage Madrid to stay trapped in her grief—it's your hold on her."

Vienna came at me in a rush, rage distorting her face, and as we were about to collide, I dropped down, reached out with both hands, and gave her ankle as hard a tug as I could manage. Then I heard her body slam to the floor as my eyes closed.

# EPILOGUE

ANY DAY NOW THE WALLFLOWERS WOULD BE OUT. AND FOR me the appearance of those sweet, simple flowers with their heavenly scent have always proclaimed that summer has arrived. It was a Sunday afternoon, and Ben and I had taken the children into the garden so that Abbey and Tam could romp while Rose basked in the sunshine dappling down through the branches of the old copper beech. I still worried sometimes about loving this baby too much, but more often about not loving all three children enough.

In the end, I learned that it wasn't Freddy's fecklessness that kept him from rescuing me on that awful day. While Abbey had been crying because I was gone and Mrs. Malloy was preoccupied looking after Rose, Tam had disappeared. He had been hiding in the herb garden, hoping to give us all a good scare that would make us realize he was every bit as important to us as baby Rose. Perhaps he was remembering how glad I had been to find him safe the day he had disappeared from Clarice Whitcombe's house. But now he had adjusted to having Rose with us and was my proud helper.

Jonas had joined us for a while, to potter among his beloved flower beds, but when the sun became too strong for his bald head he went inside to fetch his hat, which might be on a hook in the kitchen alcove, but was just as likely to be somewhere in his bedroom. Mrs. Malloy had returned to her house in Herring Street, after staying at Merlin's Court for a week to help get Rose settled in. But we didn't get many opportunities to miss her, because she had decided I needed her at least three mornings a week. On the days when she didn't come she would telephone at least twice to discuss ideas she had for more of Abigail's Housecleaning Products. Tom Tingle came quite often to garden with Jonas and Ben. Clarice Whitcombe and Brigadier Lester-Smith were now pursuing an open courtship. Sir Robert and Maureen Pomeroy had invited us over for tea one afternoon. They appeared to have rekindled their happiness, so I assumed he had forgiven her one lapse of honesty. No one talked much about the upcoming trials of the Miller sisters. But a large number of people in the village—including Clarice and Tom—now owned Norfolk terriers.

"Tam, get out of that tree before you fall," I shouted up at my son just as Abbey came skipping up to me with a tiny toad cupped in her hands.

"Mummy, can he be my pet?"

"Darling, he wouldn't like it indoors." I still had one eye on Tam and another on Rose, who was stretching, stirring as if about to wake up.

"But Daddy said . . ."

"That it was up to your mother." Ben cupped his hand over his eyes to keep the sun out and smiled at me. "Remember, Abbey, I said Mummy would be the one who'd be landed with taking the animal to vet, buying him a lead, and making sure there was always food in his bowl."

"And I expect you also told her that if she kissed that toad it would turn into a prince."

"Of course he didn't." Freddy came ambling across the grass to add his sixpenny-worth. "My friend here"—draping an arm around Ben's shoulders—"wouldn't want his pretty little daughter getting warts on her lips as well as her hands."

"Yuck!" Abbey dropped the toad without a downward glance, and it had the sense to hop away when Tam jumped out of the tree without regard for the lives or limbs of anyone in his path.

"Tell them." My son gave his sister a poke. "Tell Mummy and Daddy that you want a dog named Prince, not the stupid kind in fairy stories."

"Oh, please! Please!" Abbey clasped her hands and lifted beseeching eyes heavenward, like a holy child experiencing a vision.

"We are not getting a dog." Ben went on to ruin this authoritative statement by adding, "At least not today. I've got something even more fun in mind. Why don't we get the kite off the shelf in the old stables and see how high we can fly it?"

This suggestion was enthusiastically received, as much by Freddy as by the children, and soon they were all industriously trying to unravel the string of the kite and entreating Daddy to please not take all day. Not wanting Jonas to miss the festivities, I checked on Rose, who was again sleeping comfortably, and smoothed a hand over her downy head before going back inside. I had picked up the repaired mirror the previous afternoon and had been hoping for the opportunity to slip into Jonas's bedroom and hang it up. When I didn't find him in the kitchen I knew that he must be upstairs, and I decided to take it up to him now. This way I would get to see his immediate reaction on having his mother's long-ago present restored to him, I decided as I tucked it under my arm and tapped on his door. He didn't answer my knock. I softly called his name.

"Jonas?"

No answer. Should I take the mirror back to the study? Or hang it, as originally planned? I hadn't made up my mind when I went into the room. But the faded rectangle of rose-patterned wallpaper where the mirror previously hung had a particularly forlorn look today. So I crossed the floor, feeling as I always did that I was embarking on an obstacle course.

The mirror looked happy to be back where it belonged. Could it be that there was something magical about it, as Jonas had believed when he was a young boy? Certainly, I thought stepping back from it, the glass did seem to reflect sunlight in a special way. When I stood a little to the side with my eyes half closed, it showed the room bathed in a golden glow, and I could imagine that I was looking at a painting by one of the Dutch masters gifted in depicting homely scenes in such a way that an old man sleeping in a chair by the window acquired a dignity often denied lords and ladies.

"Jonas?" I didn't want to startle him; he looked so peaceful with his battered old hat and Abigail's book lying open in his lap. He must have dozed off while leafing through it as he often did, when he wasn't busy mixing up a batch of her furniture polish. "I didn't see you at first"— still keeping my voice low—"this chair has a high back and with it being turned to face the window . . ."

He did not hear me. I knew before I touched his hand that Jonas would never hear me again. He had slipped away without saying good-bye. A wave of desolation swept over me as I knelt beside his chair and rested my face against his knee. Life would never be the same without him. I wanted to shake him, ask him if he had forgotten that he was needed here. Wanted to tell him that little Rose was entitled to more time with him. And then something strange happened. The emptiness inside me filled with the golden glow cast by that narrow rectangle of mirror.

Getting up, I opened the window and leaned out into a breeze that smelled of wallflowers. I could see my family down below in the garden. Ben stood under the copper beech with Rose in his arms. He was smiling at Tam and Abbey, who capered in circles while watching Freddy unleash the faded kite into the clear blue sky. For a moment it seemed doubtful, almost fearful of taking flight. But then that old kite soared eagerly, joyously towards the sky, straining to touch the sun until its string broke free, and I smiled through my tears as I watched it vanish into the heavens.